THE DEVIL'S ARCHITECT

BOOK TWO OF THE *DARK HORIZON* TRILOGY

THE DEVIL'S ARCHITECT

FOUR BRUTAL MURDERS, FOUR MYSTERIOUS CHURCHES, ONE TERRIFYING PURPOSE

DUNCAN SIMPSON

Whitefort Publishing
London

Published by Whitefort Publishing.

First Whitefort Publishing edition published in 2017.

ISBN: 978-0-9932063-5-1

Printed in the United Kingdom.

Edited by Katie Simpson & Amy Butcher.
Cover design by Juan Padron.

DEDICATION

For Katie, Tamsin, Louis and Finley, with all my love.

PROLOGUE

The Minories
Central London
One Year Earlier

Professor Roland Ballard stabbed desperately at the black London soil with his trowel. Time was running out, as if the last grains of sand were tumbling through the neck of an hourglass and with them, the discovery of his career. No one had listened: not even the Board of the Museum. But he had been right all along. He knew the monument was buried just feet below from where he now stood.

A loud voice echoed from above.

'No more extensions, Professor. Four more minutes and your time is up.'

The archaeologist squinted up to the flickering outline of the suited man standing at the edge of the excavation pit.

'Damn it. I've found something here, don't you understand!'

Ballard's protests were soon swallowed by the sound of heavy machinery starting up.

The Professor dropped to his hands and knees and hacked at the London ground. He was on his own; his team had already packed up their equipment and were fighting their way through the London traffic. He glanced down at his wrist and wiped the grit from the face of his watch. Within minutes, the bulldozers would be laying waste to the site in readiness for the foundations of a new hospital.

As the sun slid behind the glass office blocks surrounding the site, a cold shadow tracked across the archaeologist's back. Ballard frantically attacked the earth with the blade of his trowel in a sprint to uncover what he could.

His trowel hit something hard, which sent a painful tremor vibrating up his forearm. A clod of soil fell from the artefact and Ballard's body stiffened. Staring up at him was a small patch of bone-white stone. He blinked, trying to make sense of the shape of the newly exposed stone design.

Soon his thumbnail was scraping away at the caked-on earth. As he worked, clumps fell away to reveal more of the detail underneath. It was a sculpture of some sort.

A cold splash of rain hit the archaeologist's face. He wiped it away, leaving a smear of London earth on his cheek. Another hit the back of his neck. Soon heavy droplets were hitting the ground around him.

A triumphant voice sounded from above.

'That's it, Ballard. It's over.'

This time the developer's voice was amplified through a loud hailer. 'Need I remind you that I have two police officers with me to make sure you exit the worksite without any trouble?'

The rain began to drum heavily on Ballard's back and sent a cold trickle of water down the inside of his shirt. He shivered, and then felt a new resolve take hold of his body.

He hauled himself upright, gripped the object and strained with all his might to free it from the ground. The joints in his arms screamed in protest. He released his grip and repositioned his feet. Gasping, he readied himself for one final effort. As he planted his boot heels in the wet soil, he heard voices approaching from behind.

His thighs juddered as he heaved upwards. Then it came free, released from the London earth that had entombed it for almost two millennia. Slipping back from the sudden release, Ballard lost his grip on the statue, which toppled onto its side.

In the hole where the base of the statue had been, Ballard spotted something that appeared incongruous with the soil. He moved closer and blinked through the deluge of rain now filling his eyes. Falling to his knees, he looked down at a small metal disc whose shape was disappearing in a muddy pool around it. The Professor scooped it out from the gritty water, and as he held it up to his face, he could see that it was a coin. A silent fork of lightning then lit up the sky, followed moments later by a tremendous roar of thunder, as if the very fabric of the sky had just been torn in two.

PART 1

Revelation 12:9

And the great dragon was cast out, that old serpent,
called the Devil, and Satan, which deceiveth the whole world:
he was cast out into the earth, and his angels were cast out with him.

CHAPTER 1

Broadmoor High-Security Psychiatric Hospital
Crowthorne, Berkshire, England
Present Day

Enoch Hart sat Buddha-like on the floor of his darkened cell. His naked body was perfectly still, apart from the gentle rise and fall of his back. The staff at the Broadmoor high-security psychiatric hospital had gradually grown to accept Hart's daily practice. In any case, quiet times at an institution that housed some of Britain's most violent and disturbed men were always welcome. But no one was complacent. Hart's history left no one in any doubt of his potential threat.

Nearly an hour had passed since Hart had effortlessly lowered himself from standing position into his cross-legged posture. His meditation practice had begun in the usual way with the silent recitation of the medieval Mantra of the Marshall: 'Inner stillness is the key to outer strength'. Within seconds, Hart's attention had turned inwards, as his breath flowed freely between the words of the mantra.

As the minutes went by, a single shaft of light appeared through a gap in the window shutters of his cell and moved across Hart's muscular chest. At first the prisoner merely accepted the narrow pencil tip of heat warming his skin. But as he continued to sit, his mind's eye was drawn down to the point of energy journeying across his flesh. With every subtle rise and fall of his breath, he felt his perception moving closer to the tunnel of light. Then something disturbed his concentration.

Hart's eyes snapped open. The sound had returned. The prisoner parted the curtains of long matted hair in front of his eyes and looked at the sink basin attached to the wall of his cell. A low buzzing emanated from the ventilation grille below the sink. He crawled over until his face was up close to the grille. The droning vibration began to rise and fall in pitch. After stealing a glance towards the door, Hart lowered himself onto his chest. The grille was a light metal mesh some six inches across and three inches high and provided air-conditioning to the small cell. Hart carefully unclipped it from its wall housing and tentatively peered behind it. A slow grin crept up his face. Today was going to be a good catch.

The small space behind the grille was alive with shadowy movement. Hart carefully slid his hand into the gap and felt the smooth surface of a plastic cup. His fingers moved around the cup's circumference and then he gently raised it upwards to trap the contents inside, before easing it out of its hiding place. As soon as the cup was free, his other hand quickly covered it.

The banana had already been overripe when delivered to his cell as part of his breakfast five days earlier. Now, it had decomposed into a pool of dark mush at the bottom of the cup. Feasting on the remains of the perishing fruit were half a dozen crawling wasps. Hart stood up and leant over the sink. He could feel the small black and yellow bodies brush against the skin of his palm. With his elbow, he opened the sink's faucet. He wrapped his thumb and forefinger around the flowing spout and directed the water into the vessel. Once the cup was full, he covered it again with his flat palm and gave it a rigorous shake. He stopped and then did it again, this time harder, before emptying the contents of the beaker into the sink. With greasy hair hanging in his eyes, he quickly picked through the detritus covering the basin like a man panning for gold.

Moving quickly, Hart plucked up a wasp and brought it close. His eyes locked onto the insect. The wasp was dazed but still alive, and for a moment he was unsure whether the gentle throbbing in his fingertips came from his pulse or the gentle rising and falling of the animal's abdomen.

With his thumbnail, he cut the insect in two at the narrow waist, dividing its yellow and black abdomen from its thorax, and discarded the upper part of the body to the floor. While carefully rotating the abdomen in his fingers, Hart held it up to the shaft of light coming through the shutter. The gentlest of pressure was all he needed for the wasp's black stinger to shoot out of its body like a dagger.

CHAPTER 2

'It's a fake,' said Blake as he returned the yellowing sheet of paper to the table.

'Are you out of your mind?' exclaimed the dealer, who stood up so quickly his chair almost fell over.

'Please calm down,' pleaded the buyer from the British Museum. 'Vincent do you need more time?'

'If you want me to authenticate this document as belonging to Wolfgang Amadeus Mozart, then no, I don't need any more time.'

The dealer smacked his fist in his palm and began to stride around the table. 'Go on, Blake, grace us with your amazing insight. How on earth can you be so sure?' he asked, his face white and furious.

Blake exchanged a quick glance with the man from the British Museum, who gave him a 'go on' look with his eyes.

After breathing out audibly through his nose, Blake picked up the magnifying glass from the table and passed it to the dealer. 'It's undoubtedly a fake,' said Blake as he kneaded his lips with the knuckles of his right hand. 'Take a close look at the paper fibres.'

Huffing to himself, the dealer leant over, his large stomach brushing the edge of the table as he examined the paper. 'No idea what you are talking about,' he said, the impatience building in his voice.

Blake rocked back in his chair. 'A good forger takes their time looking for the right type of paper, spending months rummaging around sales rooms for unframed prints or pictures. The best sources are lightly drawn sketches, as soft pencil can easily be removed by a little rubbing with dilute detergent. Another good source of original paper is antiquarian bookshops. If they're lucky, they can stumble over books with lots of end-papers. These blank pages are much more valuable to the forger than the actual work itself. Sometimes you can find unlined ledgers or account books. They are often dated to the year by their first entry.'

'All very interesting Blake, but what the hell does that have to do with Mozart?' demanded the dealer.

'It's all to do with the fibres,' answered Blake. 'All paper was made by hand until 1798, when a Frenchman, Louis Robert, invented a paper-making machine. Prior to 1798, paper was made one sheet at a time. A rectangular wooden frame with a fine wire mesh attached to its bottom was dipped into a vat of paper pulp, essentially a soup of fermenting rags. Just before the frame was dipped, the vatman would give its contents a good stir to loosen up the fibres. Once the frame was removed, and the water pressed out of the pulp, the paper was then allowed to dry. This method always left a random distribution of paper fibres.'

The man from the British Museum pinched his eyes in confusion.

'The fibres don't all line up in the same direction. Hand-made paper doesn't have a grain,' said Blake, pressing home the point.

The dealer replaced the magnifying glass on the table, his face set in stern lines. The buyer from the British Museum immediately picked up the magnifying glass; after blinking through it for several breaths, he let out a long laboured sigh.

'Ah, I see, this has a grain. You can see the parallel fibres quite clearly.'

'It's been machine made,' continued Blake. 'It must have been produced after 1798.'

The dealer slumped in his seat. '1798,' he said quietly to himself, his eyes now blinking with the dawning realisation that he had just lost a considerable sum of money.

Finally, the penny dropped for the man from the British Museum. 'And Mozart died in 1791, so this can't be his signature.'

Both men looked over to the dealer, who was now staring up at the ceiling with deep worry lines across his face. He had been well and truly screwed over. Buying the document up front from the Latvian middleman had been a gamble, even though the supporting material had appeared to confirm its provenance.

'I'm sorry, but the museum will have to pass on this one.'

The metallic beep of an incoming message sounded from Blake's phone. He dug it out of his pocket and entered his passcode. The screensaver image of his daughter cleared and he read the message. His face instantly drained.

VINCENT, I'M OUT AND HEADING
FOR LONDON. ROSALIND.

CHAPTER 3

By the time the four-man team burst into Enoch Hart's cell, the loud drone of the emergency alarm was reverberating down the corridor. Hart was writhing on the floor, his arms wrapped around his stomach, his legs flailing out in all directions. The tallest man of the team readied himself to examine the prisoner but was stopped in his tracks by what he saw.

Hart's face was almost unrecognisable. His skin was covered in a patchwork of red lumps, with sweat streaming from his forehead. The tendons in his neck were locked taut beneath his clenching jaw. After snapping on a pair of pale blue surgical gloves, the tall man edged closer. Through the white shirt pasted to Hart's body, he could see the prisoner's chest rising in fits and starts. Hart's head thrashed from side to side, leaving a smear of sweat on the floor beneath his ponytail of greasy, unruly hair.

Not looking up, the tall man shouted something and one of the guards turned and ran out of the cell. With his eyes, he then signalled to the other men to move closer. In a moment, Hart's arms and legs were pinned to the floor by the guards. The tall man grabbed the prisoner's left wrist and attempted to locate a pulse. It wasn't hard to find. The double beat pounded out from his skin like a racing train. Suddenly Hart's body went slack and foam, like egg whites, started dripping from the side of his mouth.

In unison, the three guards leaning over Hart's body turned their heads towards the door. A smartly dressed lady charged into the room, swiftly followed by a uniformed prison guard pushing a medical trolley. Moving quickly, the woman took charge and gave a series of rapid and clipped instructions to the men around her. As she leant forward to secure the blood pressure monitor onto Hart's arm, his eyes rolled backwards revealing the whites of his eyes.

CHAPTER 4

'Sarah will be down in a minute,' said the physiotherapist. 'I thought we could have a little chat before she arrives.'

Blake edged back slightly in his chair and two lines of wrinkles appeared on his forehead.

Sarah's new physiotherapist was a small woman with greying hair cut into an immaculate bob. She sat perfectly upright in her crisp white uniform, a pair of sharp elbows resting on the sides of her chair. Blake could feel her eyes sizing him up.

'Over the last few days, Sarah's attitude has become a little, shall we say, unfocused.'

'Right?' said Blake.

'She's obviously come a long way, but recovering from a coma is an unpredictable business. Her muscle strength, balance and flexibility are all improving, but they need constant work, and I mean hard work, if she's going to get full use of her legs again. There are no certainties. She had been making very good progress up until recently, but things have somewhat plateaued. Sarah needs to battle, Mr Blake. Battle long and hard.'

Blake rubbed his temple. Like a jumping movie reel, Blake's mind rewound to the months following Sarah's waking. Working with the team at London Bridge Hospital, one of the world's leading coma rehabilitation centres, his twelve-year-old daughter had slowly relearned her motor skills: first learning to roll over; then manoeuvre herself into her wheelchair; and several months ago, with the aid of a transfer board, to shuffle in and out of the bath.

Now she was learning to walk again, and it was maybe the hardest thing she would ever have to do in her life. It felt like they had slid to the bottom of the ladder again.

'Her progress has slowed,' said the woman, making a steeple with her fingers. 'She needs to grit her teeth, focus on the task in hand, and—'

Before she could continue, the doors of the elevator at the far end of the therapy room scraped open.

'Dad!' The call was loud and excited.

'Excuse me,' said Blake, quickly getting to his feet.

Half walking and half running, he was at the elevator doors before Sarah had steered her wheelchair onto the therapy room floor.

As they hugged each other hard, Sarah whispered something.

'Don't listen to what she says, she's a witch.'

Blake pulled back in surprise and looked quizzically at his daughter. Even though her clothes hung to her like a limp sail, Sarah's eyes were bright and alive. 'Pardon?'

'She's horrible and a bully,' mumbled Sarah whilst her hand smoothed down her loose ponytail of black wavy hair.

'Let's go Sarah, we have lots of work to do today,' a voice came from the other end of the room.

Blake raised his hand in acknowledgement. 'We're coming.' He gave Sarah a concerned look and lowered his head so he was almost cheek to cheek with his daughter. 'You okay?'

'I'm okay, Dad. It's just that she's a witch,' she whispered back as a slanted little smile appeared on her face.

Blake's brows unknitted. 'You going to give this a shot?'

'Just watch me,' said Sarah as her hands returned to the wheels of her wheelchair.

'We'll chat more after the session, okay?'

'Okay, pops,' said Sarah as she moved towards the parallel bars.

The bars ran the entire length of the therapy room. Surrounded on three sides by floor-to-ceiling mirrors, the walking track between the bars was made of soft padding. As Blake helped Sarah out of her wheelchair, the therapist adjusted the control console on the wall. There was a slight hum of electric motors and the bars started to lower.

'Right, young lady, let's get to work,' said the physiotherapist as she clapped her hands.

Standing upright with a stick, Sarah waited for the ache to settle in her legs. With the bars now at a height just above her hips, she licked her lips in readiness.

Blake put his arm around Sarah's shoulder and followed her line of sight down the runway of the parallel bars. 'Remember what I said princess: walk tall, tall like a tree,' said Blake.

Blake's comment was more than academic. It had been his mantra during his months of rehabilitation following the reconstruction of his knee. These were the same months of Sarah's gradual awakening from her coma. He had told his daughter that the injury to his right kneecap was the result of a fall from a motorcycle. He wondered if he would ever tell her the truth.

CHAPTER 5

Hart's eyelids flickered open. As his vision stabilised, he slowly became aware of his surroundings. The graveness of his situation then hit him with full force. A cold sweat trembled down the length of his body. He was lying alone in a hospital bed.

Instinctively, he tried to raise his hand to rub his face, but his reach was halted abruptly with a clatter. His eyes jerked downwards. His left wrist was handcuffed to the metal tubing of the bed. He tugged at the restraint again. This time the loop of the cuff scraped noisily along the length of the metal side rails.

Hart's shoulders collapsed into the pillow as if the air had been let out of him, and waves of exhaustion and nausea took hold of his body. Willing his eyes to focus inward, new voices began to echo in his head. The killing would start soon. There would be blood sacrifice. The moon will run with blood.

He needed to move fast before the window of opportunity was lost forever. His body stiffened with the weight of the moment, but seconds later he was regulating his breathing to a well-rehearsed rhythm. He had trained for this time, and this is where the war would begin. Almost instantly he could feel the thud of his heart beginning to slow.

The door handle of his room jerked downwards and in walked two policemen dressed in black military-style uniforms, followed by a female nurse. The face of the stockier of the two policemen bore the deep lines of experience; so did his uniform, which proudly displayed the three-chevron insignia of the rank of sergeant. His colleague was his junior and much younger looking, tall and lean in stature. Seeing the athletic frame of the seemingly unconscious prisoner, the Sergeant's face hardened. Moments later he was circling Hart's bed.

As the nurse busied herself checking the stack of medical monitoring equipment beside her patient, she couldn't help but steal another glance at the pistols secured on the belts of the policemen. A disapproving frown travelled over her forehead.

'How's he doing?' asked the younger policeman.

'Well, he's stable,' said the nurse, not looking up from the blood pressure machine, 'but his body has suffered a serious shock. I doubt if he's going anywhere soon. The consultant will examine him on his ward round in the morning and you can ask him then.'

Hart willed himself not to swallow. He felt a slight waft of air against his cheek, just before his left hand was dragged several inches over the tight sheets of his bed.

The police sergeant tugged at the handcuff. 'All secure,' he said over the clinking sound of metal on metal. He checked his watch. 'You okay to take the first shift?' He nodded over to the younger policeman.

'No problem, but first I need something to eat.'

The nurse looked up from her medical notes.

'The canteen is still open for another ten minutes. It's on the third floor. If you hurry you should be able to get something.'

'Sounds like a plan,' accepted the Sergeant.

With that the two policemen left the room, followed seconds later by the nurse.

Hart's eyes snapped open. Soon he was twisting and turning his body free of the tightly tucked hospital sheets. Threading the loop of the handcuff along the side rail of the bed, he managed to get his body sitting upright. He quickly scanned the room and clocked the time pulsing on the top corner of the digital blood pressure monitoring machine: 01.23 am.

At the side of his bed stood a small white cabinet. In a series of small bucking movements, Hart bounced his body closer to it. Using his left handcuffed hand as a pivot, he turned his body over the side rail and reached down to the cabinet. Fumbling fingers quickly found the handle and inched open the door. A ghost of a grin flitted across Hart's face at what he saw on the lowest shelf. He reached down with all his might, the strain squeezing the breath out of his chest. His fingertips were just millimetres away from their target, twitching in mid-air. With his face running in sweat, Hart relaxed his body just enough to take on several lungfuls of air and then tried again, this time sliding his hips square to the side rail.

The muscles of his outstretched arm trembled, and his fingertips finally touched their quarry. Seconds later, Hart's prison-issue shoe landed on the bed with a thump. He looked up at the clock on the blood pressure monitor and a sickening feeling lurched inside his stomach: 01.25 am. There was no time to lose.

To ease the tight ache numbing his hand, he clenched and unclenched his fist several times before moving it to the back of his head. He dragged the rubber band free from his loose ponytail, and his hair fell in lank sweaty ribbons across his face. The palm of his hand patted down the back of his head. It took no time to find the thin length of metal woven into the strands of greasy hair. After several concerted yanks, the hacksaw blade was free and feeling sharp between Hart's fingertips: 01.26 am.

Nothing special had been added to the plain black leather shoe that now rested on Hart's lap. Like all shoes issued to maximum-security patients, it had no laces, only Velcro straps. A pair of shoelaces in the hands of a determined patient could be used to garrotte an unsuspecting guard. The shoe had passed through countless metal detector examinations at Broadmoor; no weapon was concealed in the heel; no drugs were hidden under the insole. But it did have an unusual feature; Hart had made sure of it. Not something added, but something carefully removed.

With matted hair clinging against his cheeks, Hart secured the shoe, heel facing upwards, between his knees. Picking up the hacksaw blade between his thumb and index finger, he moved it closer to the back of the shoe. Squinting, he could see the tiny hole that he had burned into the rubber heel with the end of a blade weeks before in the prison workshop. Holding his breath, he lowered the fine-toothed strip of metal vertically down into the hole. It was a perfect fit, with half its length securely fixed in the rubber and half protruding out: 01.27 am.

Using the shoe as a saw handle with the blade fixed rigidly into the heel, he set to work on the metal tubing of the side rail securing the handcuff to the hospital bed. Hart went at a frenetic pace and soon cut a groove into the metal tube. His arm gunned in and out, like the piston of a steam engine. After several minutes, Hart's face turned slack and he discarded the makeshift saw onto the bed. He blinked through the sweat filling his eyes and examined the half-cut metal tube. His fingers touched the slit and felt heat radiating from the incision line. Only a third of the tube's circumference remained. He yanked at the side rail with all his power. It yielded almost immediately, and the loop of the handcuff clattered against the side of the bed as it slid free.

Hart swung his legs over the side of the bed and stepped down. The floor felt cold on the soles of his feet.

At 01.32 am, the police sergeant's fist hammered down upon the emergency alarm.

CHAPTER 6

Gerry Sanders breezed into the conference room and shook the hands of the two men seated by the window.

'Sorry to keep you gentlemen waiting,' he said. Sanders bounced into one of the leather chairs and glanced at his Rolex. 'I can only give you twenty minutes I'm afraid. I have to be on the other side of town in an hour to meet the councillor.'

Sanders talked like a politician, fast and as smooth as a milkshake. Over the last decade, he had built a reputation as one of London's most aggressive and successful property developers. Where there was development opportunity, Sanders wouldn't be far behind. His first million, however, had been made in the gambling industry. He was the man behind the explosion in the fixed-odds betting terminals now ubiquitous in London's betting shops: machines which were as addictive as crack cocaine. At the time, Sanders had controlled the UK licence for the distribution of the terminals. He then used his wealth to make investments in property all over the capital and in the adult film industry.

'Angelo, you're looking well, and this must be the Reverend Jackson,' he said, casually brushing the knee of his flint grey suit. 'I suspect you have both made a wasted journey. Anyway,' continued Sanders, 'as a favour to Angelo, I am willing to hear what you have to say.'

Sensing his opening, the Reverend cleared his throat.

'Mr Sanders,' he said falteringly. 'On behalf of the Trustees of the Hawksmoor City Churches, I would like to thank you for your time today.' In contrast to Sanders, the Reverend cut a crumpled figure. He was a fidgety man and looked dishevelled with windblown hair.

'As you may know, the Friends of Hawksmoor City Churches came into being a little over eight years ago. Founded by Angelo here, and other senior church representatives across the city, our organisation aims to ensure that Hawksmoor's architectural legacy is preserved for posterity and, most importantly, that his churches are kept open as places of worship. Hawksmoor's churches are a priceless heritage that need to protected.'

'From the likes of people like me,' Sanders teased.

'We have nothing against progress,' Reverend Jackson said, unconsciously raising his voice. 'But sometimes it can destroy the culture and heritage of an area. These churches are totally unique and can't be replaced. With Angelo's help, the Friends have managed to secure the long-term stewardship of five of Hawksmoor's churches, but your planned Windsor development is threatening the future of St George-in-the-East and the important work it does in the local community.'

The Windsor Development was a seventy-million-pound building project to transform the church's surrounding area into luxury apartments. Targeting wealthy Russian and Chinese business people who worked in the nearby Canary Wharf financial centre, the Windsor Development was set to return significant profits in today's superheated property market.

'St George's,' the vicar continued, 'has been a blessing to so many of its congregation, many of whom are City professionals. They are seeking comfort in the Christian faith, and St George's brings them sanctuary from the stress and anxiety of their workplace.'

Sanders pushed back from the table, a trace of a smile on his face.

'I'm sure the Church is doing lots of good work, but please forgive me for saying so, there seem to be more pews than people in there. Redevelopment won't kill the area, it will only strengthen it,' said Sanders. 'Many of the churches have fallen into disrepair and, with respect, I see them as an impediment to progress. Many are deserted and magnets for vandalism.' He locked eyes with the third man sitting at the table. 'Angelo, you know what I'm talking about.'

Angelo Ricard adjusted the orientation of the gold pen sitting in front of him so that it was parallel to the edge of the table. Exquisitely tailored in a black suit, Ricard wore gleaming tan brogues and a silk handkerchief sticking out from his jacket pocket. He was in his early fifties, but his immaculately parted hair was untroubled by any trace of grey.

Ricard had made his money in hedge funds during the crazy days of unregulated markets, but he had quickly diversified into property. His dramatic conversion to faith had been well documented in the financial press. Ricard was now seen as a philanthropist, a spokesman for good causes, and a safe pair of hands, having donated much of his wealth to inner-city projects.

'Gerry, how long have we known each other?' said Ricard, in a distinctive sonorous voice. 'Maybe ten years, give or take?'

Sanders nodded from the other side of the table.

'I'm not as young as I used to be.' He smiled. 'But I have realised that certain things need to be protected, whatever the cost. These churches are not just bricks and mortar. They are our nation's heritage.' Ricard started tapping his fingers on the table.

'Come on, Angelo, you're going to have to do better than that. This is a legitimate development opportunity. We aren't even touching the fabric of your church. We are reclaiming some of its surrounding land. Land that is overgrown and unkempt, I might add.' He took a pause to take on breath. 'Here's the thing; if you want the plans adjusted, you need to give something in return. You've got to have some skin in the game, if you will. Then maybe I could iron things out with my investors.'

The developer tried to read Ricard's face as he exchanged a sideways glance with the vicar.

'You help us here, Gerry, and I will make sure you get a good hearing with the City Corporation about that office development south of the river. I can't promise a result, but I can arrange a private lunch with you and the Chief Financial Officer.' Ricard waited for his words to take root.

Sanders's swinging foot suddenly went still, and a smile travelled across his face.

'A small gesture of goodwill goes a long way in this world,' said Sanders. He leaned over the table and offered his hand to seal the deal. 'I'll talk to my investors this afternoon.'

Two minutes later, Ricard and Reverend Jackson were outside Sanders's exclusive riverside offices nodding their goodbyes to each other. Ricard felt his mobile phone vibrate in his pocket. He read the message, and his heart went cold.

ENOCH HART HAS ESCAPED FROM BROADMOOR

CHAPTER 7

A cold blast of wind rattled through the East End car park. The six floors of tightly packed parking bays were designed around a central concrete axis, like the chambers of a giant spiral shell. By day, the car park was a prime parking location for the city's close-by financial centre. By evening, it had all but emptied and transformed itself into a high-rise echoing skeleton.

Apart from a row of bright-red payment machines and dirty tyre tracks snaking their way to the lower floors, everything had the colour of washed-out grey under the harsh overhead lighting. Next to the payment machines, a loud ping signalled the arrival of the elevator. After a short pause, the doors of the elevator clunked open and out came a black dog. It walked confidently like a leopard moving out onto the savannah, tasting the air, its head lilting from side to side, as if looking for prey. The animal dropped silently onto the circular ramp, stopped, and then looked back towards the elevator.

On the side panel next to the doors, a small downward arrow blinked on. Moments later, the elevator's mechanism burst into life again, pulling the doors shut for its journey down to the ground floor. Just before the sliding doors had fully closed, a hand darted out from inside, reversing their direction of travel. The hand was dark and weatherworn and had black lines of dirt etched deeply into the creases of the skin. Mary stepped from the elevator, her face consumed in thought. As she walked, she talked to herself, asking and answering her own questions in the same breath. Her clothes were grimy and possessed a greasy shine to them, a reflection of months of continual wear and sleeping rough. When she joined her friend, she reached down and touched the animal's head as if bestowing a blessing.

'Don't worry. We should be high enough to be safe,' she said as she stared into her friend's glistening eyes. 'For now at least.'

The dog growled an acknowledgement and moved the weight of its body into the side of Mary's leg.

'I know, I feel it too.' She gave the animal's side a friendly rub and then squatted in front of it. For a moment, they both just looked at one another, reading each other's thoughts. Mary smiled solemnly, closed her eyes and then nuzzled her cheek into the dog's muzzle. She felt the shifting weight of a heavy object in her coat.

'You don't need to take on this burden,' she whispered, her eyes still shut. 'Oh, my dear friend, you know you can get out now, before it all starts? I was the one who was chosen, not you.'

The dog moved its head away from Mary's cheek and tugged at the arm of her coat.

'Okay.' She smiled. 'You lead the way then.'

With that, the dog turned and trotted off towards the simple window set in the concrete wall on the other side of the floor. The animal's nose arrived at the protective metal bars several seconds before Mary's footsteps stopped behind him. Standing by the animal, Mary peered through the bars and gasped. The London skyline had been transformed into a dreadful spectacle. A huge blood red moon filled the sky. It was as if the entire city were ablaze and the moon was a gigantic mirror reflecting the raging flames into the very fabric of the heavens. In all her days, Mary had seen nothing like it. Her hand searched for the dog's shoulder to find a familiar anchor. The animal snapped at the giant moon hanging low in the sky. Sensing the onset of the eclipse seconds before she could see it, Mary tightened her grasp around the dog's fur.

In that moment, the sharp outline of the earth's shadow became visible against the moon like a silent advancing tide. As the black margin edged further across the moon's face, the sky darkened.

The silhouette of a lone construction crane stood like a miniature flag against the moon's receding circle. Even though the crane stood some distance away from the car park, its base lost in the silhouette of the skyline, Mary knew its exact location. Like a pointer, it marked a building site in an ancient area of London known as the Minories. The name sent a cold chill racing down her spine. Soon the outline of the crane became consumed in the eclipse's unstoppable wake.

Mary felt her heart quicken at the advancing line of blackness. The crane stood on cursed ground. The construction of the Minories Hospital had transformed the surrounding area aboveground, but nothing could erase the darkness that lurked beneath. It had once invaded her and tried to make her its own.

CHAPTER 8

The striking white-stoned profile of St George-in-the-East stood brightly in its overgrown grounds. The sound of salsa music burst forth from the small crypt window. Directly outside the narrow grass-level opening, accompanied by the big brassy sound of horns and Afro-Cuban percussion, a small dog bounded after an insect awoken by the glorious sunshine.

At this time of the morning, the Nigerian housekeeper had the place to herself. As her ample bottom moved in time to the bongos and timbales, her hands plunged into the large sink of soapy water. Every few seconds, she plucked a coffee cup from the sink and deposited it onto the drying cloth by her side. Up until now, she had had two loves in her life: Jesus Christ and Salsa dancing. Maybe a third was on the horizon, God willing.

She had met a certain gentleman at her Thursday night dance lesson six weeks ago. Since then, she had felt the happiest she had in ages. They had hit it off from the moment the music started. He worked as a tube train driver and lived in Bethnal Green with his son. Over the weeks, they had danced and laughed and laughed and danced, each week getting a little closer. As he helped her on with her coat at the end of a lesson, he confided that he had been widowed in his early forties and had recently been feeling low. She was a ray of sunshine in his life, he had told her. *Yes, a ray of sunshine,* she thought, as her fingers located a stray teaspoon within the watery suds.

All of a sudden, the sound of paws scurrying on flagstones made her turn around. A small dog with a bottlebrush tail started jumping up at her, its black and shiny eyes beckoning her to follow. She leant her head back and sighed.

'Yes, yes, my gorgeous child. You want me to play with you outside?' she said as she dried her hands on her flower-print dress.

Minutes later, the housekeeper and Reverend Jackson's dog were out in the sunshine. By the time she turned the corner into the church gardens, the dog had already disappeared, only its yapping leading the way.

'I'm coming, I'm coming,' said the housekeeper as the dog's chatter turned to a full-scale bark. She rounded the west wall and surveyed the flowerbeds for the sign of a tail bobbing between the beds of daffodils. She quickly realised that the barking was coming from a recess in the wall further up ahead.

As she got closer, a sense of unease began to build around her, like a coil getting tighter and tighter. Reverend Jackson's dog appeared from the recess in the wall. It had stopped barking and just stared back at the housekeeper, its eyes edged with confusion and panic. A strange spinning nausea churned inside the housekeeper's stomach. Then she saw it, and a scream exploded from her chest. The scene was monstrous. The whitewashed wall of the alcove was streaked with long crimson trails of blood. At the base lay the horrifically mutilated body of a naked woman.

CHAPTER 9

DCI Lukas Milton zipped up his crime scene overalls and waved back at the forensics officer at the entrance to St George-in-the-East. The church's white facade almost shone in the bright sunshine. The Afro-Caribbean police officer looked up and took in the strange and powerful profile of the building, its silhouette more in keeping with a castle than a typical church. After exchanging pleasantries, Milton and the forensics officer started walking and their conversation quickly turned to the facts.

'Female, 32, Nicola Booth, no fixed address. She was staying at a shelter run by the church.'

'Who found the body?' asked Milton as he adjusted his tinted glasses.

'The Vicar's housekeeper. She had to be sedated. It's quite a mess. The church safe was also cleared out a couple of days ago.'

'No CCTV I presume?'

'It's a church, they don't have the money for CCTV. The photography boys are nearly done, and then we'll start the sweep of the church grounds,' she continued.

They wound a route past the front of the church onto a gravel path circling the building.

'You worked the last job here?' asked Milton.

'I did,' said the forensics officer. 'We've just walked past the spot.'

The crunching of gravel underfoot stopped and they turned around.

'Just past that door,' nodded the woman, her face dappled in the morning sunlight. A heavy wooden door was set into the wall, its hinges shining with layers of black enamel paint. 'They kept the garden tools in there,' she said. 'The boss tells me that Hart escaped from Broadmoor a couple of days ago.' Her words were punctuated by long pauses while she considered her thoughts. She turned to Milton. 'That bastard needs to be taken down.'

Milton straightened up and scratched at the dusting of a beard around his chin. 'We'll get him,' he said, his voice sounding like dry leather.

'I mean permanently,' said the forensics officer. 'What that monster has done here, it's inhuman.'

A deep crease formed between Milton's eyebrows. He nodded in acknowledgement, and the two officers walked in silence along the path.

They turned the corner and Milton felt a cool breeze ease past his cheek. Ahead, standing up against an alcove in the wall, was a large forensics tent. 'Metropolitan Police, working for a safer London' was displayed on the side. Milton slowed as he approached and felt unease build in his gut. He ducked under the tent entrance and immediately sucked in air. His eyes tried to take in the scene.

'By the volume of blood, she was very much alive when her throat was cut. Probably standing,' said the forensics officer, who joined Milton in the tent. The body of a naked young woman lay some ten feet away from the wall. Long lines of dark blood daubed the white back wall like a macabre firework display. The grass surrounding the body was pebbled with large drops of dried blood.

The forensics officer followed Milton's eyes around the scene. 'The carotid artery must have been still pumping hard to make this pattern on the plasterwork,' she said. 'Her throat was cut twice, left to right.'

'Right handed,' said Milton as he scratched at the side of his face and moved around the body.

'The victim was laid on her back and then the killer—' the officer screwed up the sides of her eyes, '—performed these mutilations,' she said with chilling simplicity.

Cut deep into both cheeks were two inverted V shapes. The cuts were obviously made by a long sharp blade.

'Both upper eyelids have been removed,' she added, as small tics of revulsion fired across her face.

Milton frowned and continued to look into the large doll-like eyes staring up at him. 'This alcove provided him with perfect cover. He wouldn't have been seen by anyone walking in either direction, not until they were level with him.' He rubbed his flat nose and then tilted his head to the side. He glanced at the timeworn stone inscription set into the base of the wall. The date 1729 could still be made out in the lichen-speckled granite.

'There's something else sir.'

'Okay,' said Milton.

The officer crouched down and shuffled closer to the corpse.

'Another incision has been made into the victim's body, here.'

The forensics officer pointed to a line cut into the skin, two inches long to the right of the victim's navel. Although the cut wasn't deep, it had lifted an area of skin from the connecting tissue.

'Something had been placed under her skin.'

'Something?'

The officer hauled herself up and walked over to her forensics holdall. She picked out a clear plastic evidence bag and handed it over to the DCI.

'What the hell is this?'

'It's a coin,' she paused. 'A Roman coin, I think.'

Milton raised the bag and squinted at the metal disc adhering to the side of the plastic. It was about an inch across and dark with blood.

'Once you've tested it for DNA, I'll get Blake to have a look at it.'

'Vincent Blake?' asked the woman.

'The very same,' said Milton, not looking up from the coin. 'You know him?'

'By reputation,' said the officer. 'Does he know about these things?'

'When things get crazy like this, there's no one better,' replied Milton, handing her back the bag.

From outside the tent came raised voices, followed by the loud barking of a dog. Milton and the forensics officer exchanged glances and then moved outside to locate the disturbance.

'Just some tramp causing trouble.' The officer lost interest in the noise and stepped back inside the tent.

On the other side of the church gardens stood a dishevelled figure whose back was to Milton and who was being cautioned by a uniformed constable. Milton could hear everything.

'I'm going to have to ask you to leave. This is an active crime scene and it is prohibited for you to be here.'

A large black dog paced the two figures, all the time looking up at the tramp's face.

The tramp said nothing and rocked gently from foot to foot in a grimy full-length coat.

'This is your final warning. If you don't leave now, madam, I'm going to have to place you under arrest.'

The homeless woman shrugged her shoulders and turned to get one final look at the church.

Milton's interest in the figure sharpened when he saw her face. He had an eerie feeling of recognition. For a moment, he thought his mind was playing tricks with him. He had walked past her picture a hundred times on the incident board outside his office. Milton tore off his glasses. She was now staring directly at him. Despite greasy hair falling around her face in large tangled clumps, Milton could make out her wild and haunting eyes. He felt impaled by her stare. Without warning, Milton rushed forwards.

'Stop that woman,' he shouted to the constable as his bulky frame gained momentum.

The constable reached out to grab the woman but grasped thin air as the homeless woman slipped past him. A heavy object shifted in the pocket of her coat. She pulled it close to her, running towards the road.

As the constable turned to take chase, his path was quickly blocked by the black dog. It bristled with threat, saliva trailing from exposed fangs. It paced up and down while growling fiercely. Milton slowed to a walk and edged towards the animal through the tall shadows falling on the grass.

'Good dog,' he said hesitantly, keeping one eye on the dog and one eye on the tramp climbing over the low wall onto Cannon Street Road.

A shrill whistle sounded, and the dog pushed forward on its hind legs to sprint at full speed after the woman. It disappeared over the wall in seconds. Milton followed behind running as fast as he could. After pulling himself up onto the wall, his eyes raked up and down the busy road. His focus quickly locked onto the woman, who was half walking and half running pushing her way through a wall of pedestrians.

For a moment, Milton considered his options and then swallowed hard. The wall was only two brick-widths wide. After wiping away the salty moisture from his forehead, he raised his arms by his sides and started to run on top of the wall like a tightrope walker rushing back to safety. Soon he was moving fast, unimpeded by other people. He avoided looking down as he jumped over a gap in the brickwork. He was gaining ground on the woman. She was now only twenty feet ahead. His chest burned. He could see the dog by her side weaving through the legs of shoppers and office workers moving along the pavement. The dog noticed him first. It growled a warning. Alerted by the dog, the tramp stole a glance over her shoulder and quickened her pace.

All of a sudden Milton's foot slipped, knocking him off balance. For several tottering steps, and propelled by his forward momentum, Milton managed to stay upright. But as his body lurched out of control, his legs began to buckle. Instead of falling into the pavement, his large frame teetered to the opposite side. He came down hard onto a pile of bricks abandoned on the edge of some park ground close to the church. A jolting agony ripped through his shoulder, and his eyes screwed shut as he recoiled from the pain.

CHAPTER 10

The rain drummed heavily on the roof of Blake's red Alfa Romeo. He looked through beating windscreen wipers to the inconspicuous wooden door of the mortuary on the other side of the road.

After turning up the collar of his jacket, and cursing himself for leaving his overcoat at home, he ventured out into the deluge. Cold rain splashed into his face as he hand-locked the car door. By the time a safe gap in the traffic opened for him to cross the road, chilled rivulets of water were running down his back. Thankfully, he was buzzed through the door quickly, and he shook the rain off in the foyer. After signing himself in, he was escorted to examination room three, where Dr Sullivan, the forensic pathologist, and DCI Milton were in deep discussion, standing either side of a table of shining surgical instruments. The smell of disinfectant hung in the air.

'Still raining, then,' said Sullivan, enjoying the spectacle of Blake looking like a drowned rat.

Blake didn't answer.

'Right, let's get this thing done.' Milton walked over to the body laid out on the examination table at the centre of the room.

Dr Sullivan tapped on a floor switch and the corpse was suddenly illuminated in a strong white light from overhead.

'Shit,' Blake breathed out. Milton had warned him about the details of the crime, but the ferocity of the victim's wounds made his stomach churn.

The portly pathologist glanced up at Milton, who gave a small nod to begin.

'Right, the victim is in her early thirties, 5 feet 4 inches in height, weight 111 pounds.' Dr Sullivan circled around the table to the head. 'Working our way down the body, both eyelids have been removed and, by the lack of surrounding trauma, with a very sharp blade,' said

Sullivan. Blake looked down at the utterly empty eyes staring up at the light.

'Symbols have been cut into the cheeks, two on each side,' Sullivan continued.

'What do you make of those?' asked Blake, his eyes narrowing.

'No idea,' said Milton. 'Two sets of upside-down Vs, it looks to me,' he offered blankly.

Blake gave a shrug.

Turning the victim's head to the side, Sullivan continued. 'The lobe of the ear has been torn, consistent with the forced removal of an earring.' The pathologist returned the woman's head to its original position. 'There is also a slight laceration to the side of the tongue. Now for the major area of trauma.' The pathologist leaned forward. 'The neck has been cut through twice. On the left side, about an inch below the jaw, an incision about four inches in length which runs from a point immediately below the ear. The second incision is an inch below the first and extends all the way to the right carotid artery.' Sullivan's gloved finger annotated his commentary.

'The cuts are extremely deep. The laceration through the larynx, just above the cricoid cartilage, is down to the vertebra. The fifth and sixth vertebrae are deeply notched.'

Blake grimaced and straightened his back.

'The large vessels of the neck on both sides have been severed. The cuts must have been made by a long-bladed knife, and were obviously inflicted with a great deal of violence. Cause of death is exsanguination. The copious blood at the scene and the lack of bruising around the neck don't suggest asphyxiation. We'll get the toxicology results back soon.'

Blake took a step back from the body, relieved that the narration had apparently come to an end.

Milton shot him a serious look. 'That's not all,' he said.

'Indeed,' said Sullivan. 'There are distinct bruises, each the size of a man's thumb, just below the clavicle, here.' The pathologist put his thumb above the mark on the left side of the body. 'This position is over a pressure point. Enough force will disable a person. Two other things:

look here on the right hand.' Sullivan raised the corpse's hand several inches off the stainless-steel examination table. 'There are distinct ridges in the skin of the victim's proximal phalanges consistent with the wearing of rings. Abrasion marks around the knuckles suggest they may have been removed by force.'

'The forensics team found three silver rings in the grass next to the body,' added Milton. 'It looks like the killer tried to take them off in a hurry and then discarded them.'

The policeman noticed Blake's brow pinch forward.

'Sorry gentlemen, I still don't know why I'm here? You could have told me this over the phone,' said Blake, throwing a glance over to the policeman.

'That leads us to the last observation,' said Milton. 'Dr Sullivan, please carry on.'

'Dr Blake, look here.'

Blake followed the pathologist's gloved finger to a two-inch incision mark to the right side of the corpse's navel.

'A single shallow incision has been made to raise the skin and subcutaneous fat away from the muscle to form a pocket.'

'A pocket? A pocket for what?' Blake asked.

'For this,' Milton answered, handing over an evidence bag to Blake. 'It's okay, the forensic boys have finished their tests on it. You can take it out.'

Hesitantly, Blake peered into the bag. A dark disc of metal was nestled in one corner. He flattened his palm and slowly tipped the coin into his hand. It felt cold and heavy against his skin. Blake lifted it to the light.

'It's a Roman coin, right?' said Milton.

A silence fell as Blake turned the object in his fingers.

'Not exactly,' he finally replied. 'I know precisely what it is.'

CHAPTER 11

'Welcome to Broadmoor gentlemen,' said the senior psychiatrist as he shook their hands in the security control room. Dr Boltzmann was in his early forties and had thick hair and a close goatee beard peppered with flecks of ginger. He was well presented, lean and tall, and a faint smell of expensive cologne followed him around the room.

'I presume you have completed your security briefing?' asked Boltzmann.

The two visitors nodded.

'A necessary precaution, I'm afraid.' To underline the point, the psychiatrist pulled down on his tie, which came off in his hand. 'All staff ties are of the anti-strangle, clip-on variety. The men here can be unpredictable and violent.'

Blake and Milton had completed their security briefing in the facility's red-brick reception centre. The same security briefing was given to every visitor about the required safety protocols when in close proximity with some of Britain's most notorious criminals; people who represented a grave and immediate risk to the public. One such person was Enoch Hart, a man too dangerous to be managed anywhere else in the penal system.

During the security briefing, Blake and Milton were starkly warned about leaving objects of any kind within the areas used by the inmates. In the wrong hands, anything could be made into a weapon: the handle of a plastic spoon could be fashioned with sandpaper into a highly effective dagger; the shards from a splintered compact disc could inflict catastrophic injuries. As a result, all personal items were left at the front door.

Inmates at Broadmoor had time on their hands. Unlike a prison sentence, a stint at Broadmoor had no release date. *There's doing time and there's doing Broadmoor time* was an oft-quoted phrase within the institution. Without the hope of a release, idle hands often got up to abhorrent purposes. The threat of violence was never too far away.

Waving his hand up to the bank of screens in the control room, Boltzmann continued. 'Patients can only move at certain times of the day and in certain configurations. Flare-ups between patients and staff are commonplace. Patient movements are closely monitored via CCTV.'

Boltzmann smiled at his two visitors and then steered them out of the control room.

'My office is in the Cranfield suite at the other end of the hospital. We'll take the causeway,' said Boltzmann. 'After all, the sun appears to be shining today.'

An open-air walkway cutting through the centre of the facility; the causeway was essentially a rectangular tunnel made of heavy-duty steel mesh. The structure was used to transport staff and hospital supplies across the hospital grounds.

The psychiatrist nodded up to the CCTV camera above the heavy security door at the far end of the corridor. A buzzer sounded, and the door's internal locks snapped open. Boltzmann pulled open the door and waited for Milton and Blake to step into the fresh air before closing it. A buzzer sounded again to confirm that the door had locked successfully behind them. The psychiatrist took the lead along the causeway.

'Tell me DCI Milton, how is Chief Constable Lewis? I've played a couple of rounds with Peter from time to time, but I haven't caught up with him in ages.'

As Milton and Boltzmann chatted, Blake trailed a couple of steps behind, taking in the grounds. From the reception centre, the causeway ran through several hundred feet of well-maintained lawns before joining a block of red-brick buildings housing the Cranfield suite and Boltzmann's office. The deceptively quiet grounds gave the impression of a residential business college rather than a maximum-security hospital. The sound of bird song warbled behind Blake's shoulder. He turned and peered through the metal mesh to the ground to locate the trill notes. A small blue tit jumped out from behind a clump of grass and flew up into the faded denim sky. Blake's eyes, however, didn't follow the arc of the bird skywards but instead remained fixed on the small patches of purple flowers dotting the grass. He tugged at his ear as he squinted through the mesh to catalogue what he was seeing.

The sound of other voices drew him back into the moment. Three men had exited a door at one end of the Cranfield suite and were now walking outside the confines of the causeway on the lawn in their direction. The leading man's hands were bound behind his back whilst the other two, dressed in white hospital tunics, escorted him across the grass. The prisoner was a small man with spiked bottle-blond hair and incongruous dark eyebrows. As they walked towards him, Blake became aware that the man's gaze had locked on to him. Looking down the length of the causeway, it suddenly dawned on Blake that he was now some way behind Milton and Boltzmann.

Suddenly, a rapid movement shifted in Blake's peripheral vision. In the blink of an eye, the prisoner sidestepped his escorts and was running directly towards him. Even though his hands were tied, the prisoner's progress was rapid across the grass and easily outpaced his guards' lumbering pursuit. Blake took a couple of steps backwards until his shoulders rested on the back meshing of the walkway.

Like a missile smashing into its target, the prisoner clattered his shoulder into the meshing. His eyes flashed with fury at Blake. They were the blackest eyes he had ever seen, like circles of obsidian. Sending white flecks of spit through his clenched teeth, the man hissed something as his head lashed from side to side. Alerted by the guards, Boltzmann was already running back towards Blake, demanding that he keep his distance.

A strange rattling noise came from somewhere deep in the prisoner's throat, and his eyeballs began to flicker erratically. His bared teeth were biting at the air.

'Eve can't blink,' he growled in a strange, guttural voice that seemed alien to the prisoner's slight frame. For a moment, Blake felt a blackness creep over him.

'What?' said Blake without thinking.

'Eve can't blink,' the prisoner hissed a second time, just as the first of the two guards arrived and pinned him to the fence. He was quickly followed by the second guard.

Moments later, within the relative safety of the causeway, Dr Boltzmann approached half running and scraping a hand through his hair.

'You okay, Dr Blake?' asked the psychiatrist in a concerned tone. 'I'm terribly sorry about that.' Boltzmann shot a glance to the guards, who were already manhandling the prisoner away from the fence.

'Can you please get the duty nurse to check his medication?' instructed the psychiatrist. 'I also want an incident report to be filed.'

Blake wasn't looking at Boltzmann; his eyes were firmly fixed on the prisoner, who was now completely compliant to the guard's directions. All the fierceness had disappeared from his face. No longer rigid with hysteria, the prisoner's head hung down in quiet submission.

'Let's get to my office,' Boltzmann suggested, embarrassed by the incident. Blake nodded, and the two men walked over to Milton, whose lips showed the hint of a playful grin.

'Can't leave you alone for a second without you finding trouble,' said Milton.

Blake returned the smile and brushed off the wasp resting on Milton's shoulder.

CHAPTER 12

Two things were different about the surroundings of the Cranfield suite. Firstly, the rooms and corridors were all in muted pastel colours, apart from the bright-red panic buttons that stippled the walls like some sort of infectious disease. The second was the proliferation of signs warning staff that they must wear personal attack alarms at all times. *We've entered a war zone*, Blake thought as they approached Boltzmann's office door. It was a heavy secure door like the others in the suite and was equipped with an observation hole. Boltzmann unlocked it with a swipe of a card and beckoned his guests to sit down as they entered the room.

The psychiatrist dropped into his leather chair and wheeled himself closer to his desk. He gave a cursory look at the single open manila file lying on its top and then cleared his throat.

'Medically speaking, Enoch Hart is a classic paranoid schizophrenic,' said Boltzmann. 'Delusions of persecution, chaotic thinking, auditory hallucinations. He is also very dangerous. He was on a four-person unlock protocol.'

'A what?' asked Blake.

'His cell could only be opened with four people present,' explained Boltzmann. 'Even the most routine tasks ran the risk of violence. He's the real deal. He admitted stabbing the vicar at St George's church in cold blood, and at his trial he showed no contrition for her murder. He crossed the line and he didn't even flinch. At one of our first interviews together, he told me that she had been possessed and had to be stopped.'

'And what about the other patients?' asked Milton.

'They didn't want anything to do with him. He's the kind of man that when he stares at you, you want to look away. He used to get into their heads.' He paused a beat and stared down his nose. 'Monsters don't live under your bed gentlemen, they live in your head.'

'Did his psychosis come out of the blue?' asked Blake.

'As far as we can tell, he experienced some kind of breakdown and religious conversion during his last tour of duty with the army. He was discharged and then started working for the church.' Boltzmann checked the file. 'He was working under the supervision of Angelo Ricard, that's right,' he said, tapping the entry in the file. 'Have you interviewed him yet?'

Milton shook his head and wrote the name in his notebook.

'Through medication and psychological treatment, we can make significant progress with our patients. Those who are receptive to our interventions often end up moving forward with their lives, heading for the light, so to speak.' Boltzmann repositioned himself in his chair. 'Hart was unreceptive to everything we tried,' he said coldly.

'This is a manhunt, pure and simple,' said Milton with conviction. 'Hart stabs the vicar of St George's in cold blood, admits the crime, gets sectioned and ends up in Broadmoor. Less than a year later, he escapes and then kills again in the grounds of the same church.' The DCI shut his notebook. 'We've just got to catch the bastard now.'

'You mentioned that Hart suffered from delusions of persecution?' asked Blake, hunching forward in his seat.

'Indeed.' Boltzmann rubbed the back of his neck. 'Probably the best way to answer your question is to show you his cell.'

'Lead the way,' said Milton.

The three men rose to their feet, and Blake and Milton followed the psychiatrist out of the door.

CHAPTER 13

Boltzmann led them along a windowless corridor to a guard station next to a security door. After waving to the guard sitting behind the reinforced glass screen, the door opened and the three men stepped through, only to be confronted by yet another door some ten feet further ahead. Boltzmann gave a half-smile to each of his visitors in turn as they waited for the first door to close before walking over to the next one. An alarm sounded overhead and, after the clicking of magnetic locks, the second door opened.

'Welcome to the front line,' said Boltzmann, as the three men stepped into the foyer. The space was brightly lit from overhead, with four patient cells leading off a corridor. The psychiatrist waved a credit-card-sized key over the reader on the closest door and gestured his visitors to enter.

'You'll understand better when you see this,' he said as he took a step back to let Milton pass.

'What the hell is this?' Milton said as his eyes travelled over the walls of the cell. He turned with a troubled frown as Blake entered after him. Hart's secure living quarters were about the size of a small hotel room and had a bed, sink, simple bookcase, upright locker and small writing desk.

Blake tried to take in the sight that had just met his eyes. Pinching his lips tight, his gaze darted over the scene. The walls of Hart's cell were covered with sheets of paper of all sizes: pages of books, handwritten notes, sketches all stuck closely together, like the scales of a fish.

'Fascinating,' he muttered in a voice almost too quiet to be heard.

As Blake continued to systematically examine the walls, Milton took Boltzmann aside. 'All this needs to be photographed by the forensics team.'

The psychiatrist nodded.

'So he was transferred out of here to a local hospital the day before his escape?' asked Milton.

Boltzmann nodded again and then shifted on his feet.

'He was rushed out of here, as a medical emergency. Minutes after he had raised the alarm, he was convulsing and unconscious. His face was swollen and red. According to the medical team, his vital signs were critical.'

'And yet less than twenty-four hours later he sawed through the side of a hospital bed and escaped, under the noses of a pair of police officers,' said Milton.

The psychiatrist blew out air from the side of his mouth. 'Yes, but you need to understand who you are dealing with. Hart is a very capable, and treatment-resistant, paranoid schizophrenic. With a psychotic disorder, the patient's sense of reality is different from yours and mine. He believed he was engaged in some kind of holy war. When I first started to work with him, he told me that the vicar he murdered was possessed by a demon. He was totally unrepentant, saying that the woman's soul had already passed into hell.'

Milton glanced over Boltzmann's face as he continued, his lips feeling unnaturally dry.

'In those early days, Hart would at least talk to the other patients. He took a job in the workshop. Carpentry, that kind of thing. But soon after our rehabilitation work started, he withdrew into his own world. He spent less time in the workshop and more of the day alone in this cell—' Boltzmann paused, shuffling the words in his head, '—preparing.'

'Preparing for what?' asked Milton.

'For holy war. He had the delusion that a great battle was coming and that he would be called upon to carry out an important mission. Hart is a highly trained soldier. Damn it, he was in the bloody SAS for two years. He spent his days in here like some kind of warrior monk: praying, doing power yoga and reading. He often refused to eat more than one meal a day, preparing his body for whatever was to come.' Boltzmann's face stiffened with conviction. 'Be very careful when you track him down. He's a one-man army.'

'I need a list of the books that Hart borrowed from the library,' said Blake, causing the two other men to turn around. 'Some of these pages bear the stamp of the prison library.' Blake stepped back from the wall and pointed up to several sheets.

'Hart read so much, it almost became his personal library,' said Boltzmann.

'You think there might be something?' asked Milton.

'Possibly,' replied Blake. 'Look here.' He crouched down and pointed to a loose collection of pages stuck at waist height on the wall.

'Numbers, rows of numbers,' said Milton.

'Not just numbers,' replied Blake, 'these are extracts from the Astronomical Almanac.' He looked up at the blank expressions of the other two men. 'The Astronomical Almanac is considered the worldwide reference book for astronomical data. Several of its sections are concerned with the positional coordinates of the sun and moon: where they will be precisely located in sky at particular times of the year.' Blake turned his body so that Milton and Boltzmann could see two further pages. 'And these are to do with lunar eclipses.'

Milton's eyes widened.

'The murder at St George's took place on the night of a blood red lunar eclipse,' said Milton.

'Right,' said Blake, who then stood up and straightened his back.

'You see anything else?'

'There is one thing,' said Blake. 'There must be a hundred pages from the bible on these walls.'

'Okay,' agreed Milton, his eyes darting over the wall behind Blake.

'As far as I can make out, they only come from three different books of the bible: Acts, Joel and Revelation. Some of the pages are repeated time and time again.'

'And what is the significance?' said Milton.

'Don't know,' shrugged Blake. 'Get me copies of the photographs when they're done and I'll take a closer look. I also need a full inventory of the books on these shelves.'

Blake moved over to the small bookcase jam-packed with volumes of all different sizes. He slowly traced the spines of the books.

'He certainly had eclectic tastes,' said Blake. He began to lever out a small volume from the shelf, but his focus was drawn upwards to something lying on the top of the bookshelf. After a moment, a faint glint of recognition flitted across his face.

'The cell hasn't been touched, correct?' said Blake, looking over to Boltzmann.

Boltzmann affirmed the question as he tried to read Blake's face, which was now level with a small plant pot sitting on the top of the bookcase. A distinctive purple flower adorned the top of a velvety green stem several inches in length. Blake studied it for a moment. 'Monkshood. It's known as that because of the shape of the flower. In some parts of Europe, it's also known as Soldier's Helmet or Storm Hat.' He paused dragging another fact from his memory. 'Old Wife's Hood is the other name, I think.'

'I see,' said Milton, who took a step closer to scrutinise the single helmet-shaped flower.

Blake went on. 'I saw some growing outside. It's actually reasonably common around here.'

'Sorry, I don't understand?' said Boltzmann in a slightly bemused tone.

'Monkshood is very toxic, ingestion even in small amounts can result in severe reactions; violent tremors and rapid changes in heart rate,' answered Blake.

'Hold on, you think Hart poisoned himself?' said Boltzmann.

'I know so,' said Blake as he searched for a pen from the inside of his jacket pocket.

'How can you possibly know that?'

Blake picked up the stained coffee mug sitting a couple of inches to the right of the plant pot and tilted it so that the two other men could see its interior. With the end of his pen, he trowelled out the dark purple sludge from inside the mug onto the veneer top of the bookcase. Blake's pen prodded at the slimy gunk and prised out a wilted petal from the shiny amorphous mass. Even though the petal's original bright purple colour had blackened, its wilted shape could still be matched to that of the flower standing over it.

'You mean, he made a concoction out of these flowers and drank it down?' asked Milton.

'It wouldn't have taken much,' said Blake. 'The alkaloids in the petals are quite potent. I've heard stories of—' he swallowed, looking puzzled. Suddenly, he zoned out of the conversation, his vision lost in the middle distance.

'That's interesting,' he said as he dropped to his knees. His eye line was now parallel to the base of the plant pot. 'The level of the compacted soil is quite a bit higher than the lip of the pot. Raised up. I wonder?' he mused to himself. Quickly, Blake rustled around in his pocket and produced a handkerchief. He shook it open and then, using it as a barrier between his fingers and the stem, pulled the plant out of the pot. It came out easily along with a perfect cylinder of soil held together by a network of tiny white roots. Blake peered into the pot and took a moment to make sense of what he saw inside.

'You've got to be kidding?' Blake's face was brimming with amazement. 'You said that when Hart was rushed to hospital his face was burning, red?' he said, looking up to Boltzmann.

'Yes, red and raw, like he had reacted to something,' answered the psychiatrist, his face stiffening.

'I think I know what his body was reacting to.'

With that, Blake turned out the remaining contents of the plant pot onto the veneer top. The three men peered at the remnants of dozens of black and yellow wasps.

PART 2

Matthew 24:29

Immediately after the tribulation of those days the sun will be darkened, and the moon will not give its light; the stars will fall from the sky, and the heavenly bodies will be shaken.

CHAPTER 14

Diary Entry of Nicholas Hawksmoor
3rd May 1681

I set down in writing the events of quite an extraordinary day. For two years now, I have been the apprentice to the gentleman philosopher, Professor Christopher Wren. The Professor is undoubtedly a gentleman of the rarest genius. A man eminent in astronomy, mathematics, geometry and architecture, he has enriched many a subject with exceptional insights and has gained great favour with the King.

I have learned much from my master, but apprentices owe only a temporary postponement of their judgement till they be fully instructed, as opposed to perpetual servitude. Wren wants to parcel out wisdom into squares like a chessboard, everything ordered just so.

There is another branch of study that holds the key to a hidden world, that cannot be merely prodded and weighed out by experiment. I speak of the spirit world and its unseen agencies. For nothing is so real, as that which is spiritual.

I must be allowed to enquire and accept of both, without a breach of clarity. My mission is to bring into sight all that is most hidden and secret in the world. But Wren will not entertain a discourse on the subject. He admonishes me for my enquiries into the occult, but I have opened up the great map of knowledge and I am sailing the seas to discover new territories of hidden truth. In contrary, Wren's boat of enquiry is but bobbing in safe harbour, tied to the jetty by a tether of his own ignorance. He is a man who believes nothing, unless it is as clear as the three sides of a triangle, rejecting every esoteric notion, saying if it cannot be measured it cannot be real.

Two days ago we made coach for the great stone circle of Stonehenge on Salisbury Plain to take sight of the solar eclipse predicted by the Professor and his friend John Flamsteed of the Royal Observatory. The journey was slow and hard, and as our vehicle proceeded towards the pagan site, it rumbled greatly over the stones. The upward jerks of the axles threw our instrumentation heavily around our persons. During the journey we saw many vulgar, ignorant country people; not to mention dirty women with their infants giving suck without proper conduct or decorum. Often we understood not what they said. It is very odd to think that the Professor, supposedly one of the most learned men in all of London, could not understand what those chew-bacons in the country meant by their speech.

We arrived at our lodgings late, greatly fatigued and in need of sustenance. The innkeeper, though friendly and smart enough, was as lean as a skeleton and as pale as a corpse. Despite his hair being tidy and well combed through, his flesh was lank and had something of the colour of lead about it. After a hearty meal of ox tongue soup spiced with nutmeg and sliced lamb and kidneys topped with redcurrants, the Professor told the innkeeper the reason for our expedition.

Settling next to the fire, he mused to our host that on the morrow at the sight of the eclipse he would give test to his theory, that Stonehenge was in some fashion a pagan clock, its stones laid out at increments like the face of a timepiece measuring the movement of the heavens. He proposed that the exactness with which the Druids set the position of each stone within the circle was not the result of some chance. He supposed that their proportions fell into exact fractions and were fashioned to mark the sun's rising at the equinox and the position of the celestial bodies at important junctures of the calendar. The passing of a total eclipse, the most extraordinary event in the heavens, and so revered by astrologers, would afford a remarkable occasion for observation.

The innkeeper listened closely and after much thinking, chose to relay something his father had told him and his father before that. In the light of the flickering fire, his solemn discourse began with a playful warning not to reject too hastily the fables of the ancients, but instead to search out the latent truths that lay within.

The fire crackled loudly as he puffed on his clay pipe and spoke of what old Wiltshire folklore said on the matter. According to tradition, the Druid founders of Stonehenge built the sacred structure to a particular design to illicit great spiritual power, not as a static monument, but as a working engine of magical energy. Legend had it that the circle was so designed to counter and suppress some invisible evil force contained within the ground. The religious rites and sacrifices offered by the Druids at Stonehenge were all given in opposition to this dark subterranean presence, held in check, as it were, by the stones.

Though Stonehenge is the greatest of such rings still surviving on our island, the Druids had built other such designs, as far south as Cornwall and as far north as Scotland. It is said that a ring even greater than Stonehenge once stood in the City of London and was destroyed by the advancing Roman legions.

Swirling a draft of liquor around his glass, Professor Wren conceded that there was indeed a fable that the old stone, known as London Stone, interned in the walls of St Swithin's church off Cannon Street had once been part of such an ancient circle. Setting this aside, and whispering to me that the innkeeper's ramblings were nothing but claptrap, he bid the man goodnight and reminded me with no humour that we had to arise early.

In the morning I worked like a common pack mule carrying the master's instrumentation to the remarkable circle of stones. On arrival, their greatness and number astonished me. At first the Professor judged the ring's diameter to match the cupola of St Peter's in Rome, at 136 feet. But within the hour, we had surveyed the whole ground site and recorded that the circle had a smaller diameter of precisely 108 feet.

In their beauty and symmetry there was no denying. The presence of a single stone would have been worthy of esteem, but the boldness of the complete design was a thing of true wonder. Observing the general wear of weather upon the surface of the stones, the Professor recorded a date of some two or three thousand years of age in his notebook. Of this conjecture I have no idea, but of their remarkable antiquity there is no debate.

After our inspection of the stone circle, Wren set up his observation point exactly in the centre of the ring. I followed his line of sight to a specific sarsen stone with particularly impressive proportions. According to his calculations, the eclipse would appear directly above this stone. Whilst I took rest from my exertions, the professor set up his instrumentation in preparation for the remarkable occasion. Now I saw the reason for the weight of our luggage. Wren had brought so many devices for measurement, including wind up watches, metal theodolites of differing sizes, set squares and some strange inverted tube contraption, which I later understood was for safe observation of the discus of the sun on a sheet of paper, instead of viewing it directly with the naked eye.

Just before the hour of five in the afternoon the first intimation of the incomparable celestial event began. First the shade came freely over my right shoulder, then a murky blot broadened and heightened in the sky, advancing quickly and spreading over half the firmament. The sheep in the adjoining field bleated loudly, agitated terribly by the oncoming spectacle. Though the sun still looked very sharp, like a new moon, everything grew darker, together with the horizon on both sides of the ring.

When the eclipse came upon the sun's body, I could not in the least find any distinction between heaven and earth. It was all at once a dreadful and wonderful sight. A conspicuous circular iris moved across the sun and as it did so, the darkness became palpable, like a dark mantle, or a great coverlet of a bed, thrown over us.

I turned myself around several times, and the whole compass of the heavens and earth was inky black except for the light from Wren's lantern. Of all the things I ever saw in my life, or can by imagination fancy, it was the most tremendous. But instead of taking in the wonder of the sight, Wren was at work with his clocks and theodolite and scribbling notes into his almanac. Measure, measure, measure. Doesn't that wretched man ever take rest?

Suddenly light rays of perfect colours burst out from the edge of the circular occlusion. Moments later, after the sighting of the sun again, Wren pointed upwards to the planet Venus shining very plainly in the sky. As the light was propagated further, I heard larks chirping and singing very briskly for joy at the restored luminary. Like a morning emerging before sunrise, the natural colours of the heaven and earth were steadily re-established.

My amazement presently turned into silent anger directed towards the professor. To my astonishment, Wren was marking out the position of the total eclipse by carving his initials into the sarsen stone he had predicted upon, breaking bits off with his hammer and chisel as he worked. The sacrilege of this insolent folly saddened me greatly. This sacred structure had survived millennia of exposure to the wind and rain and now Wren, the ass, inflicted a greater destruction in that moment than in all of history.

What is the meaning of this eclipse of the sun that so exceedingly alarmed the whole nation? Wren measures the motions of the moon and the planets and then builds a very perfect model thereof, saying it is all but mechanics. How can this be, when its dreadful sight silences the animals and disturbs the spirit so? As I write out this letter; with the impression of the eclipse so vivid upon my mind, I have an obscure feeling that this extraordinary phenomenon was just a dim awakening of a hidden truth in my inner nature.

CHAPTER 15

By the signs of oxidation around the rim of the doorplate, Blake guessed that it had been attached to the oak door for some considerable time. Its once bright bronze finish had all but disappeared, and a greenish black tarnish had invaded the recessed lettering. Even so, the words were quite clear.

Professor Roland Ballard
Hunterian Museum

Though the two of them went back a long way, it was the first time that Blake had visited the Professor at his offices at the Hunterian Museum. The institution was a rarity in today's world of commercial museums. Part of the Royal College of Surgeons since 1813, the Hunterian was home to a unique and bizarre set of exhibits. Like the museum, Ballard was an anomaly, an individual who refused to be pigeonholed. He was a true polymath, with interests in Roman archaeology, London history, exonumia and anatomy. The Hunterian allowed Ballard the freedom to pursue multiple interests, unlike many other academic establishments.

Blake had come alone. He rapped firmly on the door and after hearing a muffled reply from the other side, he opened it.

'Ah, Vincent my dear boy. Come in, come in,' said Ballard getting to his feet. The academic was standing at his desk wearing an ill-fitting green and yellow tweed suit. With an enthusiastic wave of the hand, he beckoned his old friend inside.

Ballard's office had more resemblance to an antique shop than a place of scholarly work. Every horizontal surface, including most of the floor, was covered in a jumble of bric-a-brac and paper. Blake chuckled to himself; at last an office more untidy than his own. Blake's expert eye scanned the treasure trove of artefacts laid out on the sill of the large window that ran down one side of the room. One end of the ledge was reserved for a collection of medical instruments: forceps, scalpels, and antique brass microscopes. The other end of the windowsill displayed a loose grouping of brightly coloured pottery on several machined blocks of metal that looked to hail from the innards of some great mechanical engine.

The two men shook hands. Blake removed the pile of papers from the visitor's seat next to Ballard's desk and sat down.

'How are you bearing up, my dear boy?'

A shadow fell across Blake's face. His hand gave a seesaw gesture in the air.

'I am so sorry about Nomsa. What a terrible business. She was a remarkable woman. We all miss her very much,' said Ballard.

'Thank you, it means a lot to me,' he replied with a strained smile.

To change the tone, Ballard bounced up in his chair. 'You mentioned something about a coin?'

Relieved by the change in conversation, Blake pulled out a plastic evidence bag from the inside pocket of his jacket. He stretched over the desk to hand it to the academic.

'Can I?' asked Ballard.

'Be my guest, the police have already done their forensics on it.'

Carefully unsealing the top of the evidence bag, the professor turned out the coin onto his palm.

'My, my,' he said with an off-kilter grin, his other hand searching for the large magnifying glass lost in the mess of papers on his desk.

'It looked like an old Jewish shekel to me,' said Blake.

Ballard's enlarged eye blinked through the magnifying glass.

'You are partly right my boy. In fact, it's a Tyrian shekel to be more precise,' said Ballard with a serious look.

Blake watched in silence as the Professor closely examined the coin, rotating the object time and time again under the magnifying glass. Finally the Professor slumped back into his chair. 'You said it was found at a crime scene?'

'Yes,' said Blake slowly.

'In London?'

'East End.'

'Where precisely?' pressed Ballard.

'St George-in-the-East; it was found at the scene of a murder.'

Ballard's expression urged Blake to elaborate.

'A woman was brutally murdered in the grounds of the church. Her throat was cut down to the spine.' He cleared his throat. 'The killer cut a flap near her navel and placed this coin under her skin.'

'You found the coin under her skin?' Ballard said, backing away in his chair. For a second his eyes snapped shut. 'Horrible. Absolutely horrible,' he said finally. 'Whatever I can do, Vincent.'

'I'm trying to find out what the significance of this coin is and why the murderer would do such a thing.' said Blake as he leaned forward in his chair.

Ballard pursed his lips and then drew his attention back to the coin.

'Silver Tyrian shekels were minted in the city of Tyre, now in present-day Lebanon. They played a very significant role in Israel during the time of Christ. After the Roman army occupied Israel, they banned the Jews from minting their own currency. In Jerusalem, the Jewish authorities required worshippers in the Temple to pay a tax. The Talmud dictated that the tax could only be paid with a silver coin of high purity. These Tyrian shekels were the only acceptable coins available in Israel at the time that met the requirement of Jewish law. They were ten percent purer than the other Roman coinage.'

Blake nodded, riveted to every word the Professor was saying.

'And the depictions on the faces?' he asked.

'Well, there's the peculiar thing,' said Ballard as he handed the coin back to Blake. 'These silver coins presented the Temple authorities with a real problem. On the front is depicted the head of the god Baal, the chief deity of the Phoenicians, something that would have been highly blasphemous to the religious community, on the reverse is depicted an eagle.'

Blake turned the coin and restudied each face, but this time armed with the knowledge that Ballard had imparted.

'The image of Baal was a graven image and would have violated the First Commandment. Hardly an appropriate coin for the Temple if you think about it. So the Jews had a dilemma, reject the coin and have a meagre treasury, or accept it knowing that it depicted a false God.'

'So they chose to accept the money,' Blake interjected.

'Precisely, hence the growth of the moneychangers in the Temple courtyards. Worshippers would exchange Roman coinage for the Tyrian shekels so that they could pay the Temple Tax. And business being business, the moneylenders charged top dollar for their services. These were the money changers that Jesus fought with and whose tables he overturned in the bible.'

Blake leant back in his chair and quoted from the book of Matthew: 'My house will be called a house of prayer, but you have made it a den of thieves.'

'That's right, but there is something strange about these coins,' said Ballard twisting in his chair. 'If you look on the reverse side ...'

Blake turned the coin in his fingers. 'The side with the eagle perched on the pyramid?'

'Yes, yes,' confirmed the Professor. 'Run your finger over the design and tell me what you think.'

Blake's nose wrinkled slightly as his fingertips circled the coin's dull silver surface.

'An indentation?' said Blake with a furrowing brow.

Ballard nodded. 'It's the pyramid,' he said. 'It's a later addition to the coin. Tyrian shekels always follow the same design: Baal with the eagle on the reverse side. The pyramid, however, is totally out of place. My guess is that it was stamped into the coins at a later date. If you take a closer look, you can see that the eagle motif hasn't actually been designed with a pyramid in it all.'

The professor handed Blake the magnifying glass, and a moment later his enlarged eyes were blinking through it at the silver shekel.

Ballard was right. On closer inspection, Blake could now see that the eagle and pyramid did not make a coherent single design, but instead they formed two individual elements slightly out of line with each other.

'Well, I'll be,' said Blake with a streak of a smile darting across his face. His eyes continued to flick over the pyramid motif, its indentation now apparent in the coin's surface.

'The patina isn't too different between the eagle and the pyramid though. So the pyramid isn't a modern addition,' said the professor.

'I knew I had come to the right place,' Blake quipped.

'The thing is, my dear boy, I've seen this before. Twice in fact.'

Blake's smile faltered. He looked up from the magnifying glass and met the professor's eyes.

'There's another example within this museum's collection. Bring the magnifying glass. I'll show you.'

CHAPTER 16

Blake followed the professor through the Qvist gallery on the first floor of the museum to a large oak door at one end. After retrieving a key from his trouser pocket, Ballard unlocked it and flicked the light switch just inside the door. The lights blinked for a moment and then illuminated the small room in a bright white light.

Ballard offered Blake one of the two chairs parked under a modern-looking table. The room had no windows and almost all available space was taken up by shelving or by some type of specimen cabinet.

'Be a sport and put your coin on here,' instructed Ballard, his long finger tapping the table top.

Ballard slid his chair over to one of the specimen cabinets and busied himself with opening and shutting a number of its drawers. 'The Minories coin, I'm sure it's in here somewhere.'

Moments later, he clapped his hands in relief. 'Got you, you bugger.' In no time, a second coin had joined Blake's silver shekel on the table.

'Make sure you don't mix them up,' said Ballard. 'Left hand for the museum's property, right hand for the police coin, okay?'

'Okay,' agreed Blake.

Without picking them up, it was easy to see that the two metal discs were almost identical. Even the dark patina that burnished their surfaces were of similar hues and consistencies.

'Go on, turn them over,' said Ballard, handing Blake the magnifying glass. Blake carefully examined both coins. The coin from the museum displayed the same eagle motif as that of the coin extracted from the body of the church murder victim, along with the pyramid design stamped below it.

Blake returned the coins to the table and straightened out the kink in his back. 'So, Roland, where did this coin come from?'

'I dug it up,' Ballard said mischievously.

'Really?'

'During an archaeological excavation at the Minories, in the East End of the city,' said the professor as he moved his hand vigorously around his chin. 'The site was being cleared for a brand-new hospital. During the excavations for the foundations, skeletons dating back to the Roman occupation were uncovered. A protection order was raised by the City of London on the site and my team were given a month to survey what we could. For years I was convinced that the area east of the City walls had been of special significance to the Romans. In the final days of the dig, I started to uncover the outline of some kind of mausoleum. I was so bloody close.'

'A mausoleum?' Blake's tone urged him on.

Ballard passed a hand over his bald head, liberally flecked with liver spots due to years of sun exposure from archaeological digs. He stood up and shuffled past Blake's chair to the rack of shelving to the right of the door. With a tug, he pulled away the green material covering the large see-through plastic box underneath. A gasp escaped Blake's lips. Hurriedly, Blake moved the coins as the professor carefully transported the box to the table.

'This is what I managed to excavate during the last moments of the dig,' said Ballard.

Blake shifted closer, his eyes transfixed on the magnificent two-foot-high carved stone sculpture sitting in the box. The sculpture depicted a powerful eagle with a writhing snake in its beak.

'4th century AD,' said Ballard, 'made of Cotswold limestone. It probably depicts the victory of Roman power over pagan evil. Can you see inside the snake's mouth?'

'Sharp teeth,' replied Blake, his breath misting up the side of the box.

'The symbolism here is very unusual. A snake displaying sharp teeth represents ultimate evil. The only other Roman example of this eagle and serpent composition was found in Iraq in 1937. It's now in the Cincinnati Art Museum in the US. It was found adorning an impressive mausoleum that was later obliterated during the Gulf War. My guess is that this piece was part of a similar mausoleum. Our ground-penetrating radar surveys of the area had revealed the presence of a substantial structure around it.'

'It's a haunting sculpture,' said Blake his face brimming with curiosity. He shifted on his elbow while he took in the beautiful workmanship. 'Couldn't you get a temporary stop to the building?'

Ballard raised his brow sceptically.

'Bloody developers. They're all the same. I applied for three extensions to the dig, but I was rejected every time. You know the scene. Unless you have the right connections, it doesn't matter what you do. Doesn't matter if the bastards drive a bulldozer through something that hasn't seen the light of day in two millennia. It's all to do with money.' He scowled and his focus returned to the coins sitting to the side of the box. 'The Tyrian shekel I found at the site was directly underneath this sculpture. They almost came out of the ground at the same time.'

Blake sat back in his chair, and his upper lip disappeared under his bottom lip in contemplation. He looked at the eagle and then at Ballard, studying the broken veins across the academic's cheeks. After a little pause, his hand squeezed the armrest of his seat.

'You mentioned you had seen two Tyrian shekels before? Is the other one here too?' asked Blake.

'No,' replied Ballard. 'It's in the crime museum of Scotland Yard.'

Blake's mouth drew down in surprise. 'Scotland Yard?'

'Of course, that's where all the evidence is kept for the Jack the Ripper murders.'

CHAPTER 17

A wedge of hair seesawed down to the ground like a falling feather. Another snip and a new tuft glided downwards and landed on Enoch Hart's right foot. He kicked it away and discarded the kitchen scissors onto the hotel bed.

With a twist of the tap, steaming hot water cascaded into the white porcelain sink. Soon the outline of his face in the mirror disappeared in the steam. After ripping open a packet of disposable razors with his teeth, he dropped one into the sink of turbulent water. At first, the razor was caught under the pummelling stream from the tap, but it then shot out around the circumference of the basin like a small boat escaping from a storm.

Hart wiped the bathroom mirror free from steam and looked at his naked form. Would he be able to fulfil his mission? He smeared large dollops of white shaving foam across his head. Plucking the razor out of the water, he scraped it across his scalp. At first, the blade snagged small tufts of hair left by the scissors, but soon clear tracts of smooth skin became visible. After a while, Hart ducked his head into the sink and looked back at his handiwork.

He was a soldier and the war had just begun.

CHAPTER 18

Blake looked at the grainy image of his face printed on the Scotland Yard security badge around his neck. He was told by DCI Milton that visits to this museum were by invitation only and reserved for police officers, lawyers and other specialists in the field of crime. He guessed he fell into the latter camp. The white striations across his image caused by the defective printer at the reception area gave the impression that he was fading into the background; a pixelated apparition of a man. As he turned the badge in his hand, his eyes locked onto something that wasn't fading: the dark band of discolouration surrounding his left index finger, a birthmark he shared with his father. It was strange, but he could have sworn that it was becoming more pronounced.

His attention was brought back into the moment by the arrival of the museum's curator. He was a small man, wearing an out-of-date suit whose pockets gleamed with a dark shine.

'Dr Blake, I presume,' he said in a friendly manner. 'Welcome to the Black Museum.'

Blake had heard the museum's grisly nickname the night before during his daily status call with Milton. His eyes couldn't help but be drawn to the display case full of hangman's ropes. He swallowed loudly and his throat clicked. The curator followed Blake's line of sight, over his shoulder.

'Ahhh, the nooses. We hold an impressive display of ropes here at the museum,' the man said. 'The one on the far left was the one used to execute convicted murderer George Platts in 1847. We also have the ropes used to perform the last executions in Britain on 13 August 1964 of two criminals who bludgeoned a man to death to steal just £10.' Blake acknowledged the information with a reserved nod.

'But you are here for our most infamous collection.' With that, the man excused himself and disappeared into a side room before reappearing several moments later with a cardboard box file.

'Would you like to join me here at the examination bench?' The curator pulled a chair out from under the table with his foot. Blake walked across the room over to the table, and as he approached, he could make out the lettering on the yellowing label attached to the front of the box file.

Jack the Ripper
Annie Chapman

Blake sat next to the curator and listened intently.

'Between August and November 1888, five brutal murders took place in a one-square-mile area of Whitechapel in London. All the victims were prostitutes, and all except one were horrifically mutilated.' Almost reverently, the curator eased open the box file. 'Jack the Ripper may be the most infamous killer in all of British crime history. The Ripper's murders have gripped the world's attention for over a century, but the identity and motivations of the world's most notorious serial killer still remain a mystery.'

Blake took a deep intake of breath. 'I understand DCI Milton briefed you that I am particularly interested in the facts surrounding the murder of the second of the Ripper's victims, Annie Chapman.'

'Ah yes, poor Annie Chapman,' said the curator. 'Chapman's body was discovered early on the morning of 8 September 1888. Her body had been terribly mutilated, her throat cut savagely.' From the box, the curator handed Blake a copy of a black and white autopsy photograph of Chapman's body. Although the photograph had been taken with an early camera, the image clearly portrayed something of the true horror of Chapman's murder. Blake cringed at the photograph.

'The incision reached right around the neck and was applied with such force that the blade nicked the neck bone. Her throat was cut from left to right, and she was also disembowelled, her intestines thrown over her shoulders,' explained the curator.

'Very pleasant,' Blake murmured. As an officer in British Military Intelligence, Blake had seen his fair share of grisly sights, but the details of the Ripper murders were sadistic and almost beyond comprehension. He respectfully placed the photograph back onto the table and then asked the question he had wanted to ask from the moment he had heard of the Ripper connection from Professor Ballard at the Hunterian Museum. He cleared his throat. 'I understand that Scotland Yard is in possession of a number of coins found at the foot of Chapman's body.'

'You are absolutely correct. Full marks, Dr Blake. A small stack of three coins, including two farthings and a coin of foreign mintage, were found at the foot of Chapman's body.' The curator shuffled his chair closer to the box and peered inside. Silently, he picked through several brown cardboard files before extracting a small manila envelope. He opened it, and three brown coins dropped into his palm. One by one he transferred them from his hand onto the table. 'Be my guest,' he offered, sliding the shiny elbow of his jacket from the table.

Two of the coins shared identical dimensions and markings. Blake gave them a cursory examination. The small copper farthings were common currency in the reign of Queen Victoria, and the front face of each coin depicted the head of the monarch. Similarly, the reverse sides were identical, with Britannia, the female personification of Britain, sitting guarding the island nation with a lighthouse in the background.

The third coin was much larger. The face of Baal stared up to him from the Tyrian shekel, daring Blake to turn it over. With a slightly trembling hand, he reached down and felt the cold metal against his fingertips. He inhaled for a moment and then turned the coin over in his hand. Even with Professor Ballard's prior commentary, Blake could feel a spike of adrenaline hit his bloodstream. The coin had the same eagle and pyramid design as the other Tyrian shekels from the St George's murder scene and the Hunterian Museum. He brought the coin close to his face and angled it towards the bright light coming from a close-by mirrored display case of murder weapons. Although Blake didn't have a magnifying glass, he could clearly see the pyramid motif stamped into the silver.

He slumped back into his chair, his mind racing. Three seemingly identical coins forged in the city of Tyre two thousand years ago, all found in the East End of London, and two taken from horrific murder scenes. What the hell was the connection? Blake could feel the gears of his mind slipping out of control, unable to connect to anything solid.

'The other curious detail about the murder relates to Chapman's rings. On the night of her murder, Chapman was seen to be wearing her two brass rings. It would appear that the Ripper removed them from her fingers sometime during the murder. They were never recovered. All the pawn shops in the area were searched for the rings but without success.'

Blake raked his fingers through his hair. Days ago he was with Milton in the morgue looking down at the body of the woman murdered at St George's church. In his head, he could almost hear the voice of the forensic pathologist describing the abrasion marks on the victim's fingers. The marks being consistent with the forceful removal of the woman's silver rings, which were eventually found in the grass next to her body. The thought of a copycat serial killer lurking in the East End of London sent a chill running through his body.

'Why would a killer remove jewellery?' Blake asked. 'Is it always to sell them or as trophies?'

'Mostly, but not always. In certain cases, it's more complicated.'

'How so?'

The curator searched Blake's face, appraising him with his eyes. 'A few cases, the Ripper amongst them, have strong occult overtones.'

Blake raised an eyebrow.

'The museum record has interview transcripts of criminals who are involved in these types of practices. They describe certain rituals in which all metal is removed from the skin.'

Blake shook his head slightly.

'Metal is conductive, and these transcripts suggest that the perpetrators remove all metal to ensure that the dark energies called upon during the occult rituals are not disturbed by the metal's conductive qualities. Interestingly, a similar practice of metal removal is part of the Masonic initiation oath. In the ritual, the initiate is symbolically stripped of all metal objects, such as rings, watches and earrings.'

Blake looked back to the museum's coarse-grained black and white photograph of Chapman's body. 'At least there are no cuts on Annie Chapman's face,' he said in a voice intended just for himself.

'Not on Annie Chapman,' replied the curator. The man's answer hung in the air for a breath. 'There were some strange geometrical designs cut into the cheeks of the Ripper's last victim, Catherine Eddowes.'

'Designs, what designs?' Blake shot back.

'Her eyelids were cut and two upside-down capital V's were carved into both cheeks.'

'Like a pair of pyramids?' said Blake with tension in his voice.

'Mmmm, I guess so.'

'Why isn't any of this talked about?'

'There are lots of things about the Ripper case, and the infamous Ratcliffe Highway murder case before it, that have strong occult connections, but no one seems to want to go there,' said the curator.

'The Ratcliffe murders?'

'They are known as the Ratcliffe Highway murders, and in many ways they are even more bizarre and shocking than even the Ripper cases.'

'Never heard of them,' said Blake.

'They're never talked about,' said the curator. 'They happened in an area very close to the Ripper's killing ground. The Ratcliffe Highway was a road that led east from the Tower of London to Shadwell. During the ending months of 1811, two separate East End households were brutally murdered. The killings took place twelve days apart. The nature of these frenzied attacks was unprecedented and shook London to its core. The victims included a young mother and her baby who were clubbed to death with a heavy maul and slashed with a ripping chisel. You can still visit the gravestones of some of the victims. They are in the grounds of a church called St George-in-the-East. I don't know if you've heard of it? It's just off Cannon Street Road.'

'Yes, I know it,' said Blake. 'Did they get whoever was responsible?'

'Well, here's where the story takes a rather bizarre twist. Eventually, a seaman named John Williams was arrested for the murders. The night before his trial, he was found hanging in his cell. A mob gathered outside demanding Williams's body be handed over to them, convinced he had been possessed by some evil power. The body was handed over and paraded in the streets. In a ritual never seen in London before or since, Williams's corpse was bundled into a makeshift grave, and hundreds watched as his body was decapitated and a wooden stake was hammered into his heart.'

CHAPTER 19

Enoch Hart tracked the arrival of the blacked-out Mercedes four-by-four as it crept along the alley. Several seconds later, the vehicle emerged into an abandoned car park, where it made a long sweep before reversing up to a crumbling wall. Almost immediately, the front doors of the vehicle opened, and two figures stepped out onto the blistered tarmac. Enoch Hart observed the men from the darkness. He spent the morning staking out the area and assessing potential escape routes through the labyrinth of disused warehouse buildings. The location was ideal for the transaction. High fences, red-brick walls, only a single security light on a high pole in the centre of the car park. Quiet, not overlooked and, importantly, only one way in and out for a vehicle. He could easily control the angles.

Hart shifted in the shadows, moving closer to the two men leaning against the front bumper of the Mercedes. In the pale, muted light, their profiles couldn't have been more different. A thin, dreadlocked Rastafarian sharing the bonnet with a massive, white-skinned hulk of a man who looked like an Icelandic hammer thrower. He was the muscle, and the Rasta, the brains of the operation. Neither man looked like they had filed a tax return recently.

The muscle pushed himself off the bonnet and the car's suspension groaned with relief.

'Don't ya fret, he'll be here,' said the Rasta lighting up a cigarette. He sucked on its end and mouthed a ghostly smoke ring into the air. 'Everything's cool.'

From the side, Hart stepped out of the shadows, and his sudden appearance surprised both men. The Rasta immediately dropped his smoke and ground it into the tarmac with his heel. As the three men sized each other up, a cool gust of wind blew between them.

'The name is Eight Ball,' said the Rasta, tangled dreadlocks swaying in his face. 'And this is my business associate.' Eight Ball looked up at the man-mountain at his side and smiled a long, slow smile.

Even at his safe distance, Hart could smell the stench of cooking fat on the man, as if he had spent the day leaning over a roasting spit. The heavy stood tall with thick muscles and thinning, slicked-back hair.

'You come recommended,' said Hart, keen to get on with business.

'Ah yes, our mutual friend, Sidney,' recalled Eight Ball. 'You did time together?'

Hart nodded. Sidney the Spike was a psychopath with a penchant for armed robbery and torture.

'Wandsworth, right?' said Eight Ball dismissively.

'You pissing with me?' Hart's eyes tightened with suspicion.

'Where then?' Eight Ball's demeanour suddenly bristled with threat.

The hand of the hired muscle quickly tightened around the Glock 42 secreted in his coat pocket.

'Broadmoor, we were both in Broadmoor.' Hart's stance showed no sign of fear. 'The smart move would be not to play any more games,' he said coldly as he cast a scathing look at both men.

Eight Ball shrugged. 'Just wanted to check that you're the real deal.' He squeezed a handful of dreadlocks from the back of his head and let them fall around his shoulders.

'I was told by Sidney that you were the guy to talk to.'

'Any friend of Sidney's is a friend of mine,' said Eight Ball. 'We go back a long way,' he paused. 'We did a lot of business together, in the day.'

'I want to do some business now,' said Hart. He shifted closer to the Mercedes.

'Well, you've come to the right place my friend, this sweet shop is well and truly open for trade.'

Eight Ball exchanged glances with his heavy, who nodded and plodded to the rear of the car. He waited until his boss gestured to open the boot before pressing the button on his key fob. Rising on

German-engineered hinges, the boot glided open to reveal a faded green tarpaulin covering the boot well.

'Okay, what do you have?' asked Hart.

'What do we have? The only things we don't have are weapons of mass destruction.' Dragging the tarpaulin to one side, Eight Ball revealed the armoury beneath.

Hart's eyes darted everywhere to size up the cache of weapons. 'May I?'

'Be my guest, my friend. No charge for touching the sweeties, but if you want to take them home, then you'll need to talk to my accountant.' Eight Ball looked over to his hired muscle.

The boot of the Mercedes was a veritable buffet of lethal hardware. Hart moved through the inventory in his head: an Uzi complete with a mounted bayonet, a box of light anti-tank missiles, an aged AK47, three Calico 9mm submachine guns, a sawn-off Winchester pump action shotgun, a Claymore anti-personnel mine, at least a dozen Glock pistols of differing specifications, and a pristine box containing two Heckler & Koch MP7's.

Hart re-stacked some of the weaponry to one side to get a better view of the hoard buried beneath. His sight was immediately drawn to a familiar profile in the shadows. He reached down and liberated the weapon from its neighbour with a slight clattering sound of metal moving on metal.

'Ah, good choice, my friend. The Scorpion Evo 3. Light-weight, designed to be manoeuvred in tight spaces. Comes with a three-mode fire switch: semi-automatic, three-round burst, or hell-raising fully automatic. Very versatile.'

Hart locked his hands onto the grip and quickly racked the cocking handle. Nuzzling into the stock, he aimed the weapon upwards towards the security light blinking on the high pole in the centre of the car park. He pressed the trigger and a metallic sound clicked within the interior of the machine gun.

'Czech-made,' said Hart. He ran a finger down the muzzle before replacing the weapon into the boot.

Unsure whether the comment was a statement of fact or a question, Eight Ball continued with his sales pitch.

'You handle guns like a pro, my friend. Yes, Czech-made, stolen to order, direct from the ČZUB factory, 300 kilometres southeast of Prague. From there, overland to Boulogne and then sailed over the Channel, up into the Thames estuary. We are an international operation, my friend.'

Hart backed up a step and crossed his arms. 'One of the Glock 17's, the L118 sniper rifle, six grenades, the Scorpion and a silencer for the Scorpion.' Hart's eyes narrowed. 'And I'm going to need ammunition, lots of it.'

'Ammunition is no problem. Looks like you are about to start a war,' said Eight Ball fingering his dreadlocks.

'The war has already begun,' said Hart.

CHAPTER 20

Whilst the man sitting in the centre of the packed tube carriage had his eyes closed, he was far from asleep. His mind was very much alert and was rehearsing the speech he was about to give. He sensed that his juddering progress along the tracks of the London underground was about to come to an end.

'The next station will be Covent Garden,' announced the automated public address system in a comforting female voice.

Captain Sam Lambton slowly opened his eyes and immediately felt the stare of people upon him.

'I guess we're here,' he said as his frown softened into a smile.

A friendly hand from the seat next to his touched his shoulder. He gave a nod of his head and locked his hand onto the grip of his walking stick.

'Let's get started,' he said as the tube train decelerated.

When serving as an officer with the British Army's Explosive Ordnance Disposal (EOD) Regiment, the specialist unit responsible for bomb disposal, Lambton had been a striking man who stood well over six feet tall and had riveting cerulean blue eyes and thick, jet black hair.

Like all combat-serving members of EOD, he was selected for his ability to think clearly under the intense pressures of war. His role as a front-line bomb-disposal expert was reputedly the most dangerous job in the world, and Lambton had carried out his duties in two of the world's most perilous combat zones: the badlands of Iraq and Afghanistan. He soon earned a reputation as a cool operator, someone who could be trusted to make the right decisions in the most demanding situations.

In the last week of his final tour in Afghanistan, his luck finally ran out. Lambton was so good at his job that he ended up being targeted by the insurgents. They lured him in like a fish on a line.

The report of an abandoned car blocking the main road between Kandahar and Sangin in the north was enough to raise suspicions, but the two dubious-looking metal drums spotted on its backseats meant it was a job for EOD. Lambton was the obvious choice for the task. As he made the long and lonely walk to the battered Toyota pickup slewed at an angle across the desert highway, Lambton could see tell-tale wires emerging from the open drums, which had been filled to the brim with crude homemade fertiliser-based explosives, a particular favourite amongst Afghan insurgents. What he didn't see were the two additional devices made of state-of-the-art American C4 buried an inch below the road surface. Luckily for Lambton, only one of the charges detonated, but the single explosion that ripped through the right side of his body caused catastrophic injuries. He had all but lost the sight in one eye, his right arm and leg were severely damaged, and the side of his once handsome face was criss-crossed by a series of deep scars. Notwithstanding his injuries, Lambton still considered himself fortunate. He had seen many of his friends lose their lives in combat.

The army captain had forged a new life and career for himself. He was now a much-liked and respected public figure and a successful entrepreneur. His eighty-pound bomb disposal suit had been replaced by a business suit and his sometimes-present walking stick. Lambton always travelled by public transport, a rare activity for a public figure. It helped to cement his reputation as a 'man of the people'.

The ex-soldier shot a glance over his shoulder and saw the familiar blur of Covent Garden Station appear in the window. As the train stuttered to a stop, Lambton gritted his teeth and hauled himself to his feet. His knees seemed to creak in time with the carriage, and a gentle groan escaped from deep within his throat. He vigorously massaged his leg to coax some sensation back into the flesh.

The other passengers waited until Lambton secured his grip around the vertical hand rail near the doors before they started to move. Soon the sound of excited voices pulsed through the carriage.

The doors of the tube train clunked open and, after a moment, the captain's walking stick bridged the gap between the carriage and the platform. It was followed by the shuffling, stiff-legged gait of Lambton leading his stream of loyal supporters.

The captain could hear the crowds outside the Tube station even before the doors of the elevator had opened. He gave a small, self-effacing shrug and was soon corralled by his supporters through the entrance of the station into James Street.

Only then did he fully see the extent of the crowds that had gathered to hear him speak. Word of his impending announcement had spread like wildfire on social media. The news had ignited public interest in the man that many people were seeing as the new face of politics.

Lambton took in the scene for a moment and then presented himself to the crowd. Applause thundered all the way down James Street to the open piazza of Covent Garden and the stage that had been hurriedly erected for the occasion. As he moved along, the volume of the crowd rose behind him.

The audience tracked his slow progress towards the stage. Finally he emerged from the crowd and tried to take it all in. Moments later he arrived at the lectern facing a crowd of thousands. Lambton stood there and leant heavily on his walking stick before taking his familiar grip on the lectern, setting off another burst of applause.

'I am honoured to stand here today, and I am humbled by your kind welcome. Ladies and gentlemen, today marks a turning point. The beginning of a fight between two visions of our future.' His face was stiff with conviction. 'We can either forge a new path, or we can go on accepting the status quo. We can either build a future where dignity and integrity mean something, or we can refuse to confront the problem.' Lambton allowed his words to take root in the crowd for a second.

'In my London, all people are equal, from the youngest to the oldest, from the poorest and most disadvantaged, to the richest and most powerful. Everyone is equal. That is my starting position.' His voice rang out with authority.

'Who owns this city? Is it the people? Is it you or me? No, it's the faceless silent minority. It's the bankers, the media moguls, the industrialists, the hedge fund managers.' Scattered applause and shouts of approval echoed along the piazza.

'These people have perfected greed. They think they are invincible. But I stand before you today and I tell you, they are not. All of them have secret vested interests. They live in a world of protected entitlement. Where is the fairness in them receiving massive financial bonuses, large enough to fund a number of inner-city hospitals, whilst the ordinary worker is struggling to make ends meet? Inequality is rife in our nation.'

Lambton shifted his hold on the lectern.

'The powerful are living off the backs of the ordinary people and mortgaging the next generation. Let me ask you who's going to pay for it? It's the likes of you and me and our children, that's who.'

The captain, motioned to the crowd attempting to settle down the roar of applause that had just broken out.

'The present mayor of London is part of this system. He is part of the problem, not part of the solution. That is why today, I am announcing my candidacy for the mayoral elections.' Applause erupted again from the sea of faces ahead of him and swelled out through the audience.

'Today you see a battle-scarred man, a man who has to lean on this lectern for support,' he paused for effect and regripped the edges of the wooden stand. 'But today, with your support I feel strong. I humbly ask you to join me in the fight for our city. Will you join me?'

Applause blasted out from all directions. Feeling an overwhelming sense of relief, he closed his eyes and let the sound fill his body.

CHAPTER 21

'Can I get you a towel sir?' enquired the elegantly dressed male receptionist of Boodle's private members' club, the second oldest gentlemen's club in the world. Founded in 1762 and situated in the exclusive third of a square mile in London known as St James's, Boodle's was named after its austere first headwaiter, Edward Boodle. By the serious expression of the receptionist who had just handed Blake the towel, he could have been a direct descendant.

During the short walk from the tube station to the distinctive white facade of Boodle's club, raindrops the size of small marbles had started to pelt down on Blake. Now he stood bedraggled and dripping in the grand foyer of one of London's most prestigious clubs.

'Ah yes, Mr Blake. 12.30 luncheon with Mr Ricard, very good,' confirmed the man, consulting the reservation book at the reception desk. 'Sir, the rules of the club state that a tie must be worn at all times in the dining rooms. I hope this one is acceptable?' he asked, placing a plain silk tie on top of a white towel and handing them both to Blake. 'Let me show you to the bathroom and when you're ready, I'll take you to the dining room.'

As Blake was escorted across the foyer, his attention was drawn to the line of paintings that graced the walls. Noticing that they had caught his eye, the receptionist added a brief commentary.

'Portraits of notable Boodle's members. That one is of William Petty-FitzMaurice, 1st Marquess of Lansdowne,' he said, nodding up to the painting of the regal-looking man with a sword hanging from his waist. 'He was British prime minister during the reign of George III.' Blake said nothing and trailed the man. His shoes made a wet clapping sound on the polished marble floor. 'Here is William Wilberforce, leader of the abolition movement, and next to him Adam Smith, the famous Scottish philosopher and political economist.' The man stopped next to an unmarked wooden door and smiled up to the last portrait in the group. 'And Sir Winston Churchill, I think, needs no introduction.'

Blake disappeared into the bathroom and emerged a short time later, his hair roughly tousled. He pulled at the poorly knotted tie, first one way and then the other.

'Let me take you to Mr Ricard. He's waiting for you in the dining room,' said the man with a hint of disdain.

The dining room was a large airy space, filled by thirty or so mostly occupied tables and lit from above by an ornate cast-iron skylight. The percussive sound of raindrops bouncing off the glass high above filled the room. Blake could feel the eyes of the diners follow his progress through the centre of the room. As he wound a route between the tables, it became clear that their destination wasn't the open space of the dining room but a small private area off to one side.

They rounded a corner marked by a miniature laurel tree and then entered the discreet alcove. A handsome, bronzed man wearing a fine dark blue suit sat alone at the table. He peered over his glasses and then stood up to offer Blake a firm handshake.

'Mr Blake, very good to meet you. Please come and sit down,' said Ricard.

As Blake settled in his chair, the receptionist excused himself and was almost instantaneously replaced by a waiter wearing a light grey suit.

'Something to drink?' asked Ricard. 'A glass of white wine perhaps?'

'That would be nice.' Blake smiled. 'Thank you.'

Before he knew it, the waiter had draped a crisp linen napkin across his lap.

'Just a glass of wine,' said Blake returning the napkin to the table.

'Are you sure you won't stay for lunch?'

'Quite sure, thank you. It's a very kind offer, though.'

From over his shoulder, an elegant glass half-filled with straw-coloured liquid was placed close to his silver knife.

Ricard dismissed the waiter with an arch of his eyebrow. When the waiter left, Ricard leaned forward.

'Mr Blake, I read about that horrible business at St Paul's. It was simply dreadful.'

Not a day had gone by when Blake hadn't experienced some sort of flashback to the shootout deep within the foundations of the cathedral.

'I still can't quite believe that Ema Mats of all people was involved in anything so ghastly,' said Ricard, his face hardened with conviction.

The subterranean battle had left the industrialist Ema Mats and two notorious hitmen dead and Blake and a Vatican official seriously injured.

'You knew Ema Mats?' asked Blake.

'Of course, the Mat's academy is one of the best business schools in London. Ema Mats was very well known for her charity work in the East End.'

Instantly, Blake's jaw tightened. He fought the impulse to stab his fork into the table. Mats had blown a hole in his knee and was about to kill him with a hunting knife, save for the timely arrival of the tramp and her dog. Instead, Blake thumbed his chin for a second, picked up his wine glass and drained it of most of its contents.

'That's why I was so shocked to hear she had been involved,' said Ricard, with a concerned glance at Blake's wine glass.

Another waiter appeared out of thin air and within moments his wine glass was refilled. Blake mumbled a thank you and then settled back in his chair with his arms folded.

'Mr Ricard, as I said on the phone, I'm here concerning Enoch Hart.'

Ricard nodded and lined up his knife with the edge of the table.

'What can I tell you?'

'I'm sure it's no surprise, but Enoch Hart is the chief suspect in the St George's killing.'

Ricard slowly nodded in recognition.

'Hart's psychiatrist said that he was working under your supervision at the church, at the time of his first killing?'

Ricard crossed his legs and the toe of a pristinely polished black brogue poked out from under the tablecloth.

'Enoch Hart was an exceptional member of the parish. Committed, hardworking, a man who showed a great compassion for people.'

'What happened?'

'The pressures of his calling, I'm afraid. He was showing signs of exhaustion from his pastoral duties in the parish. He was given the time, space and love of his church family to recharge his batteries. At first, the church elders gave him some light administration duties.'

'He did the bookkeeping for the church?' said Blake.

Ricard nodded. 'Yes, he was a mathematical whizz and quickly got to grips with the church's finances.'

'So he had access to the safe codes in the church office?'

'Yes,' said Ricard. 'Regrettably, we didn't deem it necessary to change them after his incarceration. After all, he was in a secure psychiatric facility.'

'He cleared out the safe?'

'Some twenty thousand pounds in all,' said Ricard. 'All the church's tithes and collections for the last three months. We have had to apply for emergency funding from the ecclesiastical council just to pay the bills.'

Blake swept his gaze across the room and tried to reconcile the talk of a church funding crisis with the luxury of his current surroundings.

'And your role in the church?'

'I'm one of the lay church elders, I help where I can.'

'You were telling me about the events leading up to Hart's breakdown.'

'What do you want to know?'

'I understand you were in the church when Hart killed for the first time?'

'A terrible day, a truly terrible day,' said Ricard, his voice tinged with emotion. 'One of our parishioners was struggling with mental health issues. The church had reached out and offered her shelter and support. She had become very disturbed and asked for spiritual counselling. Hart and the vicar arranged a meeting with her at the church. I was doing some paperwork in the church office at the time.'

'Why Hart?'

'Hart was very experienced in this type of counselling and he volunteered to help. Aside from the fact that it's always best practice to have two counsellors at this type of meeting. There was nothing to indicate at the time that he would do something so awful.'

Ricard cast a worried look over the table. 'The screaming was monstrous. From what I could make out, our dear vicar tried to escape, but Hart caught up with her outside and—' he paused. 'Well, I think you know the rest. When I got there, it was too late. There was blood everywhere and Hart was just sitting there next to the body with the gardening fork in his hand.' He cleared his throat. 'And now he's done it again. Do you think we're safe? You know he was in the military before joining the church?'

Blake nodded. 'We are doing everything we can to put him back behind bars. Have you got any idea where he might be? Anything at all, no matter how small.'

'He was a private man, he didn't really socialise as far as I know.' Ricard picked up his glasses from the table and began to clean the lenses with the stylish silk handkerchief from his jacket pocket. 'I remember him saying that he was an only child and both his parents were dead. I have no idea where he could be. Do you think he is still in London?' he said returning his glasses to the table.

'Not sure,' said Blake. 'But you can stay underground for quite a long time with twenty grand in your pocket. Especially someone with Hart's type of training.'

Ricard folded his arms. 'I'm sorry I can't be more of a help.'

Blake gave a slight grimace at the dead feeling in his knee as he rose to his feet.

'Thank you for your time, Mr Ricard. And don't worry, we'll nail him. He'll make a mistake. He's probably made several already.'

Blake rummaged in the inside pocket of his jacket and located a small collection of business cards. He squared them up in his hands and handed one to Ricard, who scooped up his glasses from the table and examined it. The card was damp and the top left corner curved inwards like the ear of a dog.

'Please phone me if you think of anything,' said Blake.

'Absolutely,' affirmed Ricard.

The two men shook hands and Blake made to leave but paused and turned back to Ricard.

'Oh, and thank you for the drink.'

Ricard looked up from table.

'You are more than welcome, Mr Blake. Perhaps we can have lunch another time.'

Blake smiled and then began to weave his way through the empty tables towards the exit. It was only several hours later that Blake realised he was still wearing the tie given to him by the club's receptionist.

CHAPTER 22

Blake paused at the door to the physiotherapy suite. He had come to hate the place. Sarah's recent progress was painfully slow, and her frequent clashes with her therapist just made matters worse. Sarah was a strong-minded girl, just like her mother.

Perhaps that was part of the therapy? Engineered by the rehab clinician to ignite the desire to fight back, to prove her wrong. The sessions had often ended in tears and cursing, with the therapist and Sarah both staring coldly at each other over the no man's land of the walking bars. There had been no pleasantries during Sarah's rehabilitation of late, just the hard reality of the difficult work still to be done.

So when Blake heard laughter, like birdsong emanating from the other side of the door, he paused. It was Sarah's laugh of old, before the incident, infectious and full of fun. He was caught at the threshold, unsure whether to open the door and risk the laughter escaping forever, like air rushing out of a balloon. Blake's hand rested on the door handle, balancing on the tension of its spring. He closed his eyes and drank up the giggles of his daughter.

Eventually, he just couldn't stand it any longer and pressed down on the handle easing the door open with his shoulder. Two grinning faces turned towards Blake in the doorway, their expressions momentarily frozen before they collapsed into a fit of giggles. Blake wanted to share in the amusement, but he felt self-conscious.

'Dad!' Sarah's voice punctured the tension.

'Hello darling.' Blake walked over to Sarah. 'What's the joke?'

'Alina said I was walking like a penguin,' said Sarah, and the mention of the animal sparked off another round of sniggering.

Blake took a step backwards and pretended to examine the outline of his daughter.

'Yes, I can see that,' he said with a wink before smothering his daughter in a bear hug. A muffled cough rumbled through the folds of his coat. The sound was accompanied by the wallop of a fist against Blake's chest.

'Can't breathe,' complained Sarah, who could hardly contain her giggles.

'Mr Blake, I'm Alina,' said the young woman standing at the other end of the walking bars. 'I'm Sarah's physio for a few weeks, until a replacement is found.'

Sarah's new therapist was a pale woman in her early thirties with dyed black hair and a dash of freckles at the top of each cheek. A line of eclectic-looking tattoos wrapped around her left arm like ivy before disappearing under the short sleeve of her white hospital uniform. Her voice sounded Eastern European.

'Replacement?' asked Blake quizzically.

The new physio paused for a moment, her face turning serious, extinguishing any trace of the previous levity.

'I had assumed that Sarah's consultant had informed you?'

Blake shook his head, his brow beginning to interlock.

Alina hesitated. 'I am really sorry to say, but Sarah's previous therapist was killed in a car accident just two days ago.'

Blake's face dropped.

'What?'

'Apparently, it happened on her way home from the hospital,' she said. 'She lived in the flats just behind here. A hit and run. The police still haven't found the driver.'

'That's awful.' Blake released Sarah from his embrace. He suddenly felt that his tie had a chokehold around his Adam's apple. He pulled it loose and tried to let the news sink in. 'Did she have kids?'

'I don't think so,' said Alina, as she cupped her hands together on her stomach. 'I'm new here,' she said, 'I didn't know her.'

For several seconds, no one spoke and then Alina broke the silence. 'Sarah, shall we show your dad the progress we've been making? Then we'll call it a day.'

'You watch this,' said Sarah, turning to Blake as she shuffled over to the bars with the aid of her walking stick. Gripping the bar, she jettisoned the stick and sent it clattering to the floor. With building concentration, she pushed the hair from her forehead and readied herself for the exercise.

'Remember, no penguins,' said Alina from the other end of the bars.

Sarah's first steps were shaky, but as she moved along the runway, her movements became slowly more controlled. Blake's eyes widened. He held his breath, tension building in his chest with Sarah's every step. His daughter was walking again. His throat choked with emotion. With his jaws clenched as tight as a vice, he willed Sarah on. Three more steps. Two. One. Then, Sarah's hands snapped back onto the bars. Immediately, she turned to her dad, a sunburst of pride shining in her face.

CHAPTER 23

A line of discarded clothes snaked its way to the bath tub, where Blake lay deep in thought. The bathwater had long since lost its initial heat and was now barely above his own body temperature.

The freestanding roll-top bath stood in the centre of the large room. The walls were shabbily decorated in a washed-out green colour. In the corner next to the washbasin, a long section of wallpaper had detached from the wall leaving an exposed tract of mildewy plasterboard.

Blake had bought the crumbling Victorian townhouse with the auction proceeds for the Cabbalistic trinket he had discovered within a secret crypt beneath St Paul's Cathedral. The auction catalogue had described it as 'the earliest known example of a Jewish amulet displaying the Star of David.' The final sales price was a record six-figure sum, enough to pay off Sarah's mounting hospital bills and to put down the deposit on the house. The plan had been to do the place up quickly, but apart from an initial cleaning frenzy, the interior of the home was essentially unchanged from the day he bought it. It was on his to-do list.

Blake's eyes were alight with movement, flitting randomly in all directions. The focus of his attention was the makeshift incident board that he had constructed on the wall directly in front of the bath. Unlike much of the plasterwork in the house, this wall seemed to be more forgiving to the insertion of drawing pins. His previous attempt at architecting the pastiche of crime scene photographs, handwritten notes, maps and pages from police reports had resulted in a foot-long crack in the plaster of the dining room wall that exposed the brickwork beneath.

The centre of the montage was given over to a collection of grisly photographs of the victim: three taken from the crime scene at St George's and two from the autopsy. The sight of them set his teeth on edge, but they needed to enter his brain, for his subconscious as well as his conscious mind to work on them. An elaborate spider web of coloured wool, held tight by bronze coloured drawing pins, formed connections between elements in the collage.

Blake leaned to the side to take it all in, his movement sending circles of ripples across the surface of the bath water. On the right-hand side were two blown-up photographs of the coin found under the skin of the victim at St George's. Three taut lengths of red wool radiated from the corners of one of the images of the Tyrian shekel. The first terminated at one of the autopsy pictures showing the cadaver's pallid torso. To one side of the victim's navel, the black incision mark contrasted vividly with the surrounding porcelain white skin. The next red line ended in the centre of an artist's impression of the Second Temple in Jerusalem. He had downloaded the image from a Jewish history website that he had used before. A comprehensive article on the Temple Tax had confirmed everything that Professor Ballard had told him at the Hunterian Museum.

The last of the three red threads finished at a group of photocopies that the curator of Scotland Yard's criminal museum had made for him. The grainy images of two of Jack the Ripper's victims, Annie Chapman and Catherine Eddowes, bore frighteningly similar hallmarks to the St George's killings: throats savagely cut, strange triangular marks carved into the cheeks, eyelids lacerated.

A series of chilling questions rose up in his mind. Was this some type of copycat killing? Not only were the victims' horrific injuries similar, but St George's also stood in the East End just next door to the Ripper's killing grounds of Whitechapel. Would he kill again? The Ripper had killed five times before he suddenly stopped the carnage, Eddowes being the last and most horrific of his attacks. But this time the police knew the murderer. It was now a straight manhunt.

The top of the collage was given over to the first page of Enoch Hart's arrest report. Although the mug shot was much smaller than the other images, Hart's eyes seemed to bear down on Blake from the wall. Only those eyes knew the meaning of the secret connections; only those eyes had witnessed the horror of the killings.

Blake suddenly felt a shiver ripple down his back. He raised his heavy leg out of the water and eased open the hot tap with his foot. Letting the piping hot water surround his legs, he felt the heat permeate into his muscles.

As the steam rose from the tap, his brain strained to understand the connections. Cracking a difficult crime was about getting just the right distance from the case. But now his mind felt caught, like a bird in a tree, unable to spread its wings against the cage of branches. He scratched at his damp hair, his eyes framed with a frown.

After a shake of his head, he submerged his body under the water and sent a wave lapping over the side of the bath. The hot water enveloped his head and shoulders. For a long while, he lay motionless apart from the intermittent escape of bubbles from his nostrils. He felt something just out of reach in his subconscious. Something significant, something blinking on and off, deep within his memory. If he could just wait long enough, his conscious mind might hem the thought in. Blake tried to slow his breathing, but his chest began to tighten.

Blake's head erupted from the water, sending cascades onto the bare wooden floorboards. Gasping for breath, he gripped the side of the bath, his eyes blinking. After taking several lungfuls of air, he hauled himself out of the water and picked up a damp towel from the floor. Drying himself, he caught his naked reflection in the mirror on the far wall. He turned his back towards the mirror. The scarring on his back looked more pronounced with his body pink from the heat of the bath. The skin from an inch above his waist to the nape of his neck was a patchwork of scars from the multiple skin grafts he had endured as a boy. The burns had left his back almost completely numb, but the recollection of that night had been seared into his memory like a brand.

His happy childhood was shattered when the family antique bookshop was deliberately set on fire. The arson attack resulted in the death of his father and left his mother seriously injured. If it hadn't been for Blake's courageous dash back into the burning building, his mother would have surely perished too. The culprits had never been found.

Blake suddenly stopped drying himself and listened intently. There it was again, the sound of scampering. Something moved in Blake's peripheral vision. He turned, his eyes tracking to the direction of the bathroom door. There was nothing there. He strained to detect the origin of the sound before he saw it, its tiny head appearing from behind the doorframe. A mouse scurried forward several inches across the floorboards and then looked up at Blake. The two of them regarded each other silently for several seconds, Blake with a cocked eyebrow and the mouse with twitching whiskers. The mouse finally broke the standoff and a moment later disappeared out of sight.

CHAPTER 24

It had taken nearly a year for Joyce Khumalo to make it this far. Would London become her home? *If it was part of God's plan*, she thought. She had fled war-torn Sierra Leone in search of safety after the murder of her family. Her father had taken a stand, and he and the other members of her family had paid the price. Before his death, her father had often talked fondly about his trip to England as an exchange student. *Until you've seen the green fields of Richmond Park, you really haven't seen the colour green*, he would say. He had given her a scarf on her nineteenth birthday, saying it was the closest shade to the colour he had remembered. She had carried it with her ever since.

Joyce made the journey alone. First through neighbouring Guinea, then through Bamako and Gao in Mali, Tindouf in Algeria, then Casablanca and onto the barbed-wire fences of the Moroccan-Spanish border circling the Spanish enclave of Ceuta. Despite the fence being twenty feet high and guarded by video cameras and patrol dogs, she had managed to scale it as part of an organised assault on the barrier by hundreds of migrants. As she climbed for her life, dozens of people either side of her dropped like stones from the onslaught of Spanish rubber bullets and live Moroccan gunfire. After stowing onto a sea freighter, she finally landed in France. It wasn't long before she had reached the makeshift camp known as 'The Jungle' on the outskirts of Calais and joined more than 3,500 other illegal migrants hoping to cross the Channel. She had taken her chance and hidden away in a container lorry heading for England. That was three months ago.

A street team working for the Servant Church of London's outreach programme had spotted her sleeping rough in a shop entrance in Whitechapel. After giving her hot soup and clean blankets, the team leader invited her to attend one of the church's nightly services. Their gentle kindness was like cool refreshing rain hitting her face after a thunderstorm in her native Freetown.

Joyce eagerly accepted the invitation and, from that point onwards, the church's presence in her life was a daily gift bestowed on her by God Himself. It was undeniable proof that God had been with her all along, at her side during every step of her perilous journey.

After a few weeks, one of the church elders took pity on her and offered her a small room in the shelter. The facility provided accommodation and support for more than twenty female clients, mostly women fleeing abusive relationships or on the streets due to substance addiction. The Servant Church of London not only fed and clothed her, but gave her a cleaning job in the church's shelter. With God's grace, she had dared to hope that she could now build a life in London.

Today, the evening meal for the shelter's twenty clients had taken a little longer than usual to tidy up. After loading up the industrial-sized dishwashing machine, she collected an orange from the kitchen larder and hurried to her bedroom to read her bible in anticipation of the rapidly approaching blood moon eclipse. She wasn't going to miss it for the world.

Last Sunday's church service focused on the Book of Joel, chapter 2, verse 31. Sitting upright in her bed, she easily found the verse, the specific page bookmarked by a sheet of neatly handwritten notes. She had taken so many that morning that her handwriting became visibly smaller the further down the page she had gotten, as she utilised every inch to record the nuggets of biblical knowledge that were being imparted to her. With her finger tracking underneath the line, she read the verse out aloud in a strong African accent.

The sun will be turned to darkness and the moon to blood
before the coming of the great and dreadful day of the Lord.

She had marked the top of her page of notes with the title 'Four Blood Moons'. It was double underlined in red ink. As she read her handwritten notes, she remembered what the senior pastor had preached last Sunday to the congregation. His sermon had amazed and excited her in equal measure. Faith had brought her to believe in the literal truth of the scriptures. She knew them to be true in her heart. But hearing that the astronomical facts surrounding the four blood moons had been verified by no less than NASA was scientific proof that God had His hand on all things, even the motion of the planets and stars themselves.

Joyce had listened dumbfounded to the pastor. Up until then, she had never heard of the term 'blood moon' or heard of their significance to the Holy Scriptures, but after listening to the preacher she understood they were a sign from heaven. A moon turned blood red during a lunar eclipse, when the earth moves between the sun and the moon, casting its shadow on the moon's surface. She didn't really understand why it turned red; something about all but the red light being filtered out by the earth's atmosphere. But that didn't matter. What mattered was the significance of the tetrad, or four consecutive blood moons. This was very rare. And what the pastor said was quite astronomically rare is when a blood red moon tetrad occurs on the Jewish biblical feast days, which had happened only eight times in the last 2,000 years.

Just thinking about these celestial alignments made her pulse quicken. Each of these occurrences had coincided with times of great peril for the Jewish people. These were messages from God, coded into the very motion of the planets, announcing times of tears and tribulation. Joyce was lost in thought as she read through her notes. Three blood moon tetrads had occurred in the last 500 years.

The tetrad of 1493-94 occurred on the Jewish feast days of Passover and the Feast of Tabernacles and coincided with King Ferdinand and Queen Isabella of Spain ordering the Jews to be driven out of the country and its territories. For over a millennium, Spain had been considered a second homeland for the Jews.

The four blood moons of 1949-50 again appeared on the Jewish Passover and the Feast of Tabernacles and occurred during the first

Arab-Israeli war just after the rebirth of the State of Israel in 1948. Seven Arab nations declared war on Israel almost immediately after it announced statehood. The war lasted some 15 months and claimed over 6,000 Israeli lives (nearly one percent of the country's Jewish population). The holy city of Jerusalem was divided, with Jordan controlling the east of the city (including the Old City) and Israel, the west.

The next blood moon tetrad occurred less than twenty years after, between 1967-68, again on the Jewish Passover and the Feast of Tabernacles. This coincided with the Six-Day War, when Israel was again in great peril. Convinced that its neighbouring states were preparing to destroy the Jewish state, Israel launched a pre-emptive strike, eventually recapturing Jerusalem.

The occurrence of four blood moons was of prophetic significance. It was clear for all to see, and tonight would be the second blood moon of the tetrad, the last tetrad for 400 years. She glanced at her watch. In a few minutes' time, she would see it glowing blood red over the streets of London, a celestial signal like no other, warning God's people of impending danger.

She grabbed her coat and bible and made her way out to the garden. Settling herself onto an iron garden seat next to a sweet-smelling rhododendron bush, Joyce cast her eyes up to the large moon hanging in the sky. The eclipse would be any moment now. She picked up her bible and flicked through her notes. Reading by the light through the kitchen window, she noticed she had written another bible verse at the bottom of the page, this time from Luke 21: 'There will be signs in the sun and in the stars ... Now when these things begin to happen, lift up your heads, because your redemption draws near'. When she had finished reading, Joyce followed the instructions of the bible verse and tilted her head back. She detected a strange scent in the air; not the familiar smell of rhododendron but something else. Joyce took a sniff and held the breath in her lungs. The smell was strong and sickly and instantly transported her back to a distant but powerful memory of childhood.

For an instant, she was sitting in a dentist's chair in Freetown, her mother holding her hand telling her not to be afraid.

Suddenly a black shape shifted in the margins of her vision. From behind, a hand clamped around her throat pulling her backwards, the force of the attack lifting her feet clear off the ground. Something hard hit the bridge of her nose. Then it was around her mouth, smothering her face. Joyce gasped, drawing a chestful of thick, sickly air deep down inside her lungs. She tried to fight back, her arms flailing at her side, her feet kicking against thin air. A relentless pressure began to build in her body, like a coil getting tighter. The world began to spin. As her head was yanked backwards, Joyce caught a glimpse of a man. His face was sheened with sweat and he had the blackest eyes she had ever seen, like the eyes of the devil.

CHAPTER 25

'The MO is identical, just in a different church,' said DCI Milton as he waited impatiently for Blake to zip up his forensic overalls. 'We've just got an ID on the victim. Her name was Joyce Khumalo, from Sierra Leone. She worked here.'

'And what's this place?' said Blake nodding up to the large unremarkable red-brick office building that was reminiscent of a 1970's university campus.

'It's the headquarters of the SCL, the Servant Church of London. They're a church charity that organises accommodation and soup runs in the city. There's a shelter at the back. The victim worked in the kitchen and had a room in the shelter.'

Bracing himself, Blake followed Milton into the portable crime scene tent. The white structure was positioned tight against the tired-looking office building. The back wall of the tent had been removed so that the canopy enclosed the exterior of the office building.

Blake's face dropped at the sight of the blood bath. Wild lines of crimson were sprayed across the exterior of the office wall. The concrete perimeter surrounding the church was slicked with a large area of blood. In the centre of the carnage lay the body of a naked black woman, her throat had been savagely cut. Blake inched closer. The woman's face had been lacerated. 'Same type of triangular wounds to the cheeks,' Blake said finally, forcing the words out.

'And the eyelids have been cut, just like the St George's church killing,' replied Milton.

Blake circled the body. The corpse's features were locked into a contorted expression of dread, like those of a child looking up at something truly frightening. As he did so he couldn't help but imagine the horror that those utterly empty, unblinking eyes had witnessed.

'Jeez,' Blake said shaking his head. 'You know it was a common belief during Victorian times that an image of the final thing a victim saw was imprinted on the back of the retina, like a photograph.'

Milton cleared his throat. 'Whatever this poor woman saw, it wasn't pleasant.'

Blake pinched his eyes in thought.

'Seen something?' asked Milton.

'Maybe. There is something at odds here. There's blood everywhere,' Blake gesticulated. 'It's almost like the killer wanted to cover everything in blood. It's sprayed on the walls and all over the ground. It's wild and brutal. And yet ...' Blake trailed off as he registered a pronounced demarcation line running through the construction of the office wall, the lower parts seemingly built of large blocks of pale cut stone, the upper sections of red brick. His eyes carried on upwards towards two holes about head height in the wall. They looked fresh, with the entrance to the holes edged with brick powder.

'There's a bullet in this one,' said Blake, angling his head close to one of the holes. 'Yes, they're bullet holes.'

'Bullet holes? Shit,' said Milton, annoyed by the fact that his forensic officers hadn't spotted them earlier. 'We'll get them checked. You were saying something else before you saw the holes?'

'What?' said Blake. 'Oh yes, look at the orientation of the body.' He motioned in the direction that the body was lying. 'It's been repositioned in a very controlled way after the killing. The arms have been neatly tucked back against the side of the body. The legs are perfectly straight. It was the same at St George's. The victim's body had been reoriented after the murder. This looks like premeditated behaviour, following some kind of ritual.'

'Maybe. So what kind of ritual is Hart following?'

'Last night was the second blood red moon eclipse out of a series of four. With the murders coinciding with the eclipses and the repositioning of the bodies, I believe Hart is killing to a predetermined plan.'

Blake sat on his haunches. 'There are no earrings, no watch, no metal jewellery at all. They have all been removed.' Blake's eyes travelled down the naked corpse to a two-inch slit in the victim's skin below the navel. The skin adjacent to the cut was stretched tight in a raised circular plateau. 'Another coin inserted under the skin?' said Blake as he lifted his chin towards the DCI.

Milton was already searching through his crime scene evidence briefcase. 'Let's find out.' The police officer easily located what he was searching for within the well-ordered forensics briefcase. Holding two pairs of tweezers and a plastic evidence bag, Milton nodded over to the large flashlight standing upright on the folding table in the corner of the tent. 'Can you do the honours with the light?'

Blake picked up the flashlight and switched it on. He dropped to his knees and shuffled to one side of the DCI. Directing the powerful beam of light onto the incision mark beneath the victim's navel, Blake watched as his friend superficially examined the wound. 'Let's see.'

With one pair of tweezers, the police officer very carefully opened up the aperture in the skin and eased the second pair of tweezers into the gap. Both men heard the gentle tapping sound of the tweezers as they connected with something solid. Milton reoriented his arm and flattened the angle of the tweezers in relation to the victim's body. His fingers tightened around them. Holding his breath, he gently tugged at the object within the tweezers' jaws. At first, it wouldn't come, stuck in place by the congealed blood.

'Come on, come on,' Milton grumbled through clenched teeth as he moved the tweezers from side to side. He tugged again, and this time there was movement. Gently, he eased the circular object out from under the flap of skin and held it up.

Blake directed the beam of the flashlight onto the circular metal disc. Even though it was caked in blood, there was no question as to the identification of the object. The image of an eagle above the stamped imprint of a pyramid was clearly visible on the face of the Tyrian shekel.

A vivid green scarf fluttered in the branches of the large rhododendron bush in the church gardens.

CHAPTER 26

Blake's thumb pressed down on the dark band of discolouration that encircled his left index finger like the imprint of a large signet ring. The flesh either side of the discolouration lightened to a pale pink as he applied pressure, but the mark remained resolutely unchanged. Blake straightened his back and opened his hand flat on the armrest of the waiting room chair outside the hospital consulting room. He compared the colour of the darkened ring of skin with the chair's dark grey upholstery. It was getting darker. He had checked it a fortnight ago against the same chair whilst waiting for his regular meeting with the consultant to discuss Sarah's progress. Then, the colour almost matched the chair's fabric. Today, the mark was definitely darker.

A middle-aged female nurse with a friendly smile appeared at his side.

'The consultant will see you now,' she announced.

Snapping his hand shut, Blake thanked the nurse and got to his feet. The nurse gave the door a couple of quick knocks, waited a moment and then entered the room. Blake walked in behind, still ruminating about his finger and subconsciously wiping the back of his hand on his trousers.

'Mr Blake,' announced the nurse in a hushed tone to the doctor, who was busy typing up the notes from her previous patient.

'Please take a seat, Mr Blake.' The doctor peered over a pair of half-moon designer glasses. 'I'll be with you in just a second.'

As the consultant's well-manicured fingernails tapped on her keyboard, Blake settled himself into his chair. He had already spent far too long in these places for one lifetime. First as a boy, recovering in a burns unit for three long months from the fire that razed the family bookshop to the ground. Now with Sarah: initially with the tortuous wait to see if she would ever wake up from her coma and now the long road of her rehabilitation.

With some ceremony, the consultant's finger hit the return key and she turned her chair to face Blake.

'Well, Mr Blake, I have some very good news for you.'

Blake's eyebrow raised. He wasn't used to getting good news from the medical profession.

'At our last progress meeting, I think I said how pleased I had been with Sarah's recent progress, under the management of her new physio.'

'Alina,' said Blake.

'That's right. Sarah and Alina have been working very hard together. As you know, there are no guarantees with this type of recovery, but in Sarah's case, all the hard work is paying off. She really has come on in leaps and bounds.'

Blake wasn't sure the choice of phrase was wholly suitable to describe a patient who, until relatively recently, had been struggling to walk five yards without the aid of parallel bars.

'I was getting really worried about her, until Alina arrived,' said Blake. 'With everything that has happened, with the coma and her losing her mum, it's been ...' Blake hesitated, his voice starting to crack, '... it's been very difficult for her.' He paused a breath. 'But now she's like a different girl, like her old self again.'

'Alina knows how to motivate and get the most from her patients, and Sarah has been up for the challenge. It's been really good that she could join the department temporarily.'

'Temporarily?' said Blake quizzically.

'Alina is going back home to Bosnia, very soon.'

A concerned frown appeared on Blake's face. 'When?' he said, his voice tightening.

'Very soon. Her work visa is coming to an end, but with the progress Sarah is making, it shouldn't be an issue.'

The consultant opened a manila file.

'Sarah's scores for flexibility, balance and muscle tone are significantly higher than even a few weeks ago,' she said, flicking through the pages of Alina's patient notes.

The consultant turned back to Blake with a wide grin.

'I think you need to make preparations for Sarah to come home.'

Blake could feel a wave of emotion burst up through his chest and invade the back of his throat.

'Very good. I'll leave you to tell Sarah the good news.' She checked her watch. 'She should be finishing her physio session very soon.'

The sliding sign on treatment room five indicated the room was in use. Blake hovered outside the door for a second listening out for voices, but all was silent. Perhaps Sarah was already on her way back to the ward, he thought. Without knocking, Blake pushed down on the handle and eased open the door to the treatment room.

The scene that met his eyes sent lines of concern spidering across his temple and a pang of anxiety rattling through him. His gaze darted around, straining for some clue as to what was going on.

'Is everything okay?' he asked.

By the tears streaming down Alina's ghostly pale cheeks, everything was far from okay. Sarah and Alina were sitting together at the far end of the room. Sarah was holding her physio's hand and looking back towards her dad with obvious concern. Alina's red-rimmed eyes were staring bleakly into mid-air.

'Dad, can't you do something?' said Sarah.

'I'm sorry sweetheart, I don't know what's going on?'

Sarah gently let go of Alina's hand and shuffled forward onto the edge of her chair.

'Alina's leaving. She's being thrown out of the country.'

Blake searched Alina's drawn face. After a long breath, she started to speak.

'I have been staying at a church shelter for the last few months,' said Alina in a trembling voice. 'The police and the immigration department have been doing spot checks. My visa has expired, and they have told the hospital and the shelter,' she said, sweeping the moisture from her cheeks. 'Unless I make a new application within the week, I will have to return to Bosnia. The police have issued me a notice of deportation. Without a sponsor and a solicitor, I will have to leave. I have no money,' she said with downcast eyes. 'I have no home in Bosnia anymore; my family and my friends are gone.'

CHAPTER 27

Beads of sweat stood up on Blake's forehead as his arm took another sweep with the paint roller. There was so much to be done and precious little time. Sarah would be back from hospital in days, and whilst the condition of the house was just about acceptable for an ex-military man living by himself, it certainly wouldn't do for Sarah's return. Blake had been forced to sell their previous family home in Clerkenwell to cover the costs of her treatment. She received the best care available in London, and the family house had been a small price to pay.

Sarah's bedroom was the priority, and Blake had worked through the previous night applying coats of light pink emulsion to the walls. He was happy with his handiwork and, except for a few pieces of furniture, some soft furnishings and a new light shade, Sarah's room was finished.

Next on the list for a complete makeover was the large living room that dominated the downstairs of the tired, old Victorian townhouse. Like a windscreen wiper wiping away dirt, Blake's paint roller travelled quickly over the dreary walls. The sound of the Rolling Stones playing through the small speaker of his mobile phone and the erratic buzz of a moth dancing around the light fitting overhead were Blake's only company as he painted.

Despite the fatigue that had settled into every corner of his body, he worked on. Every so often he would offer the wall a tired smile, content in the thought that Sarah would soon be home.

He wiped the sweat away from his forehead with the back of his hand and crouched down to refill the paint tray. As he did so, his knee gave out a delicious cracking sound, relieving the dull ache that had built up over the hours. He remembered the lecture his knee surgeon had given him. Although his operation had been a success, the type of gunshot injury he had sustained tended to leave cartilage fragments and other debris floating within the joint's synovial fluid, causing intermittent pain and discomfort.

This bullet wound, Blake's third, which he sustained during a terrifying chase for sacred treasure deep within the foundations of St Paul's Cathedral, had almost cost him his life. What precisely happened in the minutes following the pistol shot to his knee was at best fragmentary: a knife at his throat; a black dog barking; the voice of the mysterious tattooed vagrant woman. Had she been the same woman that Milton had given chase to outside St George's church?

Blake heaved a large tin of paint closer to himself. With the end of a teaspoon he eased open the lid and began to pour the blue paint into the tray. As he watched it ooze into the plastic container, some thought from the shadow lands of his subconscious surfaced briefly in his mind.

Blake picked up his phone and immediately silenced Keith Richard's guitar powering through the opening riff to Jumpin' Jack Flash. Several finger taps later, Blake had brought up a map of London. The snaking shape of the River Thames was clearly visible, twisting its way through the centre of the map. He reached over to the pack of new paintbrushes and punched his fingers though the clear plastic packaging. Selecting the largest brush, Blake flexed out its fibres on the back of his hand. He dipped the brush into the paint, wiped the excess onto the side of the tray and, using the map of London as his guide, started applying paint to the wall.

Minutes later, the distinctive shape of the River Thames had been painted out with artistic flair in blue some fifteen feet across. Referring back to his phone, he found the relative positions of St George's church and the offices of the Servant Church of London against the winding profile of the river. This time he selected the smallest brush from the pack. Loading it with paint from the tray, he marked out the positions of the churches on the wall. One above the Thames and the other slightly below the loop of the river.

He stepped back and surveyed the improvised map. His fingers carefully searched for the point of the pencil sticking out from his back pocket. After tugging it free, he carefully wrote the name of each of the two locations on the wall. Blake stared at the oversized diagram for a long time. He reached for his phone and typed 'Servant Church of London' into the search window and pressed return. He picked the top result and quickly scrolled through the short introduction describing the church's mission.

Our mission is to serve the city's most needy communities. Through our pastoral outreach programmes, the Servant Church of London is committed to bringing Jesus's gospel to the most marginalised and impoverished groups within the city. Although London is a modern and cosmopolitan city, many of its citizens are isolated and struggling to provide for themselves and their families.

These people are often neglected, ostracised, and overlooked by wider society. Since its formation in 1980, the Servant Church of London has been committed to providing care across a wide range of communities and ethnic groups, including the elderly, the homeless, newly arrived immigrants, victims of domestic violence, and men and women who are battling substance addiction. Through its drop-in shelter, the Church has provided food, temporary accommodation and healthcare services for hundreds of people.

Because of its extraordinary mix of people, unique history and traditions, we consider London to be one of the most strategic cities for the world mission of the Christian faith.

The Servant Church of London is a registered charity and funded through the generous donations of its members and supporters.

Blake rubbed his tired eyes and squinted at a link labelled 'History' in the website's main menu. He clicked the link and waited a second for the page to load. The instant it had, Blake's attention immediately homed onto two words within the paragraphs of returned text. It was as if the words 'Nicholas Hawksmoor' screamed out to him from the screen. He quickly found the start of the narrative.

St John Horsleydown was built between 1727 and 1733 near the south bank of the River Thames in Fair Street (now known as Tower Bridge Road, just south of the junction with Tooley Street). The church was built as one of the last churches of the Commission for Building Fifty New Churches set up by an Act of Parliament in 1710.

The church's design was a joint undertaking between two architects. John James designed a simple square church body, to which Christopher Wren's troubled student Nicholas Hawksmoor added an unusual spire. Hawksmoor's steeple took the form of a tapered column, making it appear much taller than it actually was, topped by an extraordinary weathervane depicting a flaming comet.

The church was severely damaged by a bomb on 20 September 1940 during the London Blitz, but parts of the building remained in use for years afterwards. The church eventually closed in 1968, and the Servant Church of London (a Christian outreach organisation) bought the site from the Church Commissioners in 1982 for £27,811. The church's crypt was emptied of its dead and moved to Brookwood Cemetery and Naismith House.

Redevelopment of the site by the Servant Church of London quickly followed. Interestingly, the Mission's modern red-brick headquarters was built directly on the stone foundations of the original Hawksmoor church.

Blake's mind zipped back to the crime scene at the headquarters of the Servant Church of London. He had clocked the difference in the structure of the wall whilst examining the wild arches of the victim's blood that had been sprayed over its surface. The memory made him swallow heavily. He remembered a clear juncture line between the wall and the platform it was built upon. The platform was a plinth-like structure made of large rectangular stones, whilst the wall itself was made of much newer less substantial blocks. The larger stones must have come from the original Hawksmoor church.

All of the murders had been committed on the sites of Hawksmoor churches. The thought woke him up like a splash of cold water. It was beyond all doubt: these were ritual killings.

CHAPTER 28

Blake had trouble getting the key into the rusted front door lock. Sarah and Alina waited patiently on the doorstep behind him. They looked at each other for a moment before their confused expressions turned into a shared, playful grin. Finally, Blake turned the key in the lock and with a gentle shove, the door creaked open.

'Welcome to your new home,' he said, as he made a sweeping gesture and ushered them into the hallway. 'It needs a bit of work granted, but it's large enough and school is just five minutes down the road.'

Sarah gave her Dad a dismissive frown. 'Do we have to talk about school?' she protested with a huff.

'Alright, no more mention of school for today,' he conceded. 'Did I tell you we are really close to Farringdon and Angel tube stations here?'

Blake could see the cogs of Alina's brain working as he tossed his keys into a chipped blue soap dish that sat on top of an old bookcase by the door.

'Circle and Northern tube lines,' he said. 'We're smack bang in the centre of town here. Right in the thick of the action.'

Alina smiled at Blake's turn of phrase and followed her new boss and Sarah through the first doorway on the left.

If Blake had been religious, he might have described it as divine intervention. Whether it was destiny or just good timing, Alina's dire situation with the immigration authorities had afforded them all a mutually beneficial arrangement.

In the first place, Sarah needed regular physio sessions. She had made more progress in her short time with Alina than all her time battling with her previous physio. Secondly, if Alina was going to be allowed to stay in the country, she would need a sponsor, proof of employment and a residency address to support her visa application.

'So, what do you think, like it?' said Blake, trying to ignore the strong smell of paint fumes hanging in the air.

The three of them were standing in the middle of a large Victorian front living room with high ceilings and a bay window that looked out upon the busy street outside. At the far end of the room hung a homemade banner constructed from numerous pieces of A4 paper and threaded together with a piece of string. Spanning the length of the far wall, it bore the words 'Welcome home Sarah' penned out in different colours. It reminded Sarah of a toothy grin.

'Thanks, Dad,' Sarah said appreciatively whilst surveying the newly decorated living room with an approving eye. 'It'll do,' she said. 'It needs a woman's touch though. Some pictures, cushions, and a throw for the sofa should do it.' Sarah tossed Alina a look to coax support for her assessment.

'It's very nice, Mr Blake. Very nice.'

'Something else is missing,' continued Sarah.

Blake shrugged his shoulders.

'Books. Where are all your books? My dad is always reading. Thousands of books,' she added for Alina's benefit.

Without a pause for breath, another question came.

'What's that over there, Dad?' Sarah pointed beyond the draped banner to the oversized hairpin of blue paint that dominated the back wall.

Blake hesitated, trying to shuffle the right words in his head to give an appropriate response to his daughter.

'It's a map. A map of London. The blue paint is the shape of the Thames,' he said.

'Cool,' said Sarah dismissively, now noticing the gift wrapped in silver paper on a paint-dappled chair in the corner of the room.

'Just a little something to welcome you back home,' Blake said, a smile broadening across his face.

'Can I?' she asked through a slanted, little grin.

'Don't get your hopes up too much, it's only a little something.'

As his daughter tentatively felt through the gift wrap to the object inside, she began to giggle. It was infectious, and moments later the three of them were laughing uncontrollably together. It felt like winter had ended and the spring had finally arrived. Seconds after discarding the gift wrap to the floor, Sarah was checking out the look of her new cap in Alina's make up mirror.

'Like it?'

'You bet,' she said tucking an unruly ringlet of her hair back beneath the brim.

'Good,' said Blake putting his arm around her shoulder. 'After all, I've waited a long time to be able to do this.' With that Blake took the rim of the hat and pulled it down over her eyes.

'Dad the hair, watch the hair.'

After a short pause, hoots of juddering laughter were bouncing across Sarah's shoulders.

CHAPTER 29

'Dr Blake, come in, come in. My security manager is just leaving,' said Angelo Ricard as he beckoned Blake into his office. Ricard's security manager was a big, broad-shouldered man, well-muscled, with a low-set forehead. He got up from his seat and offered Blake a polite smile. As he passed him at the door, Blake couldn't help but glance at the prominent port-wine stain that spanned the length of his right cheekbone. Blake returned the smile and closed the door behind him.

'Take a seat,' said Ricard. 'Coffee?'

'Love some, black please.'

Ricard leaned over the table and handed Blake a cup of steaming hot coffee. The aroma wafted upwards from the stylish china cup and met Blake's nose, resulting in a satisfied murmur of pleasure. Having worked through lunch, he gratefully accepted the offer of a biscuit from the matching plate. He took a bite and brushed away the crumbs from his shirt.

'Nice office,' said Blake as he nodded in appreciation of his surroundings.

The office, located in the prestigious Middle Temple, was part of the Inns of Court, the collection of buildings and precincts making up one of London's historic legal centres. Situated close to the Royal Courts of Justice, the Middle Temple could trace its origins back to 1422 and derived its name from the nearby Temple Church. Today, most of the offices of the Middle Temple were taken by barristers plying their trade. *Obviously not all*, thought Blake as he took a sip from his cup.

The office was large by any standards, but especially so considering it was in such a prestigious old building in the heart of the city. The walls were oak panelled and decorated with an eclectic mix of paintings and photographs. In contrast to the walls, the furniture and furnishings adorning the room were bang up-to-date. Ricard's steel-and-glass desk was presidential in its proportions, with a sleek Anglepoise lamp standing to salute at its side. The rental on the lease alone would be eye-watering, but property development was where Ricard had made his money and he knew all the tricks of his trade.

'Been here long?'

'Oh, a very long time,' answered Ricard, leaning back in his chair and crossing his legs. Blake glanced at the gleaming shine of Ricard's shoes and compared them to his own. He cleared his throat in embarrassment.

Ricard was immaculately dressed in a light blue suit that hung effortlessly from his trim frame. A distinctive red pocket square tucked into the breast pocket of his jacket finished off the ensemble. Blake's suit had creases, but none of them were in the right places.

'Thank you for seeing me at such short notice,' said Blake.

'Not at all. When I heard about poor Joyce, it was the least I could do.'

The two men sat in silence for a moment.

'Would you mind me asking you a few questions?'

'Fire away.'

'Tell me about the Servant Church of London.'

'Anything specific?'

'Sorry, the reason I ask is that I was at the crime scene with DCI Milton at the church's offices in Southwark.'

'Okay?'

'I saw a plaque on the side of the building with your name on it.'

'I'm lost,' he shrugged.

'On a list of donors to the building.' The penny dropped.

'Ah, yes, I support the work of the church.' Ricard repositioned his glasses on the bridge of his nose. 'I have been very fortunate over the years, and in my small way I try and give something back, where I can. The church is a real blessing to the local community. I don't know if you saw it whilst you were there, but the church runs a homeless shelter. It does a brilliant job providing food and a roof over people's heads who would otherwise be sleeping on the streets. My contributions bless the church, and the church blesses the community. That's the way it works in the church family.'

'I see,' said Blake before taking a gulp of coffee.

'Any reason?' said Ricard.

'I am trying to work a line of enquiry linking the killings.'

'Line of enquiry? With Enoch Hart you mean?'

'My question about the plaque was more to do with the fact that the church's office was built on the foundations of an older Hawksmoor church. St John Horsleydown, I think.'

'That's right,' said Ricard.

'The first two murders took place at St George-in-the-East, another Hawksmoor church. Maybe a coincidence?'

'But you don't think so,' said Ricard.

Blake shrugged his shoulders. 'That's what I am trying to find out.'

The two men measured each other for a second, and then Ricard offered Blake some more coffee. Blake accepted, and whilst Ricard poured, he helped himself to another biscuit, this one glossy with Belgian chocolate. He took a sip from his refilled cup.

'You were saying?' said Ricard, settling back into his chair.

'I understand you have an interest in Hawksmoor churches,' said Blake.

Ricard pondered the question for a second.

'Buildings are my profession, but you could say that church buildings are my passion. You probably know that I am the chair of the trustees of the Hawksmoor City Churches. It's been a hard slog over the years, but we've managed to save several of Hawksmoor's city churches from near dereliction. Restoring churches costs millions, but through the support of our donors across the world, we have managed to fight off the speculators and transform the neglected shells of these buildings into a network of functioning churches. All of them have growing congregations,' Ricard added enthusiastically. 'The fact that I have a lot of connections in the industry helps too, I suppose,' he said with a smile. 'Poacher-turned-gamekeeper, you could say. If you want to know about Nicolas Hawksmoor, you've come to the right place.'

'The killings—do you see a connection with the churches?' said Blake.

'Until you mentioned it, it hadn't occurred to me.'

'Nor me, until I read the plaque. Hart is still at large and if we don't get to him soon, my suspicion is that he's going to kill again.'

'At a Hawksmoor church, you mean?'

'Maybe.'

'That's terrible.' Ricard pulled at the back of his hair

'The last two murders also coincided with the occurrence of blood moons.'

'I remember, they were quite unsettling' said Ricard. 'So you think there's a connection there as well?'

'That's my hunch,' said Blake as he returned his coffee cup to the table.

'I'm not sure how I can help?'

'Can you see a reason for these connections?'

Ricard thumbed his chin for a moment.

'Well, if you think of something, it doesn't matter how small. Maybe we can anticipate Hart's next move. At the moment, the police have hit a brick wall. They've no idea where he is.'

'It doesn't surprise me. Enoch Hart is a man with many talents. His SAS training will make him very difficult to find. Evasion from capture training, I think that's what they call it in the forces. I still can't quite believe what's happened to him. After finding the Lord and leaving the army, he worked tirelessly doing God's work.'

'What kind of work?' asked Blake.

'Hart worked with some of the neediest people in the city: the homeless, addicts, prostitutes, refugees. He followed the example of Christ to the letter of the scriptures. Giving himself fully to the Great Commission.'

Ricard's focus dropped to the surface of the table.

'His superiors recognised that he was burnt out and tried to limit his work, but he carried on regardless. He must have had some kind of breakdown and then ...'

A silence fell between the two men.

'All this terrible business,' said Ricard finally, shaking his head. 'I just can't believe it.'

'Can you think of anything, anything at all?' pressed Blake.

Ricard redrew his focus back from the table.

'I just can't think. The church has been fighting the powers of darkness for millennia. Good and evil are always close to each other.' A thought rose in his mind. 'Just take the names of the streets close to the offices of the Servant Church of London.'

'Sorry, how so?'

'Believe it or not, the church offices back onto a road called Druid Street. A strange name to call a street, with all its dark, pagan connotations. The bizarre thing is that, Druid Street runs directly into another road called Crucifix Lane. Good and evil running into one another if you will. I suppose every good man has a little bit of bad in him, and vice versa.'

Blake considered the matter for a second. 'Druids, in London?'

'Yes, well that's the folklore anyway. The Druids themselves never wrote anything down. There's even a tradition that at the foot of Ludgate Hill, where St Paul's Cathedral stands today, there once stood a great Druid stone circle, that extended as far south as Southwark.'

Blake nodded slowly, trying to imagine such a stone circle, then he glanced at his watch.

'Look, I don't want to keep you. If you think of anything, please give me a call.'

The two men rose to their feet and shook hands. As Blake moved to the door, he noticed a group of photographs forming a line across the wood-panelled wall. The subject of each photograph was similar: a group of women, sitting or standing in several lines, like the squad photo for a football team. Ricard acknowledged Blake's interest.

'Past residents of the shelter,' he said. 'Every year we take a picture, it's a brilliant reminder of the people we've helped through the work of the church.' He paused for a moment contemplating the faces staring back from the pictures. 'Now and again, it's good to reflect on the lives of the people that have passed through the shelter.'

Blake glanced at the picture last in the line. He recognised the face of Joyce Khumalo, the victim of the last killing. She looked happy and carefree, her hands resting on the shoulders of a fellow resident kneeling in the front row. Little could she have known of the horror that would be waiting for her on that fateful night just days ago. Blake backed away from the wall.

Ricard had taken the moment to straighten another of the photos that had been hanging slightly out of line to the others. Blake's eyes drifted over to it and widened. Stepping closer, he felt his senses sharpen.

'This woman, who is she?' he asked, his voice tightening as he spoke. Blake's fingertip singled out the lone figure standing to one side of two lines of women in the photograph.

'That lady?' said Ricard.

'Yes,' Blake confirmed, his body stiffening.

'Oh yes, that was Mary. I won't forget her in a hurry. She didn't stay in the shelter for very long. I think I mentioned her the last time we met. She was very sick for a while.'

'Sick?'

'Mentally unstable, bipolar. A lot of our residents suffer from mental illness; it's a very common precursor to living on the streets. But she was different. She complained of hearing voices and then things really got out of hand.'

'What do you mean?'

'She became deranged, started drawing things on the walls and then tried to set light to the shelter. If it wasn't for the sprinklers, the whole place would have gone up in flames.'

'What happened to her?'

'The police got involved, they took statements, a formal report was lodged, but she was never charged. She was ill and we weren't going to abandon one of our own. Even though he was exhausted, Enoch Hart volunteered to care for her. He had special experience in dealing with Mary's type of condition.'

'What kind of condition?'

'Do you believe in God, Mr Blake?' said Ricard, searching Blake's eyes.

Blake shrugged, not really knowing what to say.

'Because you won't fully understand Enoch Hart's work unless you do.'

'I'm not sure that I follow?'

'After the army, Hart trained in Rome for several years under the tutelage of a man called Father Theodore. Through his training, he discovered that he possessed a gift and a calling for a special ministry.'

'Special ministry?' asked Blake.

'He was trained to deliver the Rite.' The last word hung heavily in the air.

Blake's stomach suddenly lurched.

'What you mean, he was an exorcist? You're kidding?' Blake said incredulously.

'The Vatican gives three signs that indicate the presence of a demon: unnatural strength, the ability to speak in a previously unknown language and knowledge of facts that should naturally be unknown to the person. Mary showed all of these signs. Dr Blake, she had become very disturbed, writing on the walls of her room in her own blood. She tried to set the shelter alight, she could have killed dozens of people.'

Blake felt a strong sense of foreboding rise through his body.

'Hart performed the Rite over her, a demon was exorcised, but the strain was too great for Hart. He suffered some type of mental breakdown and in a psychotic frenzy stabbed the vicar of St George's to death. Mary fled, never to be seen again. It was a terrible scene. I saw it with my own eyes. At the trial, Hart coldly admitted to the murder. He showed no remorse.'

Blake eyed Ricard. They stood in silence for a moment and then Blake's focus returned to the photograph. His eyes drilled into the picture. His stare froze on the dishevelled woman standing to the side of a group of grinning residents, a black dog sitting by her feet.

'I've met this woman before,' he said finally with cold simplicity.

CHAPTER 30

'Lights,' Blake shouted from the kitchen. Alina hit the light switch, and the living room was cast into semi-darkness. Carefully he coaxed the plate holding the birthday cake onto his palm. The lighted candles around the cake's perimeter trembled as he edged his way out of the door, causing elongated shadows to rear up onto the living room wall.

'Happy birthday,' said Blake as he rounded the corner balancing the cake. 'This is dad's special homemade cake, not like the shop stuff we had earlier.'

As soon as he had finished speaking, he could feel the cake slide from under his hand. Twisting on his feet, he managed to follow the arc of its shifting weight and safely land the cake onto the living room table.

'That was close,' said Sarah.

'All under control,' said Blake, feigning an expression of mock surprise at the suggestion.

Sarah's birthday party was a great success. Earlier that afternoon, the living room had been full of Sarah's old and new school friends. She had been worried that the two groups wouldn't mix, but she needn't have, as both sets of friends exchanged hugs and social media addresses when it came time to go. Out of the invited guests, only their new neighbours, Dr Desai and his daughter, Noorjehan, were left. Dr Desai was a well-dressed Indian man in his late forties who lectured at Kings College London. Noorjehan was a pretty girl with large dark eyes, and was only slightly younger than Sarah.

'Don't forget to make a wish,' said Dr Desai, his hands resting on the back of his daughter's shoulders.

Blake watched as Sarah, flushed with excitement, took a deep breath and blew out with all her might. It was so good to have her back home. Blake thought of Nomsa and imagined her being there, handing out napkins and fussing over their beautiful daughter.

He allowed himself a moment to regain his composure as Sarah extinguished the last of the candles.

'Dad, the knife,' said Sarah, motioning to the kitchen knife still in his hand.

He carefully passed the knife over by the handle and watched Sarah cut large wedges out of the cake. Just then a loud knock came from the front door.

'Shhhhh,' came Blake's voice in the darkness.

Another rap echoed from the door. Alina found the light switch, and Blake pushed himself up from his chair. He wound a route around the chairs to the door, twisted its rattling handle, and opened it.

His face fell at the sight of the woman standing in the doorway.

'Rosalind,' he exclaimed. For a moment, a brief uncertainty flashed across his face.

'Aren't you going to give your sister a hug?' said the woman.

'Come on, it's time for sleep,' said Blake as he squared up Sarah's duvet. 'You can catch up with Auntie Rosalind tomorrow.'

'But Dad, I haven't seen her in ages, just five more minutes please,' said Sarah with pleading eyes.

'Bed,' said Blake, forcing a tone of finality into his voice.

Hovering at the door, Alina waved over to him. 'I'll read to her,' she mouthed silently.

'Thank you,' he whispered back, his eyebrows lifting with gratitude.

Alina stepped into the room and was greeted with Sarah's cheeky grin beaming over the edge of the duvet. Alina reached up to search the bookshelf on the far wall of Sarah's bedroom, and from her bed, Sarah guided Alina's finger to the book she wanted. As she tugged the paperback free from the shelf, Blake's eyes noticed the line of Alina's trim stomach peeping out from under her crop top. His gaze also clocked the square shaped contour of a nicotine patch stuck to her skin close to her navel.

Blake looked back to his daughter. 'Night, sweetheart.'

'Night, Dad,' said Sarah, pushing herself up on her elbows and expectantly waiting for Alina to find the page.

'Not too late,' he said. He smiled to himself and then left the room.

After making two mugs of tea, Blake found Rosalind in the living room stretched out on the sofa like a cat on the porch of a Mediterranean villa. He handed his sister a mug and, after putting his onto the coffee table, he collapsed into an armchair.

'Tired?' said Rosalind, cupping her tea in her hands.

'It's been a long day.' Blake looked over to his sister and fought down a yawn.

'If I'm not very much mistaken, you're going grey?' teased his sister.

'Just a touch of snow on the mountain,' said Blake smiling.

Rosalind looked so much better than the last time he had seen her. Her face was bright and sun-kissed, though how much of her healthy glow was down to the Californian sunshine or from a bottle, he was unsure. She was wearing faded, figure-hugging hipster jeans and a delicate checkerboard print blouse that met the soft waves of hair at her shoulders.

Despite her healthy appearance, her eyes still had something careworn about them, some trace of a troubled journey that couldn't be hidden with makeup.

'When were you discharged?' he said gently.

'Two weeks ago,' said Rosalind.

'You discharged yourself?'

'I was feeling much better, and I couldn't see the point in staying there any longer.'

'Roz, you know you have to complete the programme,' he said, casting her a worried glance.

'I'm okay, honestly,' she said.

Blake caught her eyes.

'You sure?'

'I'm fine.'

As he reached over to the table to retrieve his mug, he scanned her forearms for the tell-tale signs. He couldn't see any.

'And what about the actor? You guys still—'

'Marcus is filming in Australia. There's a lot of interest in the studio doing a spin-out TV miniseries. He got me this,' she said, admiring a distinctive silver and turquoise ring on her middle finger. 'It's Native American. Navajo, I think.'

'Nice,' he said.

For a moment, a silence filled the space between them.

Eventually Rosalind swung her legs around on the sofa and planted her feet onto the floor. She cleared her throat.

'Look, I'm really sorry about the funeral, my head wasn't in any kind of state to fly over.'

A knot of resentment tightened in Blake's stomach. He had sworn to himself that he wouldn't lose it, but he could already feel cracks forming in the dam of his resolve.

'Not even a phone call, Roz?'

Shifting uncomfortably on the sofa, Rosalind's eyes began to go gauzy.

'I don't know what to say? I know I've been a self-centred shit.' She swallowed hard and wrapped her arms around herself. 'I'm so sorry Vincent, I can't change what I've done. I know I have no right to ask for your forgiveness.' The sides of her mouth drew down and quivered.

Blake's attention turned inwards. Nomsa's death had become part of him. Time hadn't lessened the pain; it had just changed its shape. He had tried to outrun his grief through working and concentrating on Sarah's recovery, but it was still eating at him from the inside. On the day of the incident, his world changed forever. Guilt squeezed at his heart. The thought of how love could vanish in the blink of an eye hounded his dreams. Seeing Rosalind had brought it flooding back again.

'Let's put this behind us, Roz,' he said through glistening eyes.

'Okay,' said Rosalind softly.

'You are very welcome to stay here as long you like,' said Blake.

CHAPTER 31

The elevator doors opened and Blake and Milton stepped out into the basement of the police station. After dropping his coat onto the table next to the elevator, Blake glanced around the large windowless storage area. The basement provided shelving for the physical case reports that had yet to be digitised onto the Metropolitan Police's crime database. From a cursory look around, Blake could see that at least three quarters of the shelving was covered by the familiar light blue colour of Metropolitan Police case files.

Blake noticed that the air smelt like an old bookshop. A childhood memory began to surface in his mind. His father had once run an antique bookshop, and his nostrils greeted the familiar musty smell like an old friend.

Milton double-checked the writing on the scrap of paper in his hand.

'K20713,' he said, slightly perplexed. 'I'm sure the K's start over here.' He motioned to an area of shelving to their left. Whilst mumbling the location identifier to himself, Milton scoured the racks.

'Gotcha,' he said triumphantly after a short while of searching. He prised the bulging file free from its neighbours and dropped it onto the table next to Blake's coat. 'Enjoy. I'll be back with some tea after I've seen the desk sergeant.' He tossed Blake a salute and walked back to the elevator.

Soon the basement was quiet apart from the soporific drone of the air-conditioning system. Blake pulled up a chair and opened the case file. He didn't really know what he was searching for, but it was his only lead. Angelo Ricard had identified the photograph of the homeless woman in his office as Mary and apart from other scant details, he was in the dark. He said that she had suffered some kind of mental breakdown and become deranged. So deranged that she had attempted to set light to the shelter attached to the offices of the Servant Church of London. This is when Enoch Hart had been called in as a last resort to help her. Now Blake knew that Hart hadn't just provided Mary with counselling but had performed some kind of exorcism on her. She had also been at St Paul's Cathedral the day of the shootout.

Reading through the officer's statements, Blake felt a heavy sense of foreboding. As he read, he learned that the police had arrived at the scene to find Mary grunting and growling in the corner of her room like a bedraggled cornered animal. She was banging the back of her head against the wall and cursing in what sounded like Italian to the officers. Her arms were covered in blood from deep cuts in her fingertips. The wounds were self-inflicted with a shard of glass from a mirror that laid shattered on the floor. The walls of her room were covered in strange writing made with her own blood. The report noted that it had taken three officers to finally restrain her.

It also noted several other unsettling pieces of information about the police's arrival on the scene. Firstly, the police officers recorded a foul odour on entering the room, like the smell of sulphur. Secondly, a section of wood panelling next to the washbasin had been scratched raw, as if someone or something had clawed at it.

He turned the last page of the file to discover a wallet of crime scene photographs pasted to the inside back cover. Blake's mouth dried as he laid the pictures out one by one on the table. There were eleven in all. Four of the photographs were layouts showing the general configuration of the room and the position of the sparse furniture contained within it. Two others were of the strange scratching marks in the wood panelling next to the sink and the remaining five were of the bizarre blood writing that had been written onto the walls.

He moved all but the five photographs of the writings to the side of the table. Even though the water from the sprinklers had washed several areas into messy streaks of red, a patch of lettering was clearly visible in the photographs. Blake's face drained as he decoded the cryptic writing.

At the top, the word HAWKSMOOR was scrawled in crimson. Underneath it, four more lines were marked out in sharp, angular capital letters.

FOUR BLOOD ALTARS
FOUR BLOOD SACRIFICES
FOUR BLOOD COINS
FOUR BLOOD MOONS

Blake's nerves were shot through with the implications of the photograph he was holding. Blood altars, coins, sacrifices and blood moons? It fitted the pattern of Hart's killings exactly. Were there going to be four? Damn it. How could she have possibly known this? Was it some kind of prophecy? A hurricane started to blow in his mind, with thoughts flying in every direction. He appraised each line again in turn. Skipping through the photos, he noticed that one of the five photographs had been taken from a slightly different angle, from which two additional lines of writing were visible. Blake's internal radar was now on full alert.

EVE CAN'T BLINK

He thumbed his chin, trying to recall where he heard this phrase before, but he just couldn't place it. The chilling image of the mutilated faces of two of Hart's victims suddenly reared up in his mind. They had both had their eyelids cut out. Was this the meaning of the phrase? Did it refer to blinding women? That must be it, he thought as he focused vacantly onto a patch of basement wall where a window might have been.

He looked back to the photograph. The second new line was a reference to a bible scripture.

JOEL 2:31

Although he was sitting in the basement of the police station, his phone still managed a weak signal. He typed the bible reference into his search engine app and tapped the return button. The bible passage appeared instantly on his phone's display.

The sun will be turned to darkness and the moon to blood before the coming of the great and dreadful day of the Lord.

CHAPTER 32

Blake circled the incident board as Milton drummed his knuckles on the table. Suddenly his hand went still.

'Your hunch better be right my friend. Ten detectives, that's half my unit tied up on this.' A silence fell as the awful reality of the situation weighed heavy in the air.

Milton pushed back from the table and rose to his feet. He approached the board as he scratched the side of his craggy face.

'Alright, let's go over it again,' he said.

The board was taken over by a large street map of London, the distinctive shape of the River Thames winding its way across its centre. Eight large red drawing pins punctured the map at various positions across its surface.

'Hart is killing to a ritualistic plan,' said Blake. 'In his mind, I think he rationalises the killings as some kind of sacrifice. To intensify the potency of the sacrifice, he carries out the killings to coincide with the appearance of the blood moons.'

'And there lies the problem with your theory. Hart's first murder at St George's didn't coincide with anything. We've checked with the meteorological office, and the moon wasn't even in its first quarter on the date of the killing, let alone part of a tetrad that has occurred less than ten times in the last two thousand years.'

Blake swallowed loudly. 'I know,' he said, conceding the point.

Milton's eyes tracked back over the map.

'But what does match with your theory is the location of the murders. All the killing sites are churches designed by this Hawksmoor architect some three hundred years ago.' He paused. 'Tell me again.'

'I must have trawled a dozen websites by now. He was born in Nottinghamshire around 1661 and at the age of eighteen entered the service of Christopher Wren here in London. He had the reputation for being a brilliant student and became Wren's apprentice, involving himself in some of his master's building projects. Following the Great Fire of London, a commission was set up by an Act of Parliament in 1710 with the purpose of building fifty new churches for the rapidly growing City of London.

'With Wren now+ at 79 years of age, the commission appointed Hawksmoor as one of its surveyors. Due to mounting costs, only twelve churches were completed. Hawksmoor was solely responsible for the architecture of six of them and collaborated on a further two with fellow commissioner John James. Miraculously, all of Hawksmoor's unique city churches have survived to this day, apart from one.'

'St John Horsleydown, where the Servant Church of London now have their headquarters,' said Milton.

'Correct.'

'And why are they special?'

'Hawksmoor was considered a maverick and not fully accepted by the establishment. There are rumours that he dabbled in the occult.'

'Why do you say that?'

'His churches are completely devoid of Christian iconography. Instead Hawksmoor took his inspiration from the ancient pagan traditions of Rome and Egypt. How he got away with this amazes me. He was known to have had a large library that included books on the architecture of many pagan temples from the ancient world, along with the great Islamic mosques and the design for Solomon's Temple. Hawksmoor incorporated aspects of the Solomonic design into his buildings. You've seen the churches; they're strange, unsettling places.'

Milton growled an acknowledgement, his deep voice sounding like it was covered in dust. 'So there are eight churches that Hawksmoor designed outright or built parts of,' said Milton, referring to the pins on the incident board.

Pointing at each of the pins in turn, Blake's finger circumnavigated the map of London.

'St Alphege, Greenwich; St Mary Woolnoth, in the City of London; St Anne's, Limehouse; St George-in-the-East, where the first two killings took place; Christchurch, Spitalfields; St George's, Bloomsbury; St Luke's, Old Street; and finally we have St John Horsleydown, where Joyce Khumalo was murdered.'

'And you're convinced that they're all connected: the killings, the Hawksmoor churches and the blood moons?'

'Almost certainly. Hart's killings are ritualistic. A series of human sacrifices consecrated around Hawksmoor's pagan churches.'

'And the blood moons?'

'They amplify the occult significance of the sacrificial act.'

'Because they are important to the Jewish faith?' asked Milton with a dour face.

'Lots of people think the blood moons are of global significance,' said Blake. 'Some even believe that they are linked to the biblical prophecy of the End Times.'

'You believe in this stuff?' asked Milton.

'It doesn't matter what I believe. It's what Hart believes is the issue. The third blood moon of the current tetrad is tonight and he's out there roaming the streets.'

'So if he plans to kill tonight, it's going to be at one of these Hawksmoor churches. The question is which one? I have officers at each one, including a couple of other detectives patrolling outside the shelter at the Servant Church of London. If Hart is going to try something tonight, we'll be there to nail the son of a bitch.'

'I hope it's enough,' said Blake with a subdued tone.

'The unit is at maximum capacity. With the demonstrations for the city mayoral elections, we just don't have the resources.'

Before Blake could object, Milton's phone went off in his pocket. He answered it and his head dropped in concentration as a voice shouted down the line.

'Pyramid? Slow down man. What did you say, on fire?'

Blake's eyes widened. 'Where? St Anne's Limehouse?'

Milton's massive leathery hand pointed to the drawing pin marking St Anne's church on the map. He ended the call with his on-site detective and moments later was issuing orders to the duty sergeant of the control room.

'Redeploy all units. Everyone to St Anne's church in Limehouse. Get moving.'

CHAPTER 33

Her parents had christened her Janet Brenda Easton, but her clients on the escort agency website knew her by a multitude of other names. A gentleman had once called her 'Snow White' on account of her trademark crimson lips, porcelain skin, and raven hair. It was her special look, he had said.

Janet took the gold lipstick case from her handbag and reapplied the luxurious bright-red colour to her lips. Smiling at her reflection in the large oriental cherry wood mirror, she undid the top two buttons of her blouse and then closed the door of the restroom behind her.

As she returned to the dining booth of the upmarket Mayfair restaurant, she could feel eyes upon her. It was often the case. A young vivacious woman in a revealing outfit, out with an older man, regularly drew disapproving looks. She didn't care. This evening's customer was turning out to be very interesting. He was good-looking despite his advancing years, confident, expensively dressed, with good manners and a knowing smile that could have melted the ice in her gin and tonic. If she played her cards right, she might have actually hit the jackpot this time.

With a small shuffle of her bottom she wiggled herself down the length of the dining booth and returned to her place opposite her new gentleman friend.

'Did you miss me?' she said playfully. She sipped down a large measure of her drink.

'I did. It's been a very agreeable evening. A shame for it to end here.'

Very deliberately Janet leant back in her chair and crossed her long stockinged legs. The man's eyes followed the progress of her thighs under the tight fabric of her silk skirt.

'It would be a pity,' she said, biting her rouged lips.

From under the table, her slim leg reached out and met the edge of his chair. Concealed by the white linen tablecloth, she edged her foot forward, easing a gap between his thighs. She heard the click of his throat swallowing as her foot made contact with his crotch. From over the table, she threw him a stare and slowly applied pressure.

'So what do you want to do now?' she said, her finger teasing an arc around the neck of her blouse and her formidable cleavage. The man followed the path of her painted fingernail.

'I think I should get the bill. Perhaps a nightcap back at my place?' he said, his eyes bright and alive.

'I'm in your hands,' she said as she moved the ball of her foot in a small circular motion. 'Is it far? Because you seem to be getting very excited.' Her last word hung in the air like a smoke ring.

She had thought him a bit uptight when they first met, but now he was well and truly in her tractor beam. She didn't want him to explode; well, at least not yet. She slowly eased off the pressure and returned her foot to the floor.

'Hell, you really are something else,' he said, patting down the front of his fine woollen jacket.

As she got to her feet, Janet began to feel a little giddy. Almost immediately, she felt the reassuring hand of her gentleman friend at her elbow.

CHAPTER 34

A thick trail of acrid smoke cut across the outline of the full moon hanging heavy in the London sky. As Milton turned the patrol car into Three Colt Street, his mouth dropped at the scene. It could have come straight from Dante's *Inferno*.

To the side of the church gardens stood a raging bonfire, and thousands of sparks were drawn upwards from its apex into a vortex of billowing smoke. The brooding edifice of St Anne's Church was alive with the reflected light from the fire. Stretched out shadows reared up at all angles from the recently arrived firefighters who were now circling the pyre. Only when Blake and Milton had shouldered their way through the crowd of onlookers did they see its true form, a perfect dark pyramid standing at the centre of the flames.

Within seconds, Milton was being debriefed by an armed officer who had a Heckler & Koch 9mm carbine slung across his shoulder.

'What the hell is that?' shouted Milton, shielding his eyes from the heat.

'According to a local, the pyramid has stood in the church grounds for as long as they could remember. It was meant to top the church when it was originally built, but was never used. It's been here ever since.'

'It was meant to have been part of the church?'

'Apparently so,' said the officer, trying to force conviction into his voice.

Milton turned his back to the fire. 'What about a body?'

'Nothing yet. All patrols are searching the site with a fine-tooth comb.'

'Stay alert, Hart could well be very close by. I want a full sweep of the area. Call in extra units if you have to. I want this bastard off the streets now.' Milton started to cough in the smoke-choked air. He ushered the policeman away from the flames and cleared his throat.

'Didn't anybody see who started this?'

'We didn't, but a passer-by did. He's over there.' The officer motioned to a worried looking man standing next to one of the five patrol cars parked haphazardly outside the church.

Whilst Milton and the officer interviewed the man, Blake watched the firemen extinguish the flames with gallons of white foam sprayed in a wide arc from a fire engine hose. As the firemen worked, Blake studied the outline of the church. During his research, he had discovered that Hawksmoor had often employed architectural optical illusions to make his churches seem much bigger and heavier than their actual dimensions. Optical illusion or not, St Anne's, like the other churches designed by Wren's troubled apprentice, was no ordinary building. Its mere presence dominated the senses and created an unsettling aura. Blake could feel it rooted in his gut.

Subconsciously, he took several steps further away from the church and then noticed Milton striding back towards him, his face filled with concern.

'There's something not right about this,' he said loudly as soon as was in earshot.

'Less than half an hour ago, that guy,' Milton nodded over in the direction of a man giving a witness statement, 'was walking down Commercial Road and saw a man pull up outside the church on a red off-road motorbike.'

'And?' asked Blake.

'Strapped to the back of the bike were two canisters.'

'Petrol?'

'I guess so. The rider parked the bike just inside the church entrance and disappeared into the grounds with the canisters. Less than a minute later, he was back on his bike and gunning it back towards the city, with a fire raging behind him.'

Both men looked over to the fifteen-foot pyramid smouldering in the light of the blood moon. A fireman was now hosing it down with cold water.

'Let's take a closer look,' said Blake.

After checking the surface temperature of each of its four sides with an electronic thermometer, the fireman gave Blake and Milton the all-clear to approach the pyramid. The fire-fighter handed the DCI a torch.

Blake walked a circumference of the large curious object before cautiously touching the surface with his fingertips.

'Like a gravestone.' he said. 'The cold water has drawn all the heat out.'

'I thought it was made of metal?' said Milton.

'No, I think it's Portland stone, the same material as St Paul's Cathedral. There are letters engraved into it,' said Blake, squinting under the powerful torchlight.

One of the pyramid's faces was divided into five carved panels. The top panel bore an inscription. Blake's index finger traced a path underneath the letters chiselled into the stone.

'The Wisdom of Solomon,' Blake said slowly. 'It says, "The Wisdom of Solomon"', he repeated, this time more assuredly. 'Move the light down a bit.'

Milton did as instructed, and the light beam tracked downwards to the lower panels.

'There are some words, written in Hebrew I think, but they are very faint. Damn it, they're too faint to read.'

Just then Milton's phone rang loudly in his pocket as the headlights of one of the parked patrol cars flashed its headlights in their direction.

Milton handed Blake the torch and retrieved the mobile from his pocket. 'Milton,' he grumbled sourly down the phone. The control room sergeant was talking frantically on the other end of the line.

Blake watched the pressure build in Milton's face as the DCI received the information.

'Shit!' Milton hung up the phone and pretended to hurl the device into the undergrowth in frustration. Finally, Milton locked eyes with Blake. 'All this has been a diversion. He's led us to the wrong bloody church. They've just found a body.'

'Where?' said Blake.

'Christchurch, Spitalfields.'

PART 3

Mark 13:24

At that time, after the anguish of those days,
the sun will be darkened, the moon will give no light.

CHAPTER 35

Diary Entry of Nicholas Hawksmoor
14th May 1681

I received a message from Professor Wren to meet him at William Cooper's bookshop near Smithfield Market at the hour of three in the afternoon. Cooper was a man of dubious references and by reputation a dealer in illegal and highly sought-after astronomical, alchemical and esoteric manuscripts; all obtained through an underground network of merchants, occultists and experimenters throughout England and beyond. He had sent a message to Professor Wren that a fine copy of De architectura by Marcus Vitruvius Pollio had come into his possession and that he was hoping to settle upon a mutually agreeable price. As is my station as the gentleman's mule, I would undoubtedly be required to carry any purchases back to the Professor's address, saving his arms and legs from any fatigue.

I left my lodgings at Middle Temple under some trepidation. Two nights previous had seen rioting in the East End of London. Crowds of zealous weavers from Spitalfields had marched by torchlight protesting against new taxes, intolerably imposed by the City elders. The army had been called to quell the disturbance and in the ensuing agitation, two of the protesters had been shot dead upon the spot and another dragged from the crowd and drowned in a watering trough. The weavers, greatly angered, had vowed revenge. And according to the gossip of the alleys, the mob was melting pewter dishes into bullets.

As I walked with rapid step through London's stony lanes and passages, heavy clouds darkened the landscape. Soon big drops of rain came slanting in upon my face. London was lost in a great swirling fog. Sometimes I stumbled, not seeing a step before me for the thick, opaline mist.

Finally I reached Smithfield and found Cooper's bookshop. I was shown in by a well-shaped, comely woman and was met by the Professor shaking off the rain in the porch.

The bookshop was a wondrous thing to behold. Its grandeur not comprising of one thing but the unique assemblage of all things; not just books and manuscripts but knick-knacks and curios of all types. The main room was very large and furnished throughout, with shelves chock-full of old books and almanacs, ancient registers and parchment sheets.

The Professor was in full discourse with Mr Cooper the bookseller. They were flanked by the comely woman, carrying a tray of cups and a steaming pot of the Turkish drink called coffee. According to Cooper's narrative on the subject, the drink is made from a berry of the same name and is as black as soot. The berry is beaten into a strongly scented powder and is taken, in water, as hot as you can drink it. I myself, was not offered a drop to taste, but I have been told that it is a drink that comforteth the brain and the heart, and also helpeth digestion.

Cooper's discourse with the Professor was gross and full of palpable flattery, telling my master that his reading and travels had made him a great scholar of antiquity. Indeed, only a gentleman of his particular learning would be able to appreciate the fineness of the copy of De architectura he now had in his possession. He went on saluting the Professor in a very lowly and submissive manner. Then with a playful air he added perhaps only he, Professor Wren, could be trusted with those great secrets contained within.

As he talked on, I noticed a large wooden chest standing in the corner, the metal loop of its heavy padlock hanging open from its catch. Curious, I found myself edging towards it, desiring to look inside. When I placed my hand upon the mechanism, Cooper barked at me, like a demon, forbidding me to touch the chest. The outburst was as short as it was fierce, but, I will never forget the look with which it was said. Like I was striking matches over a powder keg. Taking a long draft of his coffee, he returned to blabbing a pretty contrivance with the Professor, but always with some eye over me, in case I was up to some mischief doing.

After several minutes of mutual converse, we were all alarmed by some violent rapping at the door; it was an acquaintance of Cooper who explained that a great mob of weavers had assembled and were marching northwards from the river. He had seen it with his own eyes, a large crowd shouting, jostling, cursing, in the midst of the rain. In such a prodigious confusion, he feared that there would be robbing and all sorts of villainies practiced. He implored Cooper to quickly shutter up his windows. Without another breath, the Professor hurried to his feet and offered his services. He instructed me to take station by the door in order to look out for the mob, whilst the other men and Cooper's woman took haste outside to fix the shutters.

I was completely alone in the shop, all apart from my growing curiosity as to the contents of the chest. Why so a tempestuous reaction from the bookseller? What did it contain? A legion of thoughts ensnared my mind. Soon, I could stand it no more. With briskness of foot and one eye fixed upon the door, I dropped the lock to the floor and opened the lead-lined chest. It gave out a creak so loud, it almost made me jump out of my britches. The chest was a large piece, three paces deep, very broad and filled with all manner of novelties. I spied charms and amulets crafted out of bone and wood, a hunting-whip with a talisman in the handle of it, books and manuscripts wrapped in sindons of linen and, even more curious, a tray of crystal vials filled with a dark red liquor.

In one corner, lying on an embroidered cloth, was a rather odd looking volume. I plucked it out and examined it in my hands. The cover was finely crafted in leather and expertly bound. I perceived it as a book of great antiquity, something that had most likely slept for an age in some great library or other. Impressed into the leather cover was a heathen design that set my hands trembling. It was the geometrical figure of a pyramid and in its centre was crafted an inverted cross, a motif I knew to be linked with occult practices.

For several breaths, I dared not open it. Professor Wren had warned me that some knowledge should only be approached with great caution; after all, hadn't the original temptation of man been the product of Adam's overreaching of sacred knowledge?

But isn't a man nothing but what he knoweth? I thought. Is the eye ever satisfied with seeing, or the ear with hearing? After an inward assent, I reconciled to turn the cover. What I saw written therein took the breath from my lungs, such were the revelations contained on the pages.

All of a sudden, the light from the window became occluded, sending the room into darkness. From beyond the door, I heard Cooper's voice instructing his lady to hold the shutter firm so he could securely lash it in place.

Without thought and being a man of an unbounded and impetuous spirit, I lost no time in securing the book upon my person. The small volume fitted in my coat pocket, like a hand to a glove. I took haste in closing the chest and returning the lock to its clasp just in time for the return of the Professor, who was mightily agitated. He informed me that the mob would be on us within the hour and that we should urgently depart. We bid our solemn regards to Cooper and the woman, who in return wished us safe passage back to our lodgings. With that, the Professor and I parted ways.

I ran all the way, skirting past the marching mob and arriving at the door of my lodgings in Middle Temple, breathless and eager to examine the pagan book hidden in the folds of my topcoat.

I entered the parlour of my lodgings without ceremony and found my landlady sitting before the fire with an empty gin bottle resting on her lap. Creeping past the snoring hag, I took leave to my room and locked the door. With much trembling, I reached into my pocket and tugged out the book. I sat on the edge of my bed and stared sternly down at the pyramid and inverted cross stamped into the soft leather and a devilish excitement took hold of my person; fear and expectation in equal measure.

Girding myself, I lifted the cover of the book and began to read. The volume was divided into two treatises. The first talked of a circle of standing stones that once stood between London's three ancient hills. I recalled hearing of such a legend as a boy, but nothing of their history had survived upon record; as to whether it was a trophy, or a monument of burial, or an altar for worship, or what else. Some thought the large stone displayed in the side of St Swithin's church near Ludgate Hill, also known as the 'London Stone' had been part of such a circle.

The book contained an extraordinary hand-drawn plan, showing where the mighty stone circle of monoliths once stood. The great ring of stones was drawn against the familiar backdrop of Roman London. The walls of the Roman city were clear to see and the Druidic circle was set someway east of Aldgate, outside the fortification. In the very centre of the circle was drawn a pyramid, the same design that had furnished the cover of the book.

The second treatise to the book was filled with occult incantations that promised great powers to the practitioner. Power that came from the inner and furthest recesses of nature. The power to satisfy vast desires. The text described in great detail a magical ritual that if carried out correctly and in exactly the right location could release a tidal wave of elemental power. The location, the book described, was at the very centre of the circle of standing stones. My spirit was completely unhinged by the unveiling of such knowledge. By and by, the evening turned to night and though exceedingly pleased with my discovery, my energies began to dissipate and I fell into a deep sleep.

I dreamed a very remarkable dream, certainly a prophecy cast from the spirit world. It started on a wide and desolate moor crowned with the blackest clouds I had ever seen. Suddenly, a terrifying bolt of lightning was discharged from the base of the clouds, like a fork of splintered gold against the inky blackness. Around the place where the lightning hammered into the ground, a circle of pagan stones grew quickly out of the soil, like a ring of oak trees. Both the lightning and the stones were in some strange way in opposition to each other, as if caught in magnetic repulsion. My mind was pulled this way and that.

Out of the sky a mighty eagle spiralled downwards. It landed on the ruins of an old Roman Temple where the lightning had cracked open the land. Its powerful wings blocked out the sun and in its beak writhed a ferocious serpent. Then like some infinite potter's furnace, my vision was filled with a sea of smoke and sparks, with steeples, domes, gilt crosses, and houses of all types swimming through it. When the smoke parted, the gleaming City of London appeared to me.

With no respite an earthquake shook the ground and a great rift opened up in it. The ring of stones and the Roman Temple along with the eagle were thrown into the gaping pit. Out of fiery mist four great steeples grew, like black towers of Babel, and on their stones I could discern my name written in fire, 'Hawksmoor'. Whilst I was pondering on the sight, I looked down at my hand and in it, I saw a sacrificial dagger dripping in blood.

I awoke greatly disturbed, and with the strong notion that I was at the centre of some extraordinary event that will in due course shake the very pillars of the world.

CHAPTER 36

Blake fidgeted in the passenger seat as the patrol car hurtled at full throttle down Commercial Street. Pulling himself forwards with the door handle, he craned his head at the striking profile of Hawksmoor's Christchurch. The vision that filled the windscreen sent a wave of anxiety through his body. Against the pregnant disc of the moon, the church's bone-white steeple reared up on the skyline like a sharp canine tooth. Blake's thoughts were consumed with what they would find there. His mind raced forward. He willed it to stop, but it just kept rushing ahead, questions tumbling one after another.

Milton hit the brakes and the car careered to a stop, leaving two black tracks stretching out behind it. Reaching over to a button on the dashboard, he silenced the car's sirens and answered the police radio. The words came fast down the handset. Milton barked back several orders, hung up and then launched the radio onto the backseat.

'That's the last thing I need right now.' His hands returned to the steering wheel, his face and grip tightening in unison.

'Lewis is about to land.'

Chief Constable Peter Lewis was Milton's boss. The two men came from different worlds. Milton was a seasoned detective, his reputation built on years of sweat at the hard coalface of police work in the capital. Not only had he battled some of the country's hardest villains, but he had also fought decades of institutionalised prejudice to move up the ranks of the Metropolitan Police Force. Powerfully built and thick set, he wore scars on his face from a life dedicated to crime fighting. A prominent gash, sustained during a drugs bust in Brixton, ran through his eyebrow and along the flesh of his cheek.

Lewis was a career professional. His meteoric rise in the police force was well documented and had more to do with classroom learning and political astuteness than walking the beat. A master's degree in criminology had secured him a foothold in the Force's prestigious fast-track programme, and his intelligence, ambition and determination had soon marked him out for accelerated promotion. He was shrewd, clever and ruthless: traits that assured him success within a force that had lost the public's trust and was under renewed pressure to show results. Formerly the man in charge of the Cambridgeshire Constabulary, Lewis had recently been promoted to a senior position in the London Metropolitan Police. Few doubted that one day he would get all the way to the top of the greasy pole, and rumour had it that he might eventually run for political office. It was only a matter of time before he was hoisting his name aloft at the top of the mountain.

'Shit,' scowled Milton, banging the steering wheel with the palm of his hands.

'If this situation wasn't bad enough. In ten minutes, I'm going to have Lewis breathing down my neck. As soon as he got the message about the body, he excused himself from the mayor's gala dinner. If only I hadn't given the order to divert the unit over to St Anne's church. I've been played like a fool. Goddammit.'

After retrieving shoe covers from Milton's boot, the two men strode off in the direction of a portable lighting rig that was being set up at the side of the church, gravel crunching under their bagged shoes. A huddle of three uniformed constables parted as Milton arrived at the scene.

'Don't you think you should be cordoning this…' Milton immediately felt the words drain out of him at the sight that met his eyes. For several seconds the group remained perfectly silent. Even the sound of the traffic rushing by seemed to be hushed in reverence at the horror of the scene.

An explosion of red shocked the whitewashed exterior wall of the church. Curving trails of dark red pushed out in all directions, like some grisly work of art. At the epicentre of the explosion lay the body of a naked woman, her ghostly pale skin covered in long, thick smears of blood. Her face had been mutilated, eyelids cut and cheeks punctured in triangular shapes. As before, the throat had been cut. Inspecting the pool of blood under the body, Blake could see that the killing had happened just minutes ago, the surface of the pool still trembling due to the engine vibration of the lighting rig.

Blake's eyes tracked down the body. At first the incision above the victim's navel was partially hidden by a mess of splattered gore around the midriff, but as he crouched lower, he saw it. From this new angle, he could also make out the circular edge of an object under the skin.

Blake only muttered two words, but it had the effect of breaking the wall of silence.

'Another coin,' he said.

The uniformed constables looked at him quizzically.

'Forget it,' said Milton, gesturing in the direction of the main road. 'Can you please get this crime scene cordoned off,' he scowled. 'This has just happened. Maybe interviewing some of the public milling around might be a good thing too,' he added pointedly.

The three officers didn't need any more encouragement and moments later were hurrying back up the path.

'Bloody idiots,' Milton said in a voice loud enough to be heard.

His gaze returned to Blake, who was now repositioning the lighting rig with his shoulder. Blake's attention had moved away from the body and had returned to the wall. The greatest profusion of blood was centred on a block of stone set into but protruding several inches out of the base of the wall. A small, blood-spattered plaque was screwed into the wall to one side of the block. At first, the plaque's inscription was hidden in the shadow cast by the stone standing proud from the wall line. With the aid of his phone flashlight, Blake made out the simple dedication it contained and read it aloud.

This foundation stone was laid by Nicholas Hawksmoor in 1715.

Blake stood up, his eyes still fixed upon the plaque, its inscription now returned to shadow. He stood almost in a trance for several seconds. Cocking his head to the side, Blake backed up a step from the wall and considered the position of the body. A constellation of points suddenly linked up in his brain, quickly joined by a surge of adrenaline into his bloodstream.

'I should have realised. Shit,' he said in frustration.

'What?' said Milton, his eyes appraising his friend.

'These killings are sacrifices, like the animal sacrifices in the Jewish Temple.'

'What?'

'The priest is to splash the blood against the altar of the Lord. Leviticus 17:6,' quoted Blake.

Milton tried to keep up. 'And that means ...?'

'Animal sacrifice was central to Jewish worship. Various kinds of animals were slaughtered in the temple precinct and their blood splashed onto the altar. To atone for the sins of the people.'

'You think this foundation stone was used as an altar?'

'Look at the blood spatter. It was the same at St George's and the Servant Church of London. The blood was all concentrated around a particular stone in the side of the wall.'

A spark of recognition flickered across Milton's eyes.

'Now look at the body,' Blake instructed. 'This poor woman has suffered a monstrous attack, and yet her body has been laid out in a particular direction, her hands placed by her side. The other victims were the same, all lined up in specific directions relative to the churches. Like the needle of a compass.'

'A compass?' said Milton, his eyebrow arching upwards slightly.

'Christian churches were often aligned along the cardinal points of a compass. The bodies have been aligned as well. And they're not the only thing.'

'What do you mean?'

Blake motioned the DCI to move closer to the body.

'The incisions next to the navel, they follow the same pattern. They've all been cut at different positions around each of the victim's navels. Each one is marking a point in a pattern.'

'What kind of pattern?'

'If I'm not mistaken, they are following the four points of a cross. The victims' bodies have been moved to align themselves to the same cross-like pattern.'

Blake's thoughts rushed ahead, and Milton was trying to keep up.

'The coins that Hart places under the victim's skin—'

'Old Jewish coins,' said Milton, not remembering the name.

'Tyrian shekels,' added Blake. 'These coins were minted specifically to pay the Temple Tax.'

Milton's eyes pinched forward.

'At the time of Christ, the Jewish authorities required the population to pay a special tax to worship and sacrifice at the great Temple in Jerusalem. The law dictated that the tax could only be paid with these coins. If you didn't offer Tyrian shekels to the temple authorities, you couldn't offer a sacrifice.' Blake began to tap his forehead with his curled index finger. 'Hart is making some kind of offering in human blood, using the foundation stones of these Hawksmoor churches as the altar for his sacrifices. In his twisted mind, he is authenticating each killing with a payment exactly according to the laws of the old Jewish Temple.' A clear mental progression was opening up in Blake's mind. 'Blood offerings to coincide with the incredibly rare occurrence of the tetrad of blood moons during the high Jewish feast days. The potency of these horrific offerings is being amplified, time and time again, with the lining up of these events.'

Blake heard gravelly footsteps coming up the path behind them. Both men turned to see the outline of Chief Constable Lewis, dressed in a dinner suit, marching towards them. His expression was hard as stone. Blake read Milton's face in an instant.

'I'll give you a call in an hour,' said Blake, understanding that he needed to make himself scarce. Ten seconds later he was passing the Chief Constable on the path. Lewis shot Blake a hard stare without stopping. His friend was about to feel the full force of his boss's dissatisfaction.

CHAPTER 37

As he walked to the road in search of a taxi, Blake looked back up to the unsettling profile of Christchurch, which many considered Hawksmoor's master work. It gave him goose bumps, its strange, overpowering presence drilling a dark root deep into his brain.

The site on which the church was built had a macabre history. No area of London was ravaged more by the plague than the surrounding parishes of Aldgate and Whitechapel. To dispose of the bodies, huge pits were dug to receive thousands of unfortunate victims. Hawksmoor's church was built on one such plague pit, and the foundations of the church cut deep into this reservoir of disease. Christchurch's association with death continued into the 19th century, as the dark streets around the church turned into the killing fields of Jack the Ripper. From Blake's research, he remembered how the police had often established the time of events surrounding the murders via witness statements that referenced the time on the well-illuminated clock of Christchurch.

A barking dog brought Blake back into the present. He glanced up at the source of the noise. He couldn't believe his eyes: on the other side of the road, separated by a fast-flowing river of traffic, stood Mary, the homeless lady, and her black dog. He suddenly felt breathless, as if a heavy weight had just been placed on his chest.

The last time he had seen the homeless woman was at St Paul's Cathedral on that fateful day in late November when he and a Vatican academic, Carla Sabatini had nearly lost their lives at the hands of two Eastern European hit men and a deranged industrialist called Ema Mats. *The Times* had described the incident as 'a treasure hunt for an ancient relic that had turned into a blood bath.' There was so much about that day that was unresolved in Blake's mind. One thing he knew for certain was that the homeless woman on the other side of the road was intimately connected with the events. She had met him on the steps of the cathedral and spouted some hocus pocus about the end of the world and a prophecy still to be fulfilled. He got goose bumps thinking about how she took hold of his hands and said that he had been chosen by God to do His will. Her eyes had bored into him with such intensity that they could have punctured two holes in the back of his head.

After finding the entrance to a previously unknown passage in the foundations of the cathedral, Blake and Sabatini discovered the existence of a religious staff, a sacred relic dating back to biblical times. During the ensuing confrontation, Blake came close to losing his life. Wounded and losing consciousness, Blake's final memory was the grainy recollection of the homeless woman and her dog praying over him. DCI Milton wanted to bring her in for fingerprinting, convinced that her prints would be all over a weapon found at the scene. Blake wanted to track her down for another reason: he was convinced she had somehow saved his life. During the subsequent months, Blake had scoured every homeless shelter and rough-sleeping haunt in London, all to no avail. But now, there she was, standing less than thirty feet away.

The woman looked distressed, almost as though she were chiding herself. She rocked back and forth on her feet, her back turned away from him. Blake could feel his heart beat faster in his chest. The traffic was hectic on both sides of the road; one wrong move and she would melt into the shadows and into the crowd of onlookers that had congregated outside the church. With his senses straining, Blake tried to scope out his options. But almost immediately the decision was made for him. She was on the move, and he started to follow, paralleling her on the other side of the street.

With the black dog trotting by her side, Mary set off at full speed down Brushfield Street. Half walking, half running, Blake tried to keep up and shouldered his way through a crowd of office workers who had spilled out of a nearby pub. Through the jostling, he momentarily lost sight of his target but he emerged from the horde and caught sight of a shadow disappearing down a dark alley off to the left. Jogging, he crossed the road and followed in Mary's direction. His footfall stalled at the murky entrance, but as his eyes readjusted, he made his way down the alleyway. His feet gained pace, and then the path suddenly broke off into two branches, one right-angling to the left. He stuttered to a complete stop. Panting in the semi-darkness, his senses looked for some clue as to which route to take. He didn't have to wait long for the answer. The sound of a dog barking some distance off to his left was all he needed to make the turn and move as fast as he could down the narrowing passage. The sound of traffic was getting louder in front of him. Suddenly, he exited the alleyway into the glare of bright streetlights and a pavement thick with pedestrians. Through blinking eyes, he took several seconds to work out where he was: Bishopsgate, the major road cutting through the northeast corner of London's main financial district.

He spun around, desperate to locate the woman. Then he caught a glimpse of Mary and the dog weaving their way through the crowd southwards down Bishopsgate. Spurred on by the adrenaline rushing through his veins, he turned on his heels and gave chase. Less than a minute later, he had caught up the distance.

Mary and the dog moved quickly, striding forwards with intent. The dog went first, like the bow of an icebreaker cutting through the pedestrians coming the other way. If a large black dog advancing purposefully along the pavement wasn't reason enough to step aside, the sight of Mary, with her blackened face, dishevelled appearance and electrified hair, quickly sealed the deal. Without warning, the dog veered down Cannon Street with Mary in tow. Blake followed a safe distance behind.

Several hundred yards further along Cannon Street, Mary's footsteps slowed. Initially, Blake thought that he had been spotted. He darted to a nearby ATM machine and made out that he was typing numbers into its keypad. He waited a brief moment before glancing back up along the street. Mary's attention had changed, but not in Blake's direction; instead, she was now fixed on an ugly iron grille set into the frontage of an unassuming office building.

Cautiously, the woman edged towards the grille. With every tentative step, Mary's posture tightened, as if she were pushing against a strengthening wind. Looking on, Blake could see that her emaciated frame was shaking within her heavy woollen coat. It was as if the iron grille were generating some kind of magnetic force repelling Mary back.

Alarmed, Blake stepped off the pavement and weaved his way through several parked cars to a position some twenty feet away. Advancing slowly, he tried to get a better view of the grille. From this new angle, Blake peered through the wrought iron latticework to what lay beyond the grate. What he saw sent a deep furrow of curiosity across his forehead. A rectangular block of pale stone, no bigger than a portable TV set, was set in a glass display case. Lit from above by several spotlights, the case and the iron grille gave a view of the object from the street, as if it were an expensive diamond necklace in the front of a jewellery shop. His eyes locked onto the weathered metal plaque set into the top of the grille. Even though the lines of citation were hidden in shadow, the title heading could be clearly read.

THE LONDON STONE

CHAPTER 38

Suddenly Mary's spine arched, sending a tremor along her rigid muscles. A strange guttural sound ripped upwards from deep within her. It was soon joined by barking from the dog, who was now pacing a circle around her. Mary collapsed onto the pavement, her limbs shaking and flailing violently. Blake shot forwards. Immediately the dog turned on its feet and growled up at Blake, its glistening eyes flashing with threat. It stood there, taut as a tight spring next to the convulsing woman. Blake edged forward and as he did so, he could see Mary's eyeballs disappearing upwards inside their sockets.

In the corner of his eye, Blake could see people crossing the street to avoid getting caught up in whatever was going on. He pulled his phone from his pocket and punched in the number for the emergency services. Before he could tap the green send key, the squealing sound of an engine filled his ears.

He turned his head just in time to see a red off-road motorbike mount the pavement further along up Cannon Street, hurtling in their direction. A plume of smoke billowed from the bike's back tyre, which etched a criss-crossed pattern of dark rubber behind it. Deftly the rider hauled the motorcycle around a tight arc, the front wheel now facing directly towards Blake.

The rider was dressed from top to bottom in black leathers, a tinted helmet visor obscuring the person's features. On the rider's shoulders was slung a small backpack. Blake watched motionless as the black figure slid the pack off and, with force, hurled it into the air. It whistled past Blake and came to rest in front of the metal grille with its top flap gaping open.

Quickly the rider twisted the throttle, and the massive torque of the bike's powerful engine instantly transferred to its back wheel.

The machine snarled into action and accelerated hard back along the pavement, sending whirlwinds of litter into the air and a trail of burning rubber behind it. Blake followed the progress of the machine up the road until it dipped into a side street, leaving only the sound of its engine roaring in its wake.

His eyes returned to the backpack. Something was flashing inside it. Still wary of the dog, he circled around the animal, stopped, and then continued on to the bag. He lifted the flap of the pack's main compartment and froze. A digital display unit taped to a small block of yellow plasticine-like material was counting down from the number eight. As his eyes travelled down the two wires connecting the digital readout to the block, he made out the words printed on the label attached to the yellow surface:

SEMTEX-H
PLASTIC EXPLOSIVE

'Shit!' he exclaimed, falling back on his haunches. With his feet kicking out in thin air, the readout clicked down to seven. Pivoting on his outstretched arm, Blake scrambled to his feet. Without thinking, he crouched down and took hold of Mary under her arms and pulled her with all his might away from the backpack. At first, Blake's action caused the dog to snarl, snapping its teeth ferociously in his direction, but as he continued hauling Mary towards the parked cars, it seemed to sense a more impending danger in the air.

Momentarily Blake lost his footing and stumbled backwards, his hand fumbling to regain its grip under Mary's arm. The movement dislodged something from her coat pocket. It hit the pavement with a clatter and began to roll along the pavement. As it rolled, a kaleidoscope of colours radiated out from its surface in all directions. Encrusted in precious stones, the rod sparkled under the streetlights before coming to rest inches away from a drain cover. Straining every sinew in his body, Blake hauled Mary's dead weight off the pavement.

Four ...

As the outline of Blake and the homeless woman dropped between two parked cars, Blake called out to the dog.

'Run!'

Three ...

The dog stopped barking and glanced back at Mary in silence.

Two ...

A jolt of panic, spiked in the dog's eyes and it turned and began to run towards the parked cars.

One ...

In the backpack, a simple electrical connection was triggered, initiating a controlled reaction with the detonator buried deep within the block of Semtex.

The light came first. A searing flash of energy. Then came the explosion, like a shock of white lightning hitting the ground. A colossal eruption of shattered glass and metal ripped through the air, smacking into the sides of the parked cars, raising them off their wheels and smashing windscreens. Jagged pieces of metal and concrete screamed past Blake's head, his body splayed across Mary's to protect her from the blast.

In that moment, Blake felt strangely calm, disconnected from time and space. He remembered turning his face away from the office building, snapping his eyes shut and feeling the shockwave punch into the side of his body.

CHAPTER 39

Mary's body moving underneath Blake brought him back to the present. As he struggled to open his eyes, he could feel Mary's rattling breath against his cheek. He rolled onto his side and took a moment to recover his senses. Blood ran into his open eye. He struggled to his feet and steadied himself against a vehicle. The scene that greeted him was a picture of pure carnage. A gaping hole the size of a small car had been blasted out of the side of the office building. A thick electrical cable hung down from the roof and danced in mid-air, sparks coming off its end like struck flint.

Blake tried to take a step, but a spinning nausea gripped his stomach. His knees buckled and a cascade of broken glass fragments fell from his jacket onto the road. Drawing in long painful gasps of air, he struggled onto the pavement.

Mary was up on her elbows, trying to shake the deafening ringing sound from her ears. The blast had jolted her out of her earlier seizure. Abruptly, her eyes jerked open. Her head quickly shot left and right in a desperate attempt to locate her canine companion. She tried to shout, but the breath had been well and truly slapped out of her body. Grabbing hold of a car bumper, she dragged herself to her feet next to Blake. She caught the look of concern in his eyes.

Thirty yards further up the street, next to a half-felled lamp post, lay the crumpled, motionless body of the dog. The force of the blast had launched the animal through the air, and it now lay between the wheels of a large parked truck. The side panels of the vehicle were peppered with debris, and a wedge of concrete several inches across stuck out from the fuel tank. Petrol streamed down onto the pavement, and a dark shadow had already collected around the dog's body.

Blake blinked the blood out of his eyes and his brain switched into overdrive. Before he could move, a gust of wind rattled the partially toppled lamp post, sending splinters of glass down onto the pavement.

Its light began to flicker in unison with a strange buzzing sound from within, as if a large winged insect were trapped inside. Blake's eyes quickly traced the line of the tilting lamp post down to its point of fracture about a metre above the road. Prostrate in a growing pool of petrol, the dog's limbs twitched momentarily and then fell still.

High above, a strong breeze buffeted the shell of the blown-out office building. The top section of the lamp post suddenly gave way, its pale orange light blinking as it hit the ground with a hollow ring. The freed section, still connected to the main post by two electrical wires, bounced several times before coming to rest twenty yards away from the dog's body. With a fizzing death rattle, the lamp finally went out, plunging the area surrounding the animal into shadow.

In that instant, Blake became aware of a sudden stillness; not the stillness of the dog's body, but the stillness of a moment charged with danger. He launched himself from the side of the car and started running towards the dog. Mary gasped and pulled herself onto the pavement. With his feet crunching on shattered glass, Blake swerved around the foot of the lamp post just in time to see the pale blue light of a spark leaping across the small gap between the exposed tungsten filament of the shattered bulb and the pavement surface. Ignition was almost instantaneous and a circular edge of flame radiated out from the bulb like a shockwave. Blake sprinted at full speed towards the dog, the advancing edge of flame biting at his ankles. Giving it everything, he slid down by the side of the animal and, in one synchronised movement, used his forward momentum to roll the animal forward. The push was just enough to propel the dog out of the pool of petrol that had collected underneath it. At that moment, the advancing wave of flame met the pool of gasoline and erupted in a blaze of fire. With a final rally, Blake pulled himself and the dog further along the pavement, out of danger.

The violent jarring of the dog's body roused it out of its unconsciousness. Blake felt a wave of relief crash over his body as the animal staggered to its feet. Almost instantly it started barking towards Mary, who was taking faltering steps in their direction, her eyes glistening. The dog slowly moved forward, increasing its pace with every step. Blake looked on as the two friends were reunited in an embrace of tears and muffled growling.

From the west end of Cannon Street came the sound of sirens. For a moment, Mary's body went stiff, her eyes scanning the horizon for approaching vehicles. The sound was getting louder. She didn't hesitate. Taking hold of Blake's hand, she stared intensely into his sweat-drenched face.

'There is no time,' she said. 'Thank you, Vincent Blake, I pray God will remember what you have done.'

Blake began to say something, but she talked over him.

'He is coming.'

'Who?' said Blake.

'His shadow is everywhere. I can feel him getting closer.'

Blake let go of Mary's hand.

'Look, I don't understand any of this.'

In his peripheral vision, Blake saw blue flashing lights appear in the distance.

'Crossbones Graveyard, tomorrow at midnight.'

'What?'

'Crossbones Graveyard. I'll explain everything then,' she said, already stepping off the pavement.

She turned back to him. 'No police, or everything will be lost.'

Blake watched wide-eyed as Mary and the dog hurried across the street. Within seconds they had disappeared into the shadows of a side alley, running along the side of a sports equipment shop.

Blake walked several steps towards the incoming flotilla of emergency vehicles before dropping to his knees. It had been one hell of a day. As his fingertips tentatively examined a cut to his scalp, he noticed something glinting by the side of the pavement. Caught in the grate of a nearby drain lay a rod-like object, over a foot in length, its surface encrusted in precious stones. Blake's heartbeat stepped up a gear. He recognised the object immediately, though the last time he had seen it, he was fighting for his life in a secret chamber deep within the foundations of St Paul's Cathedral.

CHAPTER 40

Milton wasn't listening to the police officer at his side. Instead he was making a beeline for Blake, who was sitting on the edge of the kerb and wrapped in a silver space blanket. Without acknowledging the ambulance man cleaning the cut on Blake's forehead, Milton dropped to his knees and locked eyes with his friend.

'You okay?'

'I guess.' Blake grimaced with discomfort as the paramedic moved to tend to a deep scratch on his neck.

'Fuck me, most people run away from trouble. You seem to be always running towards it,' said Milton. 'There's going to be a shitstorm of trouble over this. Counter Terrorism Command have been dispatched.' He looked like a man whose bag of woes had just expanded tenfold in the last ten minutes.

'Counter Terrorism? This isn't anything to do with terrorism.'

Milton looked over Blake's shoulder at the gaping hole blown in the office.

'What the hell is it about then?' he said, frustrated. 'It's turning into a bloody war zone.' Milton checked the message that had just buzzed on his phone. 'Lewis is on his way, and I need to give him something. If you know what's going on, you need to tell me.'

Tentatively, Blake brushed the side of his hand along his eyebrow. As he did so, a crust of dried blood tugged at the skin of his forehead.

'It's about a lump of rock,' he said

'What?'

Milton wasn't in the mood for cryptic clues.

'The bomb was set for the London Stone. It was kept behind an iron grille in the side of that office.'

'A lump of rock? Was it valuable?'

Blake thought about the question for a moment.

'Not conventionally, but there is a tradition that the city's well-being is linked to the stone.'

From Milton's pained expression, it was obvious that he didn't understand what his friend was talking about.

Blake nodded thankfully to the paramedic, who was now busy tidying away the contents of his bag.

'You need to get that checked out at the hospital,' said the paramedic to Blake, who was getting to his feet and brushing himself off.

'I'm okay,' he said as he handed back the space blanket.

'I can't tell Lewis that all this is to do with some old tradition. Where are you going?' shouted the DCI after Blake, who was now walking towards the blown-out building.

'I'm going to check it out. You coming? By the way, I followed Mary, the homeless woman here, before it was bombed,' he shouted over his shoulder.

'Say what?' said Milton, a deep line opening up across his forehead.

The explosion had ripped a hole some ten feet in length into the fabric of the office building. Its innards were now spread out in a chaotic trail of destruction across the pavement and into the road. Stumbling over bits of plasterboard, brick and insulation lagging, Blake reached the gaping hole.

He stepped over the mangled remains of the iron grille that had fronted the London Stone and protected it from the enquiring hands of passers-by. Disregarding Milton's protests from over his shoulder, he peered into the breached wall. From the light of a single light bulb blinking on and off in an adjacent office, Blake could make out the shattered remnants of the London Stone. The force of the blast had smashed it into a thousand pieces spread out in a plume of white limestone fragments across the ground.

Blake crouched down and reached in. With his hand at full stretch, he coaxed a piece of the shattered artefact into his fingers. After standing up and taking a couple of steps back onto the pavement, he examined the stone fragment in his palm. It was several inches in length and rectangular, its surfaces clean and white. As he turned it in his hand, a phrase emerged from the recesses of his mind.

'So long as the London Stone is safe, so long shall London flourish.'

An unsettling feeling descended through his body, as his brain spoke to him about the implications of the London Stone's destruction: 'And if the London Stone is destroyed, so will London.'

'It's not safe here,' shouted Milton, his voice sharp with annoyance.

'You're dead right,' mumbled Blake, as he dropped the stone fragment into his pocket.

CHAPTER 41

The front door clicked shut as Blake gently placed his keys in the soap dish perched on the hallway bookcase. He picked up a bright orange piece of paper on the doormat and turned it over. It was a mayoral election flier showing a smiling picture of Captain Sam Lambton with the headline 'A New Direction' adorning its top. Blake read the handwritten note next to the headline.

Vincent, Don't forget to vote (for Lambton that is!), Vijay Desai.

Blake's shoulders sagged an inch, and he placed the flier next to his car keys on the bookcase. Taking care not to make too much noise, he kicked off his shoes and headed for the living room. The stitches above his eye and forehead were stinging like hell, as the local anaesthetic had started to wear off. He scanned the room for an alternative source of pain relief. Rummaging in a cardboard box next to the window, he located a small bottle of whisky. After retrieving a mug from the kitchen and scrutinising his dressings in the mirror, he poured himself a generous measure of the amber-coloured liquid.

Collapsing into the sofa, he took a long sip and breathed out the vapours through his nose. He rested the mug on his chest and closed his eyes in search of some rest, but he couldn't switch off. All he could see was the intense flash of the explosion, as if the light had seared a white-hot disc into the back of his retinas.

A head peered around the door. It was Alina.

'Oh my God, Vincent, what has happened?'

'I had a little trouble at work,' he said with an embarrassed smile.

Alina was wearing a pair of blue chequered pyjamas, the top half of the ensemble all askew to the bottom. The side of her hair was sticking out like the arm of a cyclist signalling to turn a corner.

'I heard some noises. Are you alright?'

'I'm fine,' Blake said.

'Are you sure? You don't look very fine,' she said, moving closer to examine the cuts on Blake's face.

'You think it's going to spoil my rugged good looks?'

'Can I ask, how did it happen?'

'There was an explosion in Cannon Street. I was right next to it, when it went off,' he said with faraway eyes.

'Oh my, that's so awful. You sure I can't get you anything?'

'To tell you the truth, I think I could do with a cigarette right now,' he said half-heartedly. 'I haven't smoked since my army days, but tonight has been a little ...' his mind grasped for the right word, '... challenging.'

'I don't smoke,' said Alina with a shrug.

'Oh yes, I'm sorry I shouldn't have asked. You've given up haven't you? I saw your nicotine patch the other day.'

For an instant, puzzlement darted across her eyes, then she lightly touched her stomach and grew thoughtful.

'Yes, if I stay strong, no more cigarettes,' she said finally.

'How's Sarah?'

'She's fine. After her homework, she went over to see Noorjehan. I think she's angling for a sleepover soon. She had dinner there and was back by seven thirty. She went to bed early, something about a test tomorrow.'

'Algebra,' said Blake, taking a long draw of whisky. 'She'll kill it.'

Alina crossed her arms and smiled.

'Oh, and Rosalind is still out.'

'Still out?'

'She said she was going to a bar in Notting Hill to meet some friends.'

Blake's lips tightened, a shadow of anxiety tracing the outline of his mouth. 'Okay, thanks for letting me know. You get to bed,' said Blake. Alina turned towards the door, a yawn building in her jaws. 'Alina,' said Blake.

'Yes,' she said, stopping at the door.

'It's really good to have you here.'

'It's nice to be here. Good night,' she said with a soft smile.

'Night,' said Blake, his eyes following her out of the door.

Raising himself out of the sofa, he reached for the bottle of whisky. His attention now moved to the hard object poking at him from inside his coat. It was the rod. In the confusion of the bombing, he had grabbed it out of the road and slipped it into his pocket. Since then, it had worked its way through a hole in his pocket and lodged itself in the coat's lining.

After wriggling free from the arms of his coat, he patted down the material and located the end of the rod. He pulled it out and rested it on his lap.

His eyes tightened with concentration at the strange relic in front of him. It measured about the length of his forearm and was made from a piece of twisted wood. The rod was tapered slightly at one end and its surface was inset with a dozen or so gemstones and two rows of Hebrew symbols. Blake turned the object in his hands. Several areas had suffered damage from the blast, particularly around the red gemstone set in the thickest end of the rod. The surface there was striated with wooden splinters, and the lighter wood just below the rod's weathered exterior stood up in jagged shards. Blake shimmied himself onto the edge of the sofa to get more light, but as he did so he felt the staff's centre of gravity shift in his hands. He gave a quizzical look and then gave the rod a gentle shake. This time Blake heard the faintest of rattling. He ran his fingertip around the object's widest end. He did it again, this time while standing under the light hanging from the ceiling. There was no question; a faint junction line ran around the wood an inch or so from the end.

He bit the inside of his cheek while a thought tugged at his mind. As a trained archaeologist, he knew he should ignore it; the idea was reckless, unscientific, yet he desperately wanted to know what secret it held. The object probably dated back to the time of the Old Testament. It was an object of unparalleled historical importance. People had killed for it. He himself had almost lost his life over it. Mary, the homeless woman, would know she had lost it by now. Meet her at midnight at Crossbones Graveyard, she had said. Standing perfectly still in the centre of the room, Blake weighed all the possibilities in his mind.

Just then the front door crashed open.

CHAPTER 42

Blake quickly covered the rod in the folds of his coat and darted for the door. It was Rosalind.

'Holy shit, what happened to you?' she said loudly and more in tune with the crowded bar she had just come from.

'There was an explosion in the City. I got hit.'

'Explosion, terrorists?'

'I don't think so,' said Blake, watching his sister steady herself on the edge of the hallway bookcase.

'You okay?' she said with a slight slur.

'I'm fine, just some scratches. Shall I put some coffee on?'

'I much prefer the look of that,' said Rosalind after spying the opened bottle of whisky through the living room door.

'Do you think you should?'

'So what's good enough for my brother is too good for me. Is that what you are saying?'

He sensed she was only half joking.

'Rosalind, you are not long out of rehab. I don't think getting pissed is part of the programme.'

'I've had a couple of drinks with some old theatre school mates. You think I'm pissed?'

Blake didn't answer and instead just watched his sister weave a haphazard route into the living room and onto the armchair next to the fireplace.

Before joining Rosalind in the living room, he headed for the kitchen and filled the kettle. Returning quickly, he found his sister sitting in the armchair with one knee drawn up, a full mug of whisky resting on top of it.

'This is the brand Dad used to drink, isn't it?'

'I guess it reminds me of him.' Blake sat next to his coat on the sofa.

'I had a long chat with Sarah today. She wanted to know what you were like when you were growing up.' Rosalind took a long sip and playfully gnawed the side of her mug.

'Bloody hell, I hope you didn't tell her the truth,' he said with a wink that pulled at his stitches.

'She knows what happened to mum?'

'Most of it. Why do you ask?' he said.

'She was just asking about what her grandma was like before she went into hospital, that's all.'

After the arson attack on the family bookshop, their mother had suffered a mental breakdown and had lived in a psychiatric hospital ever since.

Rosalind took another sip. 'Dad would have been very proud of her.'

Blake gave a small nod. He cleared his throat and leant back into the sofa.

'She loves school, not like me,' he said, casting a knowing look Rosalind's way. 'I used to walk to school with a knife in one pocket and a book in the other.'

'You were always in some kind of scrape or another.' Rosalind took another draw of whisky.

After the fire, Blake and his sister had come under the care of their godfather, who had sent them away to boarding school. Though a brilliant student, Blake had often been in trouble and had been threatened with expulsion on more than one occasion.

'Always squaring up to authority,' she said. 'Don't worry I didn't tell Sarah. But I did tell her that you were always walking. Where's Vincent? He's wandered off again, looking for some castle or another,' teased Rosalind. 'What were those castles you used to go on and on about?'

'No idea what you're talking about,' said Blake. After boarding school, Blake had embarked on a year-long solo walking trip from Istanbul to Jerusalem following the routes of the Crusades, a distance of over 2,000 km. During this time, he developed a passion for medieval history and the Crusader Knights of the Middle Ages. Years ago he had shared with Rosalind the profound effect his walk across the Middle East had had on him. But tonight he wasn't going to take the bait.

Blake's attention had wavered for a moment but snapped back to Rosalind on the other side of the living room when he realised she was saying something to him.

'How's about it then? Me and you, let's go out one evening this week. Alina can babysit, can't she?'

Blake's body tensed slightly at the suggestion, but his face accepted it with a tired smile.

'Sure,' he said.

'It's a date.'

Rosalind finished her whisky and wiped her lips with the side of her hand.

'I think it's time for bed for me,' she said, getting herself to her feet. 'You going to be long? You look fried.'

'Not long.'

'Don't forget to have a word with Alina about babysitting,' said Rosalind as she negotiated the coffee table in the middle of the room.

'She's a good-looking woman,' she said, ruffling her brother's hair as she passed him on the sofa. 'See you in the morning.'

'Night,' said Blake, his cheeks slightly flushing.

He waited motionless until Rosalind's footfalls ascended the stairs and the door to her bedroom clicked shut. Then his hands were all over his coat, patting it down, hunting for the rod. For a second, he panicked when he couldn't feel its distinctive shape. But after throwing the coat onto the back of the sofa, he found the rod lodged between two cushions. He plucked it out of the gap and jumped to his feet. Quickly he felt for the junction line in the wood an inch from its end. His thumbnail clicked over the ridge in its surface.

Feeling a knot of tension build in his stomach, he heard the voice of his Oxford archaeology professor ringing in his ears: 'Vincent you are an archaeologist with a great future ahead of you, young man. Never forget: it is your responsibility to conserve and protect the archaeological record by your good stewardship.'

The words kept echoing in his mind. *It is your responsibility.*

Something in his head snapped. 'It is my responsibility to find the truth,' Blake said out loud, his words ringing in the silence of the room.

Gripping the rod like a champagne bottle, he pressed his thumbs down onto the neck of the rod just above the junction line. Gradually he increased the pressure to ease the top free. His face thickened with exertion. It wouldn't budge, cemented in place over thousands of years. His eyes were locked onto the junction line, urging it to break. His upper body trembled as the force of his arms transferred through his whitened thumbs to the rod. Suddenly, it shifted in his hands, the top section shooting free from its housing. Blake held his breath and looked down at the pieces in his hands. He was right: there was something hidden within the rod's interior bore. Tipping the rod at an angle, he shook the hidden object free from the wooden cylinder. He gasped as he held it up to the light.

CHAPTER 43

The cobblestones were slippery under foot, and Blake had to flatten his footsteps as he turned the corner into Redcross Way. A carpet of milky fog enveloped the pavement leading to the metal gates that guarded the entrance to Crossbones Graveyard. As he approached the gates, a chilly wind blew across his face. The stitches in his forehead were still sharp and raw, and the cold air made them throb with a pulsing ache.

Blake had known nothing about Crossbones Graveyard until he had typed the name into his computer's search engine. Thankfully, the search had given the location of the site and something of its sad and strange history. Blake read that even though today Crossbones Graveyard was nothing but a tiny piece of derelict wasteland tucked between Southwark Cathedral and the reconstruction of Shakespeare's Globe Theatre, the ground hid a tragic secret. Under the crumbling tarmac lay the bodies of over 15,000 people.

According to the website, the area had been part of a seventy-acre area known as the 'Liberty of the Clink'. The Liberty had been exempt from the jurisdiction of the Sheriff of London and instead had been controlled by the Bishop of Winchester, who also usually held the office of Chancellor or Treasurer to the King. Until the mid-seventeenth century, the Winchester bishops represented a major power centre in England. Blake couldn't believe his eyes when he read that, in 1161, the Bishop of Winchester was granted the authority to licence prostitutes and brothels in the area of the Liberty south of the Thames. Tragically, these unfortunate women were refused burial in consecrated ground due to their sinful profession and were found land far away from the local parish church. This land became known as Crossbones Graveyard. He read that the gate bordering the derelict land had been made into a makeshift tribute to London's outcast and forgotten dead, and sure enough the bars of the gate were adorned with countless ribbons blowing in the crisp night air.

Seeing that there was no lock, he tried the gate. He pushed against the scraping resistance of its hinges, opened up a gap, and edged through. It didn't take long to find her. Blake could make out Mary's outline, sitting cross-legged on a stack of wooden packing crates, illuminated by the streetlights bleeding through the fog. At her side stood her constant companion. The black dog barked at Blake's approach, with its eyes fixed upon his every move. Blake had to stay alert. He didn't know whether he was being played or whether he would finally find out more about the enigmatic Mary, who always seemed to be two steps ahead of him. Coming to this deserted location in the middle of the night without back-up meant he was flying blind. As he walked, he glanced to his left and right trying to discern any movement in the shadows.

'Mary,' he spoke into the chilled air as he cautiously eyed up the dog.

Her eyes snapped open. It took a moment for Mary's focus to find Blake's profile in the chalky mist.

'Vincent.' The word almost oozed from her lips. Under the sodium glare of the streetlight, she looked like a ghost, her skin not quite white, but the colour of pale lead.

'Do you have the rod?' she said, her voice turning anxious.

'It's in a safe place,' said Blake.

'Where is it? I need to get it back.' Concern clouded her face.

'Not so fast. You need to tell me what the hell is going on,' said Blake. 'Do you know where Enoch Hart is?'

At first she offered nothing, her expression rigid.

'I know you and Hart knew each other back at the shelter. The shelter at the Servant Church.'

Mary looked down at her dog and then eased herself off the wooden crates onto her feet.

'You saved our lives last night,' she said, running her hand down the animal's neck. 'We are both in your debt. I guess that makes us even.'

'You mean at St Paul's?' he said, referring to his blurred recollection of Mary's connection to his rescue deep in the foundations of the cathedral.

She nodded.

'Thank you,' he said. 'I guess it does. Now tell me what's going on?'

'What's going on?'

'What happened at the shelter between you and Hart?' said Blake.

Mary let out a long sigh, her breath visible in the cold air.

'I became very sick whilst I was staying at the shelter. Enoch Hart saved me, like you saved me last night.'

'Saved you? Saved you from what?'

'From a demon,' she said solemnly.

For a second, Blake didn't say anything. Somehow, he had hoped that Angelo Ricard's story of exorcism had been just an embellishment of Mary's mental breakdown.

'You think you were possessed by a demon?'

'I know I was,' she said. 'Since I was a young girl, I have always been sensitive to the things around me. The flows of energy that course through us and around us. I see things that other people cannot.'

'Things like?' asked Blake.

'I see auras,' she said. 'There are colours, always colours. Energy rushing and bending in the air. Things would be so different if others could see what I see. People wouldn't be judged by their exterior appearances. They would be seen in their true nature. The true nature of their souls.' She paused. 'That's how I knew you were different. When we met that day at St Paul's Cathedral.'

'You saw my aura?' said Blake.

'I saw it then, and I see it now. Your path was written long ago, Vincent Blake.'

'Is this for real?'

'It's very real,' said Mary. 'You see this city as a physical place, fixed in time and space, made of brick and concrete. I see that too, but I also feel the true nature of the place. London pulses with energy, some light, some dark,' she said, rocking from foot to foot. 'There are beacons of light in the city, sanctified places like St Paul's Cathedral. There, I can feel pure energy surging under my feet. Your aura Vincent Blake is of the same energy. Your life has been baptised in the same stream of holy power that is present in that place.'

Before Blake could say anything, Mary's rocking quickened.

'Then there are the pits of blackness,' she said, as she drifted to a faraway place in her mind. 'Ancient evil places that draw darkness into themselves. Like the Minories in the East End.'

'What did you say?' He struggled to recall what he knew about the location. Without giving Mary time to reply, he said, 'The Druid stone circle?'

Mary nodded.

'The ancients knew of the terrible, dark power that lay in the ground there. They built a great magic circle of unhewn stones around the place to keep the evil locked in the earth. Once the Romans came, they tore it down, thinking it to be a temple of pagan witchcraft. The London Stone was the last remnant of the circle. A great Roman mausoleum was built, its foundations located at the centre of where the circle once stood. But with the circle gone, the darkness in the ground began to seep upwards again into the city.'

Blake could hardly believe what he was hearing.

'I felt its power the day I fell sick. It was somehow connected to the shelter.'

'The shelter of the Servant Church of London?' said Blake.

She nodded. 'I didn't know then, but the shelter had been built on the foundations of a church built by Nicholas Hawksmoor.'

'St John Horsleydown,' said Blake.

Mary nodded.

'There, I felt a line of dark energy surging through the very fabric of the church building and heading off northwards through the ground. We followed it,' she said, glancing down to the dog. The tone of her voice turned grave. 'Eventually we came to the Minories. The direction of the dark energy led us off the main road and onto a piece of disused land with an iron fence. As we squeezed through a gap in the fence, a large black raven landed directly in front of us. I can remember to this day, its small black eyes staring right through me. It flew off to the side of a grassy bank running along one side of the disused plot. The bird disappeared behind a large rock embedded in the side of the bank. As we walked closer, I could see a dark recess lying further behind the rock. I hacked away at the undergrowth and saw that it was actually an entrance to a small tunnel into the bank. I could feel the dark energy being drawn into the tunnel.' She took down a gulp of air and composed herself. 'I had a cigarette lighter with me, so we could see a little in the dark. Together we travelled down the tunnel. As we scrabbled through the passageway, a burning smell like sulphur came off the walls. Then I felt something fly out from the shadows. It was the raven.

'It clawed at my hair and its beak drew blood from my neck. Its talons dragged me backwards onto the floor. As I lay there with my friend snapping up at the bird, I saw something take form in the darkness, all twisted and misshapen. It came closer and soon I felt a growing circle of darkness envelop me. I couldn't move, my will powerless to fight such a force pulling me down.' Mary's eyes glistened with tears.

'What happened?' said Blake gently.

'I don't know. The next thing I remember clearly was Enoch Hart praying over me at St. George's church. He had just performed the exorcism to drive out the demon that had entered me on that day. It felt as if a dark fist that had been clenching at my heart was suddenly released.'

Out of the corner of his eye, Blake caught the outline of a figure spring out from the shadows. He tried to whip his head around, but his motion was halted by a gun barrel at the base of his neck. From behind his shoulder, a cold voice whispered, 'Give me the rod.'

CHAPTER 44

Blake shot Mary a white-hot glare. She had set him up. Milton had been right all along. She had been part of the problem, not the solution. He chided himself for not accepting it. Hell, he should have known better. He had taken the bait and now was getting reeled in to have his throat cut.

'Turn around slowly,' the voice said from behind his head.

Blake complied with the instruction and was soon staring down the barrel of a gun into the face of Enoch Hart. Rubbing away the soreness in his neck where the gun had been, Blake sized up the UK's most wanted man.

Enoch Hart, ex-SAS soldier and hunted serial killer. Searching through dozens of police photos as Blake had over the last few months, Hart's face had become imprinted onto his brain. Even though his unruly beard was gone and his hair was now razored close to his scalp, his features were unmistakable.

He was athletically built; not bulky, but lithe like a triathlete. His skin was swarthy, and deep lines bracketed his mouth and forehead. His nose looked like it had been broken a multitude of times, and his eyes were chilling in their intensity. With his free hand, Hart pulled something from his back pocket and handed it to Mary.

'Cuff him,' he said.

Blake stood rigid as he watched Mary push the arms of the handcuffs tight around his wrists. As the cuffs' ratcheted teeth locked firmly into place, a surge of anger roared up through Blake's body. Had Hart and Mary been working together all along? Is that why she had been seen at the crime scenes? His fists tightened, railing against the chain. Was he going to be executed here and now? He thought of Sarah and his neck turned rigid with fury.

'Calm your ass down,' said Hart pushing his Glock into Blake's forehead.

'I'm here for the rod,' he said. 'Where is it?'

Blake said nothing, weighing his options in his head.

As Hart pressed the cold circle of metal further into his temple, Blake realised he hadn't got any.

'Don't screw with me.' Hart's voice was edged with threat.

'In my coat pocket,' said Blake. 'But I warn you, it was damaged in the blast.'

'Damaged?'

Blake spied concern in Hart's eyes, as the serial killer glanced over to Mary. Keeping the gun pushed against Blake's head, Hart patted down the pockets of his captive. He found the outline of the rod within the coat's material. Slowly Hart pulled the rod from the coat pocket. Once he had the object, he relaxed his weapon and took several steps away from Blake. He examined it closely.

Even in the soft amber glow of the streetlights, the damage to the rod's outer wooden casing was obvious. Splinters of pale wood stood up from the rod's time-stained surface. He turned it in his hands and looked down its length, as if it were a pool cue. With the gun still in his hand, he began to work the top section of the rod, left and right. Through gritted teeth, he eased the upper part of the rod free, just like Blake had done the night before. He carefully slid out a thin black cylinder and then held it up to his face. An eerie silence filled their ears, as Hart studied the object for damage.

'Thank God, thank God,' he said finally, his expression softening by the smallest fraction.

Shuffling the gun and the black cylinder in his hands, his focus now returned to the rod's outer wooden casing. Blake watched as Hart traced its pitted exterior with his fingertips.

'One of the stones is missing?' he said, a coldness returning to his eyes. 'There should be twelve, and there are only eleven here.' The gun was raised again towards Blake. 'Don't screw with me, where is it?' A second later the barrel of the gun was being pressed between Blake's eyes. 'You have one chance. Where is it?'

'I don't know I swear,' said Blake, his voice shredded with desperation.

'Don't make me do it. Three.' Hart started counting down. 'Two.'

The dog was on its feet, it's large eyes glancing up at Mary.

'One.' Hart's finger tightened on the trigger.

'Pocket, check the pocket again,' exclaimed Blake, his voice echoing around them.

With his eyes drilling into his prisoner's face, Hart dug his hand deep into the pocket of Blake's coat. His expression broadened as his fingertips made contact with something hard in the creases of the lining. Coaxing it upwards into his hand, Hart pulled it free and inspected it under the streetlight. A pale red light shone over Hart's hand as he turned the square ruby between his thumb and index finger.

'*In nomine Patris et Filii et Spiritus Sancti*,' said Hart to himself.

Blake immediately recognised the Latin trinitarian formula: In the name of the Father, and of the Son, and of the Holy Spirit.

A visible sense of relief travelled across Hart's face as he pocketed the stone along with the other parts of the rod. Lowering his weapon, Hart stared at his captive through his penetrating eyes.

'I had to make sure,' he said. 'After Mary realised that she had dropped the rod in the blast, we went back to the scene to see if we could find it. It was bloody dangerous, what with the police everywhere, but I guess they weren't expecting us to be around. We thought you must have picked it up.'

Blake didn't say anything, his stance defiant.

'You know Dr Blake, we are all on the same side here.'

'How the hell do you figure that?' said Blake. 'Killing innocent women isn't being on my side,' he said, his wrists straining against the chain of the handcuffs.

'I didn't kill those women,' Hart said pointedly.

'You even admitted killing the poor vicar of St George's at your trial. Or did you forget that?' said Blake. He hesitated. Goading a convicted killer when he had a gun in his hand probably wasn't his smartest move.

Hart looked down to the ground.

'You are stepping into a world you don't understand,' he said slowly.

CHAPTER 45

'Then educate me,' said Blake defiantly. Hart looked him up and down.

'Time is short Blake. What do you want to know?'

A perplexed look came to Blake's face. A moment ago, he thought he was going to end up with a smoking hole in the centre of his forehead and now he was being invited to ask questions?

'What happened with you and her?' said Blake, nodding over to Mary.

'You really have no idea what's going on, do you?' Hart gave the side of his scalp a vigorous rub. 'I'm sure you know I was in the army. In the SAS to be precise. I was in Iraq, working undercover when something happened that made me question everything.'

'What do you mean?' asked Blake.

'That's not important. Let us just say, I discovered my faith and my vocation. I left the army and trained to become a priest. During my training, I was singled out to come under the supervision of a man called Father Theodore.'

'Singled out?'

'He recognised in me the signs of the charism.'

By the confusion that had broken out on Blake's face, he decided to elaborate further.

'Charism are the fruits of the spirit described in the bible. Gifts that God chooses to bestow on His faithful. Father Theodore saw in me the gift of discernment of spiritual agents. It is like having the holy light of God lighting the way on a dark night,' he said. 'Discernment is often associated with a spontaneous pigmentation of the skin, like the stigmata, a phenomenon well known in the Roman Catholic church.'

Passing his gun from one hand to another, Hart splayed open the fingers of his right hand. From his knuckle upwards, the skin of his index finger was darkened to almost black. It took a moment for Blake to register the significance of what he was seeing. When he did realise, he shifted uncomfortably on his feet, trying not to look at his own hand.

'You appear to have the beginnings of it too.'

'It's a bloody birthmark,' said Blake pointedly. 'Just a bloody birthmark.'

Hart didn't press the point home.

'Through my work with Father Theodore, I came to realise that true spiritual evil does exist in the world, and we are all under threat. He showed me things that defy the natural order of this world.'

'You mean demons?'

'Let me assure you, Dr Blake, demons are real.' His voice turned deadly serious. 'They are not like those depicted in children's stories and comic books. They are out to destroy every living soul on this planet. They are incapable of feeling love and only satisfied by the desire to do evil. The same kind of satisfaction that people feel when they get revenge on an enemy, a satisfaction filled with hate. With Father Theodore, I learned how to practice the Rite, the holy prayer of liberation and over time I became initiated.'

'You became an exorcist?'

'That was part of it,' he said cryptically. 'The word exorcism comes from the Greek *exorkizo*, meaning to bind with an oath. During the exorcism, a demon is commanded to come out of the person it is occupying, in the name of God. You must realise that the demon is a created being, just like you or I, and therefore ultimately subject to God's power. An exorcism is only conclusive when it is performed in the name of God. It tells us in the book of Matthew that Jesus gave this authority to his twelve disciples.' Hart then quoted from Matthew 10:1: 'Jesus summoned his twelve disciples and gave them authority over unclean spirits, to cast them out, and to cure every disease and every sickness.'

'The demons, where do they come from?' asked Blake.

'They are found in every culture and every religion around the world,' continued Hart. 'In the beginning before mankind, God created the angels to honour and worship Him. Since love not freely given is not love at all, the angels were given the ability to choose. Some of the angels chose love, some chose sin. The ones who chose sin were stripped of their everlasting grace and expelled from heaven. First Satan was thrown down to earth in a lightning bolt and he was quickly followed by his hordes of fallen angels. Cut off from the grace of God, the very natures of these spiritual beings became twisted and deformed. According to the Christian tradition, after the angels fell from heaven, God created the first humans. When this happened, Satan turned his vengeance on mankind.'

Hart toted his Glock towards the sky.

'We are at a turning point, Dr Blake. A darkness is coming. These killings will be just the start.'

'If you didn't commit the killings, why don't you just hand yourself in?'

'I can't, I have to stop this,' said Hart earnestly. 'Through Mary, information was revealed to us by the demon that possessed her at the Minories. There will be four killings. Four killings to release a great evil into the world. Yesterday's killing at Christchurch was the third, one more and I fear that a great evil will invade the world. We are all sleep walking into the abyss.'

Blake's brain was churning. His mind replayed the words that Mary had written in her own blood on the walls of her room at the shelter. He had been able to make out most of the blood writing in the photographs.

FOUR BLOOD ALTARS
FOUR BLOOD SACRIFICES
FOUR BLOOD COINS
FOUR BLOOD MOONS

'You've seen the police report of the arson?'

Blake nodded. 'What happened at Mary's exorcism?' he pressed.

'There were three of us. Mary, myself and the vicar of St George's. It is quite normal for a practitioner of the Rite to call upon the services of another to assist in an exorcism. Strength in numbers, you might say. It can be a long and arduous process and it places great physical and mental demands on the people involved. I hadn't met the vicar before, and I sought assurances from the church elders that she was strong enough in faith to withstand such a spiritual onslaught.' For a moment, Hart's eyes turned downwards. 'An exorcism is a crusade against a very clever and dangerous enemy. If the demon detects a weakness in a practitioner's spiritual armour, it will use it to its advantage.'

'Go on,' said Blake.

Hart continued, but as he did so, Blake could see that Mary's eyes were filling up with tears.

'A room was prepared at St George's for the exorcism, and Mary was brought to us. She was in a very bad way.'

'A bad way? How?'

'Disturbed, hearing voices and seeing dark visions. She refused to look at us. This is one of the signs of possession, that the subject is unable to look into the eyes of the exorcist. Another criterion to discern possession is the subject's aversion to signs of the sacred. I asked her to say the word 'Jesus' and offered her communion, both of which she refused to do. Her face was vacant, shut up, as if she were no longer present. After saying prayers, I opened my bag and retrieved a bottle of holy water. When I sprinkled it over her head, she began thrashing out and screaming as if the water were burning her skin. A deep, grating voice erupted out of her, nothing like that of a woman. Then the temperature in the room suddenly dropped, and with it came the smell of sulphur. She was like a trapped animal, howling and spitting.'

Blake could feel a sickening feeling spread through his body. His throat tightened.

'We carefully moved closer, all the time asking God for His protection. As we approached the demon, it kept chanting over and over, "Shut up you stupid priest, you have no authority over me. My master is coming, my master is coming." I tried to reach out with my crucifix and touch her head with it, but as I did so, I started to feel hard blows to my shins, as if someone were kicking me, but it wasn't Mary, it was something else. Her face was so contorted, you couldn't recognise her anymore. We backed off, realising the great strength of the demon inside her.

'We locked her in the room and rested outside for an hour to fortify our spirits and pray for God's protection over each other. When we went back in, we found Mary sitting on a metal chair in silence. As we edged closer, we could see although her eyes were shut, her eyeballs were moving rapidly beneath her eyelids. With duct tape from my bag, we carefully tied Mary's arms and legs to the chair. With her body restrained, we began reading passages from the bible. Recognising the sounds of the scriptures, her eyes snapped open and she began to fight against her bindings.

'"You don't really believe in those kid's stories do you?" she sneered to the vicar in a high-pitched voice. These are the tactics demons use to rattle their opponents. They are liars, trying to find any chink in the spiritual armour of their adversary. The demon started goading the vicar about her personal life and her struggles with her vow of chastity. That's another sign of possession, the knowledge of facts that should not be known. I knew time was running out, and so I started to recite the prayer of liberation.'

Blake watched on as Hart's face replayed the scene.

'"Be humbled under the powerful hand of God. I adjure you, accursed beast, in the name of Jesus Christ, depart from this creature of God," I exclaimed. Thrashing and screaming, the demon started spitting in my face. I knew I was close. "In the name of Jesus Christ," I commanded, "I order you to stop and leave this woman." The demon started screaming and biting at the air. "My master is coming. No one can stop him, not you, not anyone".' Hart took a breath and stared at Blake square in the eyes. 'The more an exorcist sincerely invokes the help of God, the fiercer the evil fights back. Then it started reciting the phrase that Mary had written in blood on the walls of the shelter. "Eve can't blink, Eve can't blink," it sneered with pure hate in its eyes. In one final effort, I planted my crucifix onto her temple and shouted, "In

Christ, I command you to be gone".' Hart took a gulp of cold air. 'Then it departed her,' he said, throwing Mary a strained smile.

'As I untied her from the metal chair, I remember noticing that the back legs had been bent completely out of shape.'

'How could you tell for sure that it had left her?' asked Blake.

'The shadow.'

'The shadow? What do you mean?'

'It's like a stain that gets left behind. I found it under Mary's chair. When a demon is commanded out of a person, it leaves an angular mark on the inanimate surface nearest to its exit point from the body. These marks are usually found on floors or walls close to the victim. It marks the point where the demon leaves this world and enters the void looking for a new host.'

'It isn't killed?'

'According to Father Theodore, once they have been expelled from their victim, they survive for a short time in the void, searching for a new body to possess.'

Blake tried to say something, but a knot had formed at the top of his throat.

'After we had made Mary comfortable and informed Angelo Ricard and the church elders that the exorcism was successful, I went out into the church gardens to get some air. I can remember the sounds of the birds singing in the trees, and I gave thanks to God for His mercy.' He paused. 'Then it happened.'

Hart dropped the hand holding the gun down by his side. Blake heard him swallow hard.

'The spikes of a gardening fork came out of nowhere. If I hadn't turned in time, they would have skewered three holes in my neck. Pivoting around, I came face to face with the vicar, her eyes blazing with sheer hatred. In her grip was a gardening fork she had taken from the shed, and she was jabbing at my body. She was demented with rage and unbelievably strong. I tried to defend myself as best as I could, but as she lunged at my face with the spikes, I lost my footing and fell backwards onto the ground. Within moments she was on me, like a rabid animal.

Her strength was unbelievable, like nothing I had experienced in all my years in the military. Unnatural power,' Hart said coldly. 'I grabbed at her wrist, the one holding the fork, and with her drool falling into my eyes, I managed to slowly twist the spikes back upwards. Shouting up to God, I pushed against her with all my might. Suddenly, the fork jerked free and its metal blades plunged into the woman's neck. That's when Ricard arrived. I was covered in blood, holding the weapon.'

'Didn't you tell this to the police?'

'Of course, I told them everything, but what were they to believe? I had killed in self-defence. In self-defence from what? A demon? The police, the jury, my legal team, no one believed a word of it. I was sectioned and sent to Broadmoor. I broke out, not to continue the killing, but to stop it. There are things you don't understand, Dr Blake. Monumental things that happened at the Minories long ago. The very soil of that place is steeped in evil. The seeds of darkness have started to germinate in the ground there.

'The area surrounding the Minories has been cursed for millennia. History only records a fraction of the murders that have taken place in a circle around the Minories. The Jack the Ripper Murders and Radcliffe Highway murders are the most infamous, but now a new wave of sacrifice has started, and again around Hawksmoor's pagan temples.' Hart waved his gun in a long sweep in front of himself.

'Here at Crossbones Graveyard are buried the bodies of London's forgotten people. The poor, the dispossessed, the rejected. These are people that our Lord Jesus Christ set his ministry to serve. The victims of all the Hawksmoor murders are the same struggling people. A homeless woman, an immigrant, a prostitute. The person carrying out the killings is perverting Jesus's ministry of hope into a sacrifice to evil. It has to be stopped before an even greater darkness is released into the world.'

'If it's not you, then who's doing the killing?' asked Blake sternly.

'I don't know. Hawksmoor's churches are the key. On the nights of the blood moons, Mary and I have camped out at several Hawksmoor churches, guessing which one might be next. We guessed right on the second eclipse in the tetrad.'

'At the Servant Church of London?' asked Blake.

'I got several shots off at the killer whilst he was fleeing the scene, but I missed. It was dark and the wind was up. I couldn't see his face; it was covered in a ski mask.'

Blake flashed back to the bullet holes in the walls of the church's office. Had he been wrong all along? Had the police been hunting the wrong man? His mind was reeling with the possibilities.

'The killer just needs to sacrifice one more victim to complete the hellish pattern. They will stop at nothing to make this happen. The London Stone could have been used against the evil, but last night it was blown up.' Deep lines were etched across Hart's face.

Just at that moment, the air was filled with the sound of sirens shrieking close by. With his eyes raking the skyline, Hart shouted over to Mary.

'We've got to get out of here now.'

Blake watched as Hart plunged his weapon into his coat pocket. His hand came out minus the gun but holding a small ring of keys. A fraction of a second later, they were flying in Blake's direction. His bound hands grabbed them out of the air.

'Wait,' he shouted over the cold breeze, but Mary and Hart were already disappearing into the thick darkness.

'What about the rod?' he shouted. 'What's it for?'

Hart shouted back over his shoulder, but his words were drowned out by the sound of sirens.

CHAPTER 46

Blake worked the key to his front door and shouldered it open. His mind was racing, swirling with thoughts. He had returned from Crossbones Graveyard with more questions than answers. Was it beyond imagination to think that Hart was telling the truth? His description of the events surrounding Mary's exorcism might be difficult to accept, but that didn't make it untrue.

Before, he and Milton had been operating in the dark, convinced that Hart had been the killer. Had they got the whole thing wrong? Deep in his mind he sensed that now at least, he had found a handhold to help pull himself out of the darkness. He could only hope that he read the ex-special forces soldier right.

He headed for the kitchen and tried to wash away his headache with some cold water from the sink. He was worn out by fatigue and worry, but his mind refused to slow down, trapped in a maze of guesswork and assumptions. Watching the water drain from the sink, he considered again the shocking writing that Mary had written in her own blood on the walls of the shelter.

HAWKSMOOR

FOUR BLOOD ALTARS
FOUR BLOOD SACRIFICES
FOUR BLOOD COINS
FOUR BLOOD MOONS

And what was the other thing that had been written underneath the quatrain?

EVE CAN'T BLINK

After retrieving a bottle of beer from the fridge, he hunted in a kitchen drawer for a pencil. He found one, slid it into his back pocket, and made his way quietly back into the hallway. Seeing the chipped soap dish perched on the bookcase in the hallway, he dug his hand into his coat pocket for his keys. Instead of the familiar outline of the key fob of his Alfa Romeo, his fingers met the jagged edge of something hard in his pocket. His hand momentarily recoiled, and then he remembered the fragment of the London Stone he had retrieved from the blown-out remains of the office building. Carefully he plucked it out of his pocket. If Mary was right, then the piece of white limestone in his hands had been used by the Druids thousands of years ago. Had it been part of a huge stone circle?

Not wanting to make too much noise, he crept up the stairs and along the landing to his bedroom. The landing light made a loud click when he switched it on. Rounding his bed, he placed the stone inside his bedside table and lifted an old leather briefcase from the floor.

A minute later he was sitting on the sofa in his living room with the beer in his hand and the briefcase on his lap. He gulped down a swig of strong Belgian beer and swept a hand over the cracked surface of the leather briefcase. It felt old and rough, like sunburnt skin. Straining forwards, he placed the bottle on the coffee table and clicked open the lock to the briefcase. Blake rummaged through its contents and pulled out the police case file for the Hawksmoor murders.

With the events of the last few hours playing in his mind, he skimmed through the pages of the report, pausing at the grisly crime scene photographs in a wallet stuck onto its back cover. The scenes of carnage were horrific beyond belief. But they weren't random acts of brutality; these were premeditated and precise. He edged himself off the sofa and discarded the file next to the bottle of beer on the coffee table. His attention drifted to his makeshift map on the far wall. It had become something of a familiar feature of the room.

He stepped closer, his eyes darting between the positions of the murder sites marked on the wall. He ticked them off in his head: St George-in-the-East, St John Horsleydown, Christchurch Spitalfields.

According to Hart and Mary's prophetic blood writing on the walls of the shelter, there would be one more murder. But where? Time was running out. The final blood moon of the tetrad was just days away. It would take place at a Hawksmoor church, that was certain, but which one?

During his career, the enigmatic architect had built eight churches in London. Six as sole endeavours, two jointly as a collaboration with another architect. Three of these churches had already been used for killing. It would make sense for one of the other five to be the intended site for the completion of the killer's diabolical scheme.

A thick vein throbbed in his temple, which he tried to rub away with the heel of his hand. From out of nowhere something zipped across his mind. It was something that Mary had said when she had described the line of dark energy that had led her from the shelter to the Minories. What did she say exactly? That the very fabric of the building had been connected to the Minories by a line of dark energy?

Within a second, he was on his phone, pulling up a map of the Minories and checking its relative location to the three murder sites. His fingers fumbled for the pencil in his back pocket. Working quickly, he marked the locations on the wall. With an artist's hand, he drew a perfectly straight line linking the shelter, the old site of St John Horsleydown, to the Minories. He could feel his heart quickening. Then he drew another line linking St George-in-the-East to the Minories. This time his hand had started to tremble. He held his breath and then placed the tip of the pencil on the blue blob of paint, marking the position of Christchurch, Spitalfields in the north. With his mouth tightly pinched shut, he drew his pencil downwards towards the mark indicating the position of the Minories.

His heart was in his throat as he stepped back and surveyed the wall. All three churches were exactly equidistant from the Minories, which was at the very centre of the pattern. But something was missing. One line linked the east to the centre, one line linked the south to the centre, and the line from Christchurch to the Minories connected the north to the centre. Blake's gaze automatically zoned in on the imaginary line linking the Minories to a point equidistant and to the west of the centre of the pattern. He moved back to gain perspective. Blake then marked the missing position on the map and drew a corresponding line to the other three. The four lines now formed a perfect cross with the Minories at its middle.

With his mind steaming forwards, he referred back to his phone. He pecked at its keyboard for several seconds. Moments later, a map of the area indicated by the end of Blake's imaginary line popped up on its display. He quickly resized the map with his fingertips and orientated it with his drawing on the wall. His eyes scanned the screen, looking for a familiar place name. Next to a logo indicating the location of Bank Tube Station was the familiar cross sign motif indicating the position of a church: St Mary Woolnoth. The name screamed up at Blake from the centre of the phone's display and exploded in his mind like a flare going off over the sea. He knew where the fourth killing would take place. Whoever was carrying out these brutal crimes was killing his victims at locations that formed a massive cross across London. He stabbed a finger on the spot at the middle of the cross on the wall. The Minories had been the missing link. It was at the centre of everything. He was mad with himself for not seeing it sooner.

Another piece of the jigsaw dawned on him. He rushed to the coffee table and shook out the crime scene photographs from the back of the police file. His eyes darted over each picture in turn. Elements in the photos that had once seemed random were now forming connections in his brain: the orientation of the victim's bodies, the positioning of the bizarre coins implanted under the victims' skin.

Not only had the killer chosen to murder his victims at locations that formed the points of a cross, but Blake guessed that he had also carefully orientated their bodies along the axis of the cross too. He had noticed that even though the killings had been frenzied, the bodies had been deliberately repositioned afterwards. Blake surmised that if checked, their orientation would follow the cardinal points of the cross. Not only that, but the positioning of the coins around the victim's stomach would also follow the same cross-like pattern. If the victim's navel corresponded to the Minories central position on the map, each of the cuts opening a pocket in the skin followed the same pattern as the actual murders.

'Well I'll be damned,' he whispered in the stillness of the room. Blake stared at the wall for a long while before collapsing on the sofa as if his legs had given out. He waited until the first streak of dawn appeared outside his living room window before phoning Milton.

CHAPTER 47

The sky was a mural of billowing white clouds set against a background of perfect blue. As the sun made its way across the sky, shadows grew on the sides of the buildings of the Middle Temple. Blake had power-walked his way from DCI Milton's office. He had welcomed the brisk exercise, but it hadn't cleared his head. Milton had greeted Blake's discovery of the underlying pattern behind the killings with a gaping mouth and a celebratory smack of his fist in his palm. He had been much less accepting of Blake's postulation that Hart hadn't been behind the murders. Talk of evil spirits and blood writing held little sway in the analytical mind of a seasoned detective, especially since Hart had been on record admitting responsibility for the first murder at St George's. With a sceptical arch of his brow, Milton had reminded Blake that Hart had carried out a daring escape from a maximum-security prison. He was an extremely dangerous and resourceful man on the run and would remain the UK's most wanted man.

Patting him on the back, Milton had suggested that Blake check his theory out with Angelo Ricard. Milton's assistant would clear the way for a meeting. Less than an hour later, Blake was sitting on a bench in Fountain Court, only a minute's walk from Ricard's office.

The impromptu meeting wasn't the only appointment he had arranged for the morning. Rosalind had playfully reminded him of his commitment to take her out. She had also dropped into conversation that most of her clothes were back in California. Blake had taken the hint and tentatively agreed to not only fund but also act as bag carrier for a brother-and-sister shopping trip. However, with the introduction of a new appointment into the morning's schedule, Blake had called Rosalind to suggest that they postpone their trip for another day. Rosalind had insisted, saying something about how an agreement was an agreement and that he wasn't going to wiggle out of theirs so easily.

It was settled that they would meet at Fountain Court, one of the picturesque squares in the Middle Temple, and go together to Ricard's office. He would have his meeting and she would stay in the reception until his business was concluded. They would then have lunch, and the afternoon would be dedicated to shopping. As soon as he had hung up the phone, he knew it was a mistake. She was bound to be late.

A gentle gust of wind rustled the leaves on the trees, as Blake checked his watch for the second time in less than a minute. Rosalind was already twenty minutes late. Tucked away from the hustle and bustle of the city, the peaceful courtyard oasis of Fountain Court was one of Blake's favourite places to sit and think. Located in the centre of the Middle Temple, the small paved quadrangle was surrounded by four elegant wrought iron benches. Sitting alone, Blake had a good view of the alleyways leading in and out of the courtyard.

A small fountain had stood in the middle of the courtyard for around three hundred years, but the surrounding gardens had a much older history, possibly dating back to the late twelfth century, when the Knights Templar established themselves in the area. Blake looked over to Middle Temple Hall standing at the edge of the court. He remembered that Shakespeare along with his Chamberlain's Men gave their first recorded performance of Twelfth Night there in 1602.

He scanned both directions with annoyance and felt relief at the sight of Rosalind turning the corner. She was taking short, sharp drags from a cigarette and instantly registered the annoyance in Blake's face.

'Really?' said Blake.

Pouting around her cigarette, Rosalind shrugged and blew out smoke from her nostrils.

'Don't be mad,' she said dismissively. 'I had stuff to do.'

After taking a final drag on her cigarette, she let it fall to the ground and killed it with the heel of her boot.

Blake led the way through the maze of buildings and alleyways of the Middle Temple. As they tossed words back and forth, Blake's temples slowly unknitted themselves. By the time they reached Ricard's office, they were laughing. They checked in with the receptionist and took a seat next to a beautiful oil painting of the London skyline.

At that moment, Angelo Ricard appeared. As usual, he looked the picture of a successful executive. He was stylishly dressed in a blue suit, topped off with a coordinated pocket-handkerchief that stood crisply to attention in his jacket pocket.

'Good morning, Dr Blake,' said Ricard, glancing at his ultra-thin Swiss watch.

'Sorry we're late,' said Blake.

'We?'

Ricard looked over to the woman sitting next to Blake.

'Do I detect a family resemblance?' asked Ricard.

'He's my brother,' said Rosalind, getting to her feet. 'Aren't you going to introduce us?'

For the briefest of seconds, Blake felt a flush of embarrassment heat his cheeks.

'Angelo Ricard, this is my sister Rosalind Blake.'

'Charmed to meet you,' said Ricard, reaching out for Rosalind's hand.

'Don't keep my brother long,' she said. 'He's got a party dress to buy me.'

Blake forced a smile. His sister always talked too much.

'I'll do my best,' said Ricard. 'Dr Blake, we need to use our time judiciously. Our late start means that time is pressing, I'm afraid. I have an important business appointment in less than half an hour. If you'll excuse us, Rosalind, I'll get my PA to look after you with some refreshment.'

'That's very kind of you,' said Rosalind, nodding her approval and smiling.

On entering Ricard's office, Blake was first struck by the piles of paperwork spread out over his expansive desk.

'The office has a lot on at the moment,' said Ricard, placing a cup of steaming hot coffee on a small corner of the desk in front of Blake. 'So how can I help you?' Ricard lowered himself into his seat. 'Have you found Enoch Hart?'

'No,' said Blake. An earnest look swept over his face. 'But I think I understand the pattern of the murders and I want to check my theory with you. You probably know more about these churches than anyone.'

'Whatever I can do. You mentioned a pattern?' said Ricard.

Blake got up and spent the next five minutes sketching out the alignment of the Hawksmoor churches on a piece of paper next to Ricard and talking through his hypothesis.

'You see, if the Minories is the centre of the cross, that leaves St Mary's as the site of the final murder.'

Ricard said nothing in response.

'It will take place on the last blood moon in the tetrad. And that's only in a matter of days, unless we can stop it.' Blake returned to his chair and picked up his cup from the table. As he savoured a sip of coffee, he eyed the wording stamped onto the cover of a file on Ricard's desk. Returning his cup to the table, Blake read the title more closely.

London Underground
Architectural Drawings
Bank Station

'Interesting theory,' Ricard said, as he tapped out a constellation of dots onto Blake's sketch with the tip of his pen.

'What do you think?'

'If you assume the Minories is somehow connected to this, then I guess you can make out a cross pattern with St Mary Woolnoth being the final point.' He clicked down on the end of the pen with his thumb. 'So you know the time and the place; all you need to do is catch Hart.'

'It might not be Hart we're after,' said Blake.

Ricard looked intently at the man sitting on the other side of the desk. 'Not Hart? What does that mean?'

'I'm sorry, I'm not at liberty to tell you any more,' said Blake. 'Let's just say, some new information has come to light which might make us re-examine our original assumptions.'

'What information?' pressed Ricard.

'I apologise, Mr Ricard, but I can't say any more.'

A brief flash of annoyance flashed across Ricard's face. 'I see,' said Ricard, straightening out his watch on his wrist. 'I'm sorry too, my next appointment is about to arrive. If I think of anything else, I'll be sure to phone you.'

Ricard watched as Blake got to his feet. Politely, he ushered his guest out of his office and side by side the two men returned to the foyer area.

They found Rosalind deep in conversation with the receptionist, who quickly trailed off her conversation upon seeing her boss's return.

'I haven't kept your brother for too long,' Ricard said, a smile returning to his face.

'That's good. Now it's time to do some serious shopping,' chuckled Rosalind, glancing over to the receptionist.

'That's right, the party frock,' said Ricard, his eyes flicking over Rosalind's face. 'If you're looking for a good night out, we have a table at the annual Power of Music charity dinner this evening. We've been sponsoring the event for years. You are both very welcome to join us. The music is a bit young for my tastes, but lots of show biz types turn up. It's a fun evening and it's all in a good cause.'

Rosalind gave her brother a sideways glance.

'Vincent, you did promise,' she said before he could object.

Blake hoisted his eyebrows in protest but was met by his sister's pleading eyes.

A few minutes later, Blake and Rosalind exited the Middle Temple and stepped into the bustling thoroughfare of the Strand. Blake suddenly stopped in his tracks and turned his face skywards in annoyance. 'Tickets,' he said, palming his forehead.

After agreeing to meet with Rosalind again in five minutes outside a nearby coffee shop, he marched back off into the Middle Temple.

Blake entered Ricard's office building and walked briskly up to the receptionist. She glanced up from her computer. 'Back so soon?'

'I'm really sorry,' said Blake with a rueful shrug. 'I forgot to ask him something.'

'Let me have a look,' she said as her fingers pecked at the keyboard and her brow crinkled in concentration. 'You might be in luck. Mr Ricard's next appointment is running a bit late.' She snatched a glimpse at her watch. 'Go on through and I'll give him a call to let him know you're here.'

At that moment the mobile phone next to her keyboard vibrated loudly, and she answered with an enthusiastic greeting. Pausing a beat, she shot Blake a cursory glance and then nodded in the direction of Ricard's office before returning to her conversation. Blake hesitated and then left the receptionist to her call.

The door to Ricard's office was ajar and so Blake walked in. Ricard was with his security manager, and they were talking quietly with their backs towards the door. The two men were standing next to an open wall safe behind Ricard's desk, its existence normally hidden from view by an old oil painting of a church now hinged outwards from the wall. Blake approached the desk as Ricard reached into the safe and removed a wooden presentation box about a foot in length. He was about to hand it over to the security manager when Blake announced his entrance. 'Sorry, I should have knocked.'

Surprised by the unexpected voice, Ricard turned around sharply. His sudden movement caused him to lose grip on the box. It fell from his fumbling fingers and bounced off the hard edge of his desk before landing with a heavy thud onto the floor. Blake rushed forward and picked it up. Immediately his eye was drawn to a wedge-shaped dent in the box just above its brass lock. Small flakes of translucent lacquer came off in his hands as he handed it back to Ricard.

'I'm so sorry,' said Blake awkwardly.

'Don't worry, no harm done,' said Ricard as he passed the box over to the security manager. 'Did you forget something?'

'It completely slipped my mind, but the tickets for the charity dinner, do I pick them up from the venue?'

'Don't worry,' said Ricard. 'Leave your address with the receptionist and I'll get them dropped over to you later.'

CHAPTER 48

Blake and Rosalind were introduced to each member of their table in turn. Blake could hear little of Ricard's introductions over the urgent vocal performance of the West London rapper who had just taken to the stage. Instead he nodded politely at the faces around the large circular table. He had been placed opposite to Rosalind. She sat between Ricard and the lady receptionist from their meeting earlier that day. Blake had been positioned between a music promoter called Martin and an overweight partner of a management consulting company who had come along for the free booze.

Rosalind gave her brother an antagonistic look from across the table. She was already half cut when she slid herself into the taxi, and Blake's gentle words of concern had been met with a frosty reception. *Just like old times*, he thought, forcing a smile at the waitress who had just filled his glass with champagne. It was going to be a long night.

'So, what line of business are you in?' said the management consultant seated next to him as he spiked a scallop with his fork.

'I'm in the art business.' Blake fought to make himself heard over the ambient noise of the hall. He had long given up trying to explain his career to strangers. His profession wasn't traditional by any means, and his route to it had been unconventional to say the least.

At Oxford, he had worked at the university's research laboratory for archaeology and art history. There, he pioneered a number of revolutionary sample dating techniques. After Oxford, Blake was recruited by British Military Intelligence, where he spent four years in the Middle East working with international security agencies to dismantle smuggling networks set up in the aftermath of the Second Gulf War. One of his assignments was recovering priceless objects looted from the Museum of Baghdad. Following an honourable discharge, Blake was headhunted by the British Museum, where he became an authority in document authentication. Thanks to his unusual combination of skills and unparalleled knowledge of the illegal trade in rare and antique objects, Blake now acted as a special advisor to the police. Yes, much easier to say he worked in the art business.

'In the art business, you say? Excellent,' said the businessman. Small beads of sweat stood proud on his forehead. 'I might be on the lookout for a few pieces myself. Just bought a rather large apartment overlooking the river and the walls are looking a little bare. Give me a call,' the man said, dabbing his face with his napkin.

Blake nodded and took a sip of champagne.

'It's bloody hot in here.'

Blake agreed and gave a long sigh. He sat back in his chair and observed the scene around the table. Rosalind was holding court with Ricard and the receptionist. In her early thirties, the receptionist was pretty and had a small turned-up nose. She was sheathed in a tight-fitting dress and wore thick black eyeliner slicked across each eyelid. An enormous ring sparkled from her hand. Gesturing to a waitress to refill her glass, Rosalind finished off her anecdote and drained the glass in two gulps.

Blake could feel himself zoning out into the middle distance. People around him were talking in torrents, but no one was listening to each other. It was like having a particular note playing in one ear whilst a different discordant note played in the other. Tuneless and dissonant. Nothing real, just the sugar rush of glitz and show. It made his blood run cold. For a moment, a feeling of loneliness swept over him, before the sound of breaking glass grabbed his attention.

The sound had come from the other side of the table. Rosalind was tilting back on her chair, playing with the buttons of her new dress, as a hard-lipped waitress cleared up the broken glass from about her feet. Once the waitress had finished her work, Rosalind dropped the chair back onto four legs and reached for an empty water glass from the table. It was enthusiastically filled by the receptionist, and large splashes of white wine lapped over its brim onto the table cloth.

All through dinner, Blake kept a watch over his sister, trying to catch her eye. But she was on a mission. Blake had seen it so many times before. They were travelling though the eye of the storm, but the winds would hit soon. It was just a matter of time, and when they did they would be hurricane-force. He had to get her out of there.

Abruptly the music from the stage stopped and the voice of the celebrity host began to explain the proceedings for the evening's charity auction. At that moment, both Ricard and the receptionist gave their apologies to Rosalind, having recognised a local councillor waving at them from another table. Quickly taking the opportunity, Blake got to his feet, rounded the table and took Ricard's seat next to his sister, his face scrunched with concern.

'I know that bloody look,' she slurred.

'I think it might be time to go,' said Blake.

Blake's sister brushed the comment away, trying to make eye contact with a nearby waiter.

'Come on, you've had a skin full,'

'Is that right?' she said loudly. 'Don't think your sister is capable of controlling herself?' There was suddenly dead air between them. Blake could feel the eyes of the table looking at them as the celebrity host droned on from the stage.

He leant forward and put his arm around her.

'Let's go home,' he whispered.

She pulled herself away, letting his hand drop from her shoulders like a heavy coat slipping to the floor.

'Piss off,' she said, her eyes throwing daggers at him. 'Always trying to get in the way. '"Must look after little sister"', she jibed. 'Well, I don't need your help. Why don't you fuck off back home and leave me to enjoy myself with my friends?'

Blake retreated to his chair, his hands raised in mock surrender. 'Okay, Rosalind, I'll leave you to it. I'm going home,' he said getting to his feet. 'I'll give you a call later.'

'Don't bother,' she said.

With that Blake retrieved his jacket from the back of his chair and negotiated his way across the hall towards the exit. Through clenched teeth, he glanced back to the table to see the receptionist return to her seat. Blake stopped and watched as she took Rosalind by the hand and pulled her to her feet. Giggling to themselves, the two women staggered off in the direction of the ladies' restrooms. Blake started off again towards the doors. This time he didn't look back.

Ten minutes later, the receptionist arrived back at the table alone as a boy band walked onto the stage to thunderous applause. The backing track for their opening number started to fill the cavernous hall, and the receptionist took the opportunity to subtly open her purse and show Ricard a small vial half-filled with white powder. Before she sat down, she whispered, 'She's out cold.'

Ricard nodded.

CHAPTER 49

'Noorjehan is so excited to have Sarah stay over,' said Dr Desai, smiling over to his wife, who was tapping on her laptop in the kitchen.

'Sarah hasn't stopped talking about it all week, have you sweetheart?' said Blake, handing his daughter her overnight bag.

'Bye, Dad,' she said quickly, giving him the briefest of hugs before disappearing upstairs.

'Be good,' he shouted after her.

'Don't worry, she is always very well behaved,' said Desai reassuringly.

'I was thinking of taking the girls over to the Bank of England for the mayoral election results. I think it's good for their education to see the political process in action,' said Desai. 'As long as Captain Lambton wins of course,' he smiled. 'Is that okay with you?'

'No problem,' said Blake.

'It's going to be quite a night tomorrow, and that's not even including the super-sized blood red moon,' said Desai enthusiastically.

Blake's fingers played with the change in his pocket as his mind flashed with thoughts of St Mary Woolnoth and the Hawksmoor killer. Stepping towards Desai's front door, his attention returned to the here and now. 'Thanks again,' said Blake.

'No problem. Anytime,' said Desai. 'Don't worry about a thing here. She'll be fine.'

'Really appreciate it,' Blake thanked him as he stepped onto the pavement.

'Remember to vote for Captain Lambton,' Desai shouted through a grin.

Half walking, half running, Blake returned home. He unlocked the front door, stepped inside and immediately headed for his living room. A second later, he fired up his computer. Alina popped her head around the door. After checking that Sarah had been successfully dropped off with the Desais, she handed Blake a folded piece of paper.

'Rosalind asked me to give you this before she went out.'

'Gone out? Any idea where's she's gone?'

Alina shrugged her shoulders.

'Didn't say, but an expensive looking car picked her up.'

Blake eyed up the paper quizzically and then opened it. He hadn't seen Rosalind since the charity dinner. The sheet contained a single word.

Sorry

After the word, Rosalind had drawn a circular face with a sad, downcast mouth on it. Blake rolled his eyes. 'Have we any wine?' he asked.

'Some white wine in the fridge, I think. Do you want some?'

'Please,' said Blake. 'Help yourself too.'

Alina thought about it for a moment and then smiled.

'That would be nice. I'll take it up to the bath with me.'

Moments later, she reappeared holding a glass, its sides already condensing from the chilled liquid within.

'I'll leave you to it,' she said, depositing the glass next to the computer. 'My bath awaits.'

'Enjoy your time off,' he said, taking a sip and then giving Alina a small toast.

As the staircase creaked with Alina's footfalls, Blake looked back to his computer screen. He clicked open an internet search window, typed in 'St Mary Woolnoth Hawksmoor' and hit the return key. He moved the cursor over the first of the returned searches and selected the link.

Standing within the triangle formed by the junction of Lombard Street and King William Street is the remarkable church of St Mary Woolnoth. The site has been a place of worship for over two thousand years, and the present church stands on the site of a Roman Temple dedicated to the Roman goddess Concordia. The present Christian church is at least the third to have been built on the site. A church dating back to 1445 was badly damaged during the Great Fire of London of 1666 and was completely rebuilt by Nicholas Hawksmoor between 1719 and 1727. Christian iconography is noticeably absent on the exterior of the building.

The interior of Hawksmoor's St Mary Woolnoth is based on the motif of a perfect cube, a very unusual design device for a Christian church. Several commentators have connected the form of the church with that of the cubic stone or 'perfect ashlar', a central symbol in speculative Freemasonry. It is said that St Mary Woolnoth is located 2,000 cubits from Christchurch Spitalfields, another of Hawksmoor's strange and unique city churches. The Old Testament Book of Numbers includes the measure of 2,000 cubits in its rules for city planning. St Mary Woolnoth is also unique because it has a station beneath it.

Blake shook his head. The more he learned about the enigmatic Nicholas Hawksmoor, the more uncomfortable he felt. Before his mind became lost down another rabbit hole of conjecture, he rallied his thoughts together in search of some firmer ground.

He turned over Rosalind's note and searched for a pen around the table. Only after reorganising several piles of bills and bank statements did he find one. He coaxed off the pen top with his teeth and began to copy out the lines of writing that Mary had scrawled in her own blood onto the wall of the shelter.

HAWKSMOOR

FOUR BLOOD ALTARS
FOUR BLOOD SACRIFICES
FOUR BLOOD COINS
FOUR BLOOD MOONS

Taking a large gulp of wine, Blake surveyed the makeshift map that he had sketched out on the living room wall at the far end of the room. The Minories had been the key to unlocking the cryptogram of the

Hawksmoor churches. Tomorrow, on the day of the last blood moon of the tetrad, the killer would attempt another sacrifice at St Mary Woolnoth. Milton would have the place surrounded. The trap would be set, and finally the identity of the brutal Hawksmoor killer would be discovered. He felt a cold chill as he recalled the horrific wounds suffered by the victims: throats sliced down to the spine, terrible mutilations to the cheeks, eyelids cut from the face.

And then there were the additional words that Blake had discovered in one of the crime scene photos. He wrote them out underneath his earlier lines on Rosalind's note.

EVE CAN'T BLINK

He sat back in his chair and pondered the puzzling line. The image of the victims' hollow eyes kept invading his mind. Finally, he gave up and tossed the sheet of paper onto the pile of bills stacked on the table. Returning to the keyboard, Blake spent the next ten minutes studying photographs of St Mary's and street maps of its surrounding area.

'Shall I open another bottle?' said Alina, scrutinising Blake's empty wine glass. She was standing at the doorway in a dressing gown, brushing her hand through her wet hair. Her cheeks were flushed from the bath.

'Better had,' smiled Blake.

A minute later she was back at the table with a new bottle along with her glass. She poured enthusiastically and quickly filled their two glasses. As she did so, Blake studied her face. Her skin looked almost faultless in the dying light of the evening, like a painting. A lock of dark hair tumbled over her eye as she poured. She blew it back, her pressed lips directing her breath. She smelt good, like honeysuckle.

Gathering up the glasses and the wine bottle, Blake walked over to the sofa and transferred them to the coffee table. Alina sat next to Blake on the sofa. They began to chat and within minutes were sharing stories of growing up. Soon they discovered a shared love of painting and portraiture. On the computer, they took turns showing each other photographs of their hometowns and then shared stories of long-lost school friends. Glasses were filled, refilled and filled again, and smiles turned into belly laughs. Blake could feel a weight falling from his shoulders.

'More vino?' laughed Alina.

'Rude not to,' said Blake.

They both reached at the same time to collect the empty bottle. Their hands touched. A moment passed, their fingertips still touching. Staring directly at him, she slipped her fingers through his. She pulled his hand closer and momentarily placed it on her glowing cheek before holding it on her lap. Blake began to say something, but as the words left him, she leant over and pressed her lips to his mouth. Alina moved closer, her head tilting upwards. At last Blake kissed her, tentatively at first. As their lips brushed, he felt energy coursing over his skin. He could feel her heartbeat against his ribs as their kisses quickened. For the briefest of moments, he pulled back.

'Are you sure?' he breathed,

'Never been so sure.'

With eyes alive with desire, Alina began to kiss Blake's fingertips, one after the other, gently moaning with pleasure as she did so.

'Let's go upstairs,' he said.

Moments later they were climbing the stairs and were soon in Blake's bedroom. Wrapping his arms tightly around her waist, he lifted her high off her feet and carried her to the bed. Alina laughed in small breathless gasps as she landed on the covers. Blake began shedding his clothes, his trousers hitting the ground in a jingle of coins. After stepping out of them, he moved to the edge of the bed.

'Vincent, your back!' exclaimed Alina, noticing his scars from the arson attack.

'Shhhhhh,' he said, moving closer to her on the bed.

His hand stroked the inside of her perfectly smooth leg and continued upwards. Her body shuddered at the progress of his fingernail. A gasp escaped from Alina's throat, and she pulled him up onto her. Blake's body pressed into hers. Their hips started to move in unison. Gnawing at her bottom lip, she turned Blake over onto his back. She was soon astride him, shaking her hair free, her dressing gown gaping open at the front. Blake pulled at the gown's cord, and Alina shook it from her shoulders to fully expose her naked body.

Then he saw it, and his world suddenly stopped turning. To one side of her navel was the nicotine patch he had spotted before. It was hanging loose from her skin due to the action of the hot bath water. Dangling by just a corner, the disfigured flesh underneath the patch was now exposed. A cut had been made into Alina's white skin and formed the entrance to a kind of pocket on the surface of her stomach. Standing proud from under the skin was a circular object the size of a coin.

He almost choked at the sight. Fear spiked through him, his heart leaping into his throat. His legs kicked against the covers as he tried to pull himself out from underneath her. Twisting his body, he yanked himself free and fell to the floor with a thud. He scrambled back on his hands against the wall. Alina didn't move and sat ramrod straight astride the bed. He edged forward to catch sight of her face.

Suddenly she looked at him with a wild stare. He gasped with shock at the tight murderous expression on her face. Her teeth were bared and her eyes flashed with pure hatred. In a rush of movement, her hand shot out to the bedside lamp next to the bed. With a jolt, she ripped the plug out of its wall socket and rounded on Blake. Her movements were fast, almost a blur. Painted fingernails flashed across Blake's vision, and then the hardwood base of the lamp smashed into the side of his head, sending him reeling and the light shade spinning off into the air. A rush of pain roared across his head. He steadied himself against the wall, his face darkening. She came at him and jabbed the end of the light into his face. A jagged glass edge, the shattered remnants of the light bulb, shot past his right eye.

'Eve can't blink, Eve can't blink,' she taunted, spitting the words at him. Her voice was changed, deep and rasping. She stabbed at his face again, her eyes blazing. Pivoting on his heels, Blake pulled his head first this way and then that, his cheek missing the serrated edge of the bulb by millimetres.

Lightning quick, Blake's hand grabbed at her wrist and disabled the weapon. He pivoted on his feet and then, like a hammer thrower unleashing a projectile out into space, launched her against the bedroom wall. Her body smashed into the bedside table, sending it and its contents shooting out across the floor. Within the blink of an eye, Alina was back on her feet, her eyes filled with fury. Blake readied himself for another onslaught, but this time the offensive didn't come.

Breathing hard, Blake scowled at Alina, but she was no longer looking in his direction. She was rooted to the spot, her eyes fixed in a terrified expression towards something on the floor. Blake followed Alina's line of sight down to the carpet and the small lump of London Stone that he had placed inside his bedside table after the bombing at Cannon Street. It was as if she were impaled by its very presence. Blake edged forward, his eyes never leaving Alina's brooding stare. Squatting down, he picked up the stone.

'Keep it away from me,' growled Alina through unblinking eyes.

Blake took a step closer with the stone and she recoiled into the corner of the room.

'What, you mean this old rock?' said Blake.

Pushing forward against her thrashing hands, he drove the stone into her forehead. A gut-wrenching scream erupted out of her. As she shook violently, a strange sulphurous odour seemed to exude from her body. Suddenly, she went limp and fell to the ground like a puppet whose strings had been cut.

After a second of stillness, Alina's eyes blinked open. With her senses slowly returning, she stared up at Blake. She raised herself onto her elbow and wiped away the sweaty hair hanging in her eyes. Her face was drawn and pale. As she pushed her back against the wall, Blake rubbed the side of his head. The force of Alina's blow with the lamp had been incredible, almost lifting him clean off his feet. Hard to believe, looking at the frail, trembling body in front of him.

He knelt beside her and mustered the courage to ask.

'You okay?'

She nodded numbly back to him.

He reached for the abandoned dressing gown on the bed and wrapped it around her.

With the thump of his heart finally slowing in his chest, Blake sat next to her, his back propped up against the wall. He glanced down at the cut in the skin of Alina's stomach.

'Who the hell did that to you?' he asked, through pained eyes.

Drawing her knees up to her chest, her mouth began to tremble.

'A man came to the shelter,' she said, swallowing a lump in her throat.

'Shelter?'

'I told you, before I came here. I stayed at the Servant Church of London.'

Blake felt himself turn cold. 'What man?'

'I was in the church gardens when a man attacked me from behind. I was drugged and he put this in me,' Alina pointed to the object under her skin. 'I had never seen him before.'

'Why didn't you go to the police, or take it out?'

'He said he would kill me. I believed him. He was pure evil, as bad as they come.' He heard the terror in her voice. 'His eyes were so black, like poison.'

'You're safe now,' said Blake, putting a hand on her shoulder.

'Safe,' she said, hugging her knees. 'You have no idea.'

Blake put his arm around her shaking shoulder.

'You shouted something at me.' he said. '"Eve can't blink." Do you know what it means?'

'I don't know,' said Alina, shaking her head. 'When the darkness comes, it takes control, choking off my senses.' Tears were welling up in her eyes. 'I'm so sorry, Vincent.' She squeezed his arm. 'Sometimes I hear a voice shouting in my head "Eve Can't Blink, Eve Can't Blink" when it sees you. It's almost like it's taunting your name.'

Blake's eyes widened. Moments later he was on his feet bounding down the stairs, clearing three steps at a time. Sliding into the living room on his bare feet, he searched for Rosalind's note and the lines of Mary's blood writing that he had written on its reverse side. His eyes fixed on the last line he had written, as he patted down the table top searching for a pen. He quickly found one, and after clicking off the top with his teeth, he wrote his name underneath it.

EVE CAN'T BLINK
VINCENT BLAKE

With his heart pounding like a steam train, he ticked off the letters one at a time. They matched exactly.

CHAPTER 50

Blake placed his travel mug into the Alfa Romeo's dashboard cup holder and watched a plume of condensation materialise inside the windscreen. He turned the ignition key and the engine coughed into life. Adeptly, he shoehorned his car out of its parking space and into the side street.

Leaning over to Alina, he repositioned the blanket that had slipped from her lap.

'You okay?' he said.

Alina nodded her assent and strained a smile.

'The hospital is only ten minutes away. Best get checked out,' he said reassuringly.

As Blake indicated to turn into Clerkenwell Road, a red off-road motorcycle fired up its engine and emerged out of the shadows behind them. As the world whipped by the window outside, his mind returned to the bizarre fact that Mary had written an anagram of his name in blood long before their paths had actually crossed. Every time he thought about it, he felt ripples of unease sweeping down him, like spiders running down his back. Somehow he was connected to all of this; he just didn't know how. Tomorrow night would be the last blood moon of the tetrad. Someone out there would be on the hunt again for another victim. He had to nail them.

The traffic in front slowed and Blake eased on the brakes. As they crawled forward, he saw the obstruction. Substantial roadworks were going on ahead for the laying of fibre optic cables. Parallel lines of large concrete blocks were positioned either side of the road to protect deep trenches running parallel to the pavements. A bright yellow digger was parked close by, abandoned for the night. The two wide lanes of traffic travelling east along Clerkenwell Road were being funnelled into narrower lanes a little further ahead. Just beyond the roadworks, traffic lights regulated the flow of vehicles approaching the busy junction with Farringdon Street heading south towards the river.

Craning his head, Blake saw the traffic lights thirty feet ahead change to green. Seconds later, he was idling forward, edging his car alongside the wall of concrete blocks on the passenger side. He eased the car to a halt. As he did so, in his wing mirror he noticed a red off-road motorbike weaving through the stationary traffic behind them. Soon the bike disappeared behind a blacked-out people carrier that had just drifted up alongside his car. Blake kept an anxious look out for the safety of his wing mirror, as the people carrier was coming precariously close. Blake's precious Alfa Romeo was hemmed in tight, with the concrete blocks on the left and the people carrier crowding in from the right.

The lights turned green, and the vehicle in front crept forward again. Blake guided the gear stick into first and let out the clutch. The Alfa inched forward, its progress closely paralleled by the people carrier. Just as Blake's car reached the lights, they turned red. Blake let out a groan and watched the traffic whizz by in both directions along Farringdon Street.

From the other side of the people carrier came the loud snarl of a revving engine. The red motorcycle shot out from the right-hand side and screeched to a halt directly in front of Blake's Alfa, hugging its bumper. Almost casually the rider kicked out the bike's stand, dismounted and searched for something in the motorcycle's rear pannier bag. Blake squinted to get sight of the rider's face, but the tinted visor of the helmet betrayed nothing of their features underneath. The rider launched himself onto the bonnet of the Alfa and scrambled to stand up, heavy motorcycle boots pummelling large dents into the metal. Blake's body stiffened with alarm.

'Get out!' he shouted to Alina, whose senses were reactivated by the threatening figure standing bolt upright on the car's bonnet and holding a spray can. She fumbled for the door handle, found it and pushed. It opened several inches then crunched into the concrete block beyond the door. She couldn't get out. Panic took hold of her. Just at that moment, it started getting darker. The rider's outline through the windscreen soon disappeared under an opaque slick of black paint. With several long reaches of the rider's arm, the entire surface area of the windscreen was quickly sprayed black. Instinctively Blake grabbed at the wiper controls, but the rapid sweep of the wiper blades did nothing to clear the slick. With the concrete barrier to his left, the people carrier boxing them in on their right, and a line of queuing traffic behind them, they were trapped.

Blake caught a movement off to his right side. He whipped his head around in time to see the heavily tinted passenger side window of the people carrier slide open just feet away from them. What he saw inside sent confusion and panic lancing through his brain. The face of a man wearing sunglasses and a baseball cap stared back at him through the open window of the people carrier, his hand brandishing a Glock 17 pistol complete with sound suppressor. Slowly he raised the weapon towards Blake, his face alight with a murderous grin.

'It's a kill squad!' Blake shouted.

He jerked his head back just as the driver's window shattered into a thousand fragments. A bullet blazed past his cheek. He twisted around in his seat, glancing across to Alina as another bullet pinged off the dashboard, spiderwebbing the windscreen. Blake snatched the steel mug he had brought along for the ride and launched it ferociously at the gunman, like a backhand tennis smash. The projectile slammed into the shooter's face in an explosion of hot liquid, sending his sunglasses spinning into the air.

Blake's throat clamped tight as he recognised the face of the man who was trying to kill them. A dark port-wine stain ran along the top of the gunman's cheekbone; it was Angelo Ricard's security manager.

Alina's face was filled with sheer terror. 'He works for the man who cut me at the shelter,' she shrieked back, cowering in her seat.

After wiping his scalded face with the back of his jacket, the gunman levelled his Glock again towards his targets. His finger tightened on the trigger and a muffled crack sounded as the gun recoiled against his hand.

Alina slumped in her seat. For a millisecond, Blake felt immobilised, unable to process the cascade of sensory information overflowing in his brain. His eyes filled with shock as he saw the single smoking bullet hole in the centre of Alina's forehead. Another bullet droned a millimetre past Blake's ear, the round ricocheting off the steering wheel, shattering the passenger window and slamming into the concrete block beyond. He was a sitting duck.

His brain rammed itself into gear, then his hand did the same with the Alfa Romeo. His jaw tightened and his foot dropped hard onto the accelerator pedal. The engine screamed and the car bolted forwards like a whipped stallion, sending the motorcycle rider bouncing off the bonnet.

The motorcycle was bulldozered forward past the traffic lights into the lines of oncoming traffic speeding along Farringdon Street. Blake couldn't see a thing. He was hurtling forward, but with no forward vision. Tyres screeched and smoke bellowed as car and motorbike slewed across the busy road.

He heard car horns and then a colossal force impacted the side of the car, sending it spinning. Blake's insides lurched forwards. With all his might, he gripped onto the steering wheel. The blur of a fast-approaching car entered his vision out of the shattered remains of the passenger window. He braced himself for another heavy collision. But this time the oncoming vehicle just glanced off the front of the Alfa and was lost behind the paint sprayed windscreen.

Finally, the Alfa came to rest in a cloud of steam. With the breath slapped out of his body, Blake took on ragged gulps of air, accompanied by the repetitive swish of the windscreen wiper blades and the sound of blaring horns outside the car. His hand fumbled for the seatbelt release and then the car door lever. Wrenching himself free, he kicked open the door and staggered out of the car.

He stood and steadied himself on the side of his smashed Alfa Romeo. Farringdon Street looked like the aftermath of a motorway pile up. Bits of motor vehicles and shattered glass littered the road. A trail of cars cut a jagged line into the distance. The force of the collision had thrown Blake's Alfa onto the opposite pavement.

With adrenaline still boiling inside him, Blake looked back to the far side of the road. His eyes locked onto the people carrier. As he focused in, he could see that its doors were open and its occupants had fled.

He staggered across the road, weaving an irregular path between the stationary jam of vehicles towards the people carrier. Cautiously he peered into the open front passenger door. In the foot well, surrounded by spent bullet cases, was a wooden box. It took a moment for Blake to remember where he had seen it before. Then it came to him. He bent down and picked it up. Directly above the box's brass lock was a triangular dent in the wood. He recalled the box falling from Angelo Ricard's hands and hitting the edge of his desk. Blake felt the growing thud of his pulse in his neck. He stared at the box for a moment and then flicked the lock open. Slowly he lifted the lid as anger knotted his insides. The box contained a red felt insert and cut into it were the perfect silhouettes of a Glock 17 semi-automatic pistol and a tubular sound suppressor. His fingers slackened their grip and the box fell onto the passenger seat.

Blake stood up and punched his fist down onto the roof of the people carrier. Quickly finding his mobile in his pocket, he dialled a number. As the phone rang, he tried to blink away the vision of Alina's slumped body in the passenger seat of his Alfa Romeo.

After an age, Milton answered the phone.

'The Hawksmoor killer,' said Blake, emotion welling up from his chest.

'Vincent, is that you?'

Silence.

'Vincent?'

'It's Angelo Ricard,' he said finally.

PART 4

Revelation 2:17

Whoever has ears, let them hear what the Spirit says to the churches.
To the one who is victorious, I will give some of the hidden manna.
I will also give that person a white stone with a new name written on it,
known only to the one who receives it.

CHAPTER 51

Diary Entry of Nicholas Hawksmoor
15th May 1681

Even to deliver and explain what I bring forward is no easy matter; for things in themselves new can only be apprehended with reference to what is old. But after today, all is forever changed. The old world is no more.

According to the scriptures, man forfeited the happiness of this life by eating of the tree of knowledge. But I say, that knowledge itself, in all its guises, is more powerful than any cage that the church can put on it. Of knowledge there is no satiety, but satisfaction and appetite are interchangeable. I will not be led away from seeking the true reality of things and I will accept nothing that is but examined and tried.

There is an unseen spiritual world, as real as the equally unseen agencies of the lodestone and electricity in the natural world. I commit to paper not some vain babbling doctrine about the nature of things, I have seen it with my own eyes, and heard with my own ears. Today, I have glimpsed the highest link in nature's chain, where human knowledge and supernatural power meet in one.

But first, I must turn back to the events that brought me to this revelation. It is extraordinary to think that just yesterday, I first read the pages of the remarkable volume from Mr Cooper's bookshop. I now wonder whether the rioting in the streets had not been merely the result of chance, but instead guided by some invisible hand.

As I lay awake in my bed, contemplating my dream and listening to the heavy rain outside, I resolved to search out the location of the stone circle described in the book. Whether it was true or fancy, I would find out.

In the first light of dawn, I stole away from my lodgings carrying the book and the sharpest knife I could find, and headed into the thick fog. With sober and grave mind, I walked along the banks of the Thames, turning northwards at the church of St Magnus the Martyr and onto Canning Street. As I moved along the street towards the building site that was once the great cathedral of St Paul's, I thought of Wren and his grand vision for a new cathedral following the Great Fire. He keeps the details of his plans secret and only shares them with one other, the dour and ill-tempered Isaac Newton, during his visits to the Royal Society.

I reached the newly built church of St Swithin's and crossed to the south side of the street. On arriving there I examined the spectacle of the London Stone, its whiteness almost glowing in the quickening light of dawn. Hard like flint, it had been excavated as a single block and stood much higher than my shoulder. Its position had been marked on the map and by its location, and from other landmarks described in the book, I could orientate my direction towards the centre of the stone circle long since gone that had once crowned London's earth.

Guided by the map, I headed east out of the Old City towards the Minories, a place I knew well. Wren had often engaged the work of a fine Jewish instrument maker who had a workshop in the area, and I would frequently run errands between the two gentlemen. The map showed the centre of the sacred stone circle to be in close proximity to an ancient drinking well that I had on previous occasion visited. I knew its position and reached the old well in good time.

Some distance away from the well, I came across a very curious object in a spot covered by thick undergrowth. It was a pyramid forged from a material like Portland stone. I looked down at the book in my hands and I realised that I had found the centre of the circle. The pyramid and inverted cross design stamped into the book's soft leather cover stared back up at me, confirming my supposition.

Even more curious than the discovery of the pyramid however, was the small outcrop of rocks only feet away from it, surrounded by a dense thicket of brambles and catch weed. Hacking my way through the brier, I could see that the outcrop marked the entrance to some fashion of passageway.

Less than a quarter turn of my pocket watch later, I had collected a torch from the instrument maker's workshop and was venturing under its flickering light into the bowels of the earth. It was a strange and fearful passageway, the first part dropping away steeply into blackness. Guided by the torch and with head hunched, I crept ever further down through the narrowing tunnel.

Suddenly, the tunnel opened up into a deep pit. I must have been at least twenty yards under the ground, in a hole as deep as the roof of St Swithin's church. In the centre of the pit stood an amazing sight. A stone mausoleum, impaired with age, but still recognisable as a fine monument, perfectly preserved beneath the busy streets of the Minories.

The structure was of Roman design and topped with an imperial eagle statue. With my torch, I could make out that held within the eagle's beak was a writhing serpent. Soon I reached the floor of the pit and saw that the mausoleum was square in form, with a pyramidal roof held aloft by choice pillars of black marble. The building was a stately structure, echoing an age of ancient Roman glories.

Under the light afforded by the torch, I edged myself through the arched entranceway to the mausoleum. With my heart pounding in my ears as loud as a church bell, I stepped into the melancholic blackness of its interior. The centre of the space was given up to a black marble altar. Spread out on the top of the altar, like soldiers in a Roman legion, were three lines of coins. Ten in each line, thirty coins in all.

Notwithstanding reading of their existence in the pages of the book the previous evening, I couldn't believe I was now standing close enough to touch them. How this curiosity had been kept a secret for so long, and its antiquities not ransacked, I shall never know. They had been brought from the Holy Land by the Emperor Constantine to be interred in this mausoleum. The silver coins were objects of dark power, tokens of sacrifice to the God of Sulphur.

All that I had found had been laid out exactly as described in the book. I felt something strange and fearful about me, my senses sharpening in the darkness. Did I have the courage to complete the journey? Wretched feelings held carnival within me. I tried to keep the door carefully shut on them, but I could not. If I made a vow, a vow unto the Dark Lord and swear an oath to bind His soul to mine, I would not be able break that bond.

But the book promised great temporal power and knowledge beyond my understanding if I did so.

Why shouldn't I take all knowledge to be my province? For isn't knowledge like the branches of a tree, once started, infinitely multiplying outwards at right angles. I was about to awake dark powers in order to attain the mysteries of all things. To have both a longitude and latitude. Wren rebukes me often for being curious of knowing everything to excess. He says I am so frequently diverted, with inclinations towards new trifles. My inquisitive appetite should be tempered with sober devotion to practice, he admonishes.

But my great endeavours with the Professor have given me scanty success. He holds all the knowledge, and only throws me scraps, as if I were some lap dog. Of the plans for the new St Paul's Cathedral he shares nothing, of the experiments he conducts with Mr Hooke in the great stone column built to commemorate the Great Fire, he tells me less. I have come to realise that Wren gives nothing but a false lecture, that is worth naught. Whereas the book in my hands holds the promise of nothing less than the secrets and mysteries of nature itself. In that moment the plan was thoroughly settled in my mind.

With haste, I stripped myself naked to the waist and then retrieved the knife I had brought with me. As instructed in the book, and with awe and trembling, I cut a shallow line into my flesh an inch above my navel. Taking one of the coins from the black altar, I squeezed it under the flap of skin created by the cut. This hurt me greatly and many times did I cry out in pain and agony into the darkness. Gasping, I leant over the black altar and let my blood fall onto its surface like drops of rain. Then I opened the book and recited the incantation instructed in its pages. Its words held incomprehensible power and as I spoke them out loud into the echoing chamber, I felt a dark presence rise about me.

Then a cloud of glowing sulphurous particles rose up from the floor, like the glowing embers of a fire caught in a putrid wind. By the hand of some unseen agency, the particles began to spin in the air. Faster and faster they went like a twisting vortex, until the very air itself took fire. Before me stood a column of flames suspended in mid-air, like the blazing eye of a snake. My mind was consumed with fear and my body began to convulse violently.

Like a lens that causes all sunlight to meet in a single focus, the power of the flames came together onto the coin deposited under my skin. My flesh swelled, and my veins felt like liquid fire. I shook greatly in pain and agony and strange visions of black churches invaded my mind. Then as quickly as the flames had appeared in front of me, they were gone. I fell to my knees in exhaustion, utterly undone.

I will never forget the panic that followed. A loud rumbling rifled through the bowels of the earth, and then an earthquake jolted me with such violence that it shook the breath out of my body. Struggling to my feet, I was shaken to and fro, as if a ship tossed upon the sea by a tempest. Cracks and pits began to open up in the ground either side of the mausoleum. I had to escape from this place or be likewise entombed. With wildness and terror swirling all around, I grabbed my coat and filled my pockets as well as I could with the strange coins from the altar. Some tumbled to the floor in the confusion of things, as I ran for the passageway. It seemed like the very earth was turning itself inside out in front of my eyes, as I fled for my life.

Gasping for breath, but escaping without much hurt, save the slit around my stomach, I was delivered to daylight with tremendous relief. My body had survived intact, but my soul had been altered forever. I walked home a changed man; a man admitted to the secrets of arcane knowledge. My courage had been sharp enough to pierce the veil, and now with new purpose, I had been reborn. To celebrate, I bought a pleasing silk handkerchief from a hawker plying his trade near the river.

I retired to my lodgings in Middle Temple to rest. When I placed my head on the pillow, I did not sleep, nor could I be said to think. My unbidden imagination was gifted successive images that arose in my mind with an acute clarity. I saw, with my shut eyes, a powerful vision of four black churches, towering over the rebuilt cathedral of St Paul's. My name was written on each of them in fire. The Dark Lord was returning from the place to which he had been cast down and I had been chosen to prepare the way.

CHAPTER 52

Blake opened the blinds of his living room window and watched the headlights of one of the two police cars disappear into the cool London night. The other patrol car was stationed outside his front door and would be for the foreseeable future. Blake's immediate concern was for Sarah, and he insisted on seeing her before making his statement. His arrival at the Desais doorstep, flanked by police, had understandably caused them great concern, but as the police officer explained the extent of the security measures now in place, they agreed that the best place for Sarah was with them, at least in the short term.

The statement he had given at the police station had initiated countrywide manhunts for Angelo Ricard and his security manager. Searches had already been made of both Ricard's office and his exclusive London residence in Belgravia, but neither had found any trace of him or his henchmen. They had disappeared from the face of the earth. Would the police be able to nail Ricard before tomorrow evening's blood moon?

Blake had arranged to meet Milton the following day to discuss the planned security arrangements for St Mary Woolnoth. He should sleep, but his brain wouldn't let him rest. It kept blinking on and off like a neon sign. His body still felt the echo of the adrenaline that had recently sped through his veins. He tried to keep his anger in, but it kept rising to the surface. The shock of the events surrounding Alina had turned his world upside down. Blake guessed that Ricard had sought her out at the shelter and performed some kind of bizarre initiation ritual on her, implanting a Tyrian shekel beneath her skin. Had Alina's arrival at Sarah's hospital been part of a plan to keep tabs on him? Had it all been a sham? The fire of rage was burning brightly in Blake's heart.

In search of a distraction from his dark thoughts, Blake walked over to the television and switched it on. Whilst he poured himself a mug of whisky, he became aware that the programme was all about the mayoral election. According to the well-known political pundit who was presenting the show, voting had ended three hours ago and the counting of the votes was now well underway. The final result would be announced at around six o'clock that evening. Only then did Blake remember that he hadn't voted, as the events of the day had somewhat spiralled out of control.

He switched off the television and savoured a gulp of the golden spirit. Placing the mug onto the coffee table, he darted out of the room with a determined look in his eyes. Five minutes later he returned, cradling a number of items in his arms. He laid them out one by one onto the coffee table, ticking them off in his mind: a hammer, a pestle and mortar, an empty plastic medicine bottle that had recently contained painkiller tablets for the stitches in his head, and the lump of London Stone salvaged from the Cannon Street bombing.

Before setting to work, he walked over to the window and closed the metal blinds. He could feel the anger swell in him again as he grabbed the blinds and twisted them in his hands. The rules had changed. With his face hardening, a new resolve became forged within him. He just needed one chance. Then he would kill that son of a bitch.

CHAPTER 53

Blake had introduced DCI Milton to the pub years ago. Hidden off a back alley to Ely Court, and a stone's throw from London's famous diamond centre of Hatton Garden, Ye Olde Mitre Tavern had stood on the site since 1546. Although the drinking establishment was tiny compared to its modern counterparts, its out of the way location meant that conversations could be held in relative privacy. Milton had called ahead to reserve the smallest of the alcove drinking rooms. He wanted a quiet place to talk to Blake. He needn't have worried; the lunchtime rush had ended and the place was nearly empty.

After ending his phone call to Sarah outside the pub, Blake ducked his head and walked into the bar. He immediately made a beeline for Milton in the alcove.

'You slept any?' said Milton.

'I don't sleep much these days,' said Blake solemnly.

'Look man, I'm really sorry about what happened yesterday. I don't know what to say, Vincent,' he said shaking his head, the tone of his voice turning sober out of respect. 'If I can help out in any way?'

The two men silently looked at one another.

'We've got to nail this bastard Ricard,' said Blake.

Milton could read a hardness in his gaze. 'He's gone to ground for the moment, but I can't have you going lone ranger on this one. You'll end up getting yourself killed. You understand?'

Milton noticed Blake's hesitation in response.

'You know that, right? We've got to do it the right way.'

Blake said nothing.

'That lowlife isn't going to get within twenty feet of St Mary's church tonight. It's being secured as we speak. All doors and windows are being padlocked. I'll have officers stationed outside. No way in or out. If it wasn't for the mayoral elections, I would have twenty more officers there.'

'What do you mean?' said Blake.

'The official announcement,' said Milton, raising an eyebrow. 'For the mayoral elections. The final results will be declared outside the Bank of England. We've had to divert some of the team to manage the inevitable crowds.'

Blake nodded, unsure as to where he had heard the information before. But he knew that the Bank of England was just a stone's throw away from the church of St Mary Woolnoth.

'The exit polls are all indicating a landslide victory for Lambton. A new mayor usually means a new police commissioner for London. There's a good chance that our friend Lewis may be up for the top job. If that happens we'll all be in the shit,' he grumbled sourly. After shooting a cursory glance around the pub, he carried on. 'How a snake like Lewis could be put forward for a job like that beats me. He's just a talking head, not a real policeman. He couldn't piss into a pot.' His voice dropped a notch. 'Look, Lewis doesn't want anything to go off tonight that could jeopardise his chances of making it to the top of the food chain.'

'You do know Ricard will stop at nothing. This is his final chance to complete the pattern,' said Blake, staring at the DCI with a hard, unbending look. 'There won't be another blood moon tetrad for centuries.' Blake glanced up at the clock behind the bar. 'What time do you want me at the church?' said Blake.

'Here's the thing,' said Milton, rubbing his chin. 'I don't want you anywhere near the church tonight. You've gone through a hell of a lot over the last couple of days, and to be honest, I'm not sure all your wheels are on the road at the moment. Look, don't sweat it. If Ricard gets within walking distance of the church we'll hammer him. Anyway, I want you to focus your attention on Ricard's house in Belgravia. We need to get some clue as to where he might be hiding out.'

CHAPTER 54

'So, this surprise you wanted to show me?' asked Rosalind, staring into space. 'When can I see it?'

Ricard returned to the room, carrying a backpack and something that looked like a woman's purse in his hand.

'It had better be worth it,' she teased.

Since the charity event, Ricard had taken quite a shine to her. He had bought her flowers and even invited her to have lunch with him at his luxury home.

Now they were together in one of Ricard's other London properties, this one just off Green Park. He said he wanted to collect a bag before unveiling the 'big secret' to her. This apartment wasn't as impressive as his Belgravia home, but it was perfectly adequate. If the truth were known, she had started to take a shine to Angelo Ricard too. He was a good-looking, confident man. The type of confidence you get from a hefty bank account and being very well connected.

Things were getting interesting, she thought to herself, as Ricard placed the backpack on the floor and sat next to her on the sofa.

'Patience, patience. All in good time,' he said, looking amused with himself.

'And how do you want to kill the time?' she said moving closer and touching his hand.

'Thought we could have a little fun,' he said, slowly shaking the purse in front of her eyes and withdrawing his hand.'

'And what's that?'

He unzipped the black leather purse and opened it up. A knot clenched in Rosalind's throat when she saw the familiar outline of hypodermic syringes. She sat in silence, biting at her lips, staring at the needles. After a pause, she nodded to Ricard who leaned forward and tied a rubber tourniquet around her arm. When he was finished, he placed a syringe into her hand.

'Enjoy the ride,' he whispered into her ear.

Rosalind found a vein in her forearm and felt the sharp scratch of the needle enter her skin. Ricard released the tourniquet and she pushed the plunger home. She felt the cool liquid pass into her bloodstream and her body greeted the drug like an old friend. Rosalind grabbed out for Ricard's shoulder and then her head snapped back. An explosion of white light had just filled her vision. Within seconds she was staring up to the ceiling with a blank, expressionless face.

A smile curled on his lips. 'You scrawny bitch,' he said fiercely, with a cruel glint in his eye. He checked his watch and resisted the temptation of opening the backpack.

CHAPTER 55

Angelo Ricard's exclusive Belgravia residence was teaming with police officers and forensic specialists. Blake straightened his back against the wall, as two uniformed police officers began to squeeze past him in the corridor. Both officers were carrying heavy-duty transparent bags containing a cache of computer equipment, laptops, and hard drives.

'Where's Ricard's office?' asked Blake to the trailing officer, who stopped, repositioned his grip on the bag, and nodded down the corridor.

Blake thanked him with his eyes and hurried on along the passageway into the office. Like everything else about Ricard's house, it was on an impressive scale, the footprint of the room probably larger than the entire ground floor of Blake's own house. For a moment, his eyes took in the office and its high ceilings, thick carpets and ornate sash-style windows overlooking a private courtyard.

Recognising the plain-clothes detective sitting at Ricard's expansive desk as a member of DCI Milton's special response unit, he headed over to the man.

'Just been told, looks like Lambton has won by a landslide,' said the detective, reaching his hand out towards Blake's.

'Really?' said Blake, in a non-committal way.

'They've just announced the results outside the Bank of England. Let's hope he's going to be better than the last mayor,' he said with a frown. 'Lambton's going to be leading a victory march from the Bank of England to the new hospital that's just opened up in the Minories. Nice touch, I thought. It's about time a mayor focused on looking after the sick instead of sucking up to those parasite bankers, don't you think?'

Blake didn't answer, the mention of the Minories jarring in his mind.

'The city's going to be jam-packed for the next couple of hours,' said the detective. 'Me and the boys are going for a drink after we finish up here to miss the crowds, if you're interested?'

'Maybe another time,' said Blake, his focus settling onto the objects laid out on the table.

The detective observed Blake's interest. 'From the safe,' said the man as he pointed to the far wall. Blake's eyes were initially drawn to the oil painting leaning up against the wall, but they quickly moved upwards to the wall safe some four foot above the painting. Its door was ajar, and the space inside was completely empty.

'So, what have we got here?' asked Blake, shouldering forward to take a look.

'Not really sure,' said the detective. 'The DCI suggested we wait until you got here. The boss thought you might be able to shed some light on them.'

He recognised the first of the three objects laid out on the table. They were the same architectural plans of Bank Tube Station that he had spotted on Ricard's desk in his office in the Middle Temple. The drawings were detailed blueprints of the elevators and stairwells running through the centre of the tube station. A single feature had been circled in red pen in the top left-hand corner of the plan. He craned forward to get a better view. The shape looked like a door. Inset above it were several words printed in small faded typeface: 'To St Mary Woolnoth'. An arrow above the words directed the eye off the page, presumably in the direction of the church. Blake's eyebrows pulled together in thought.

'You might find this of interest,' said the detective, moving the map to one side. He pulled a flat wooden presentation box closer to the edge of the table. Fashioned out of maple wood, the box had been made by a master craftsman. Adorning its lid and expertly executed in inlaid walnut and rosewood veneers was the design of a pyramid.

Blake's eyes motioned for the detective to open it, which he did carefully.

'I bet they're worth a pretty packet? What are they, Roman?'

'Something like that,' said Blake, picking up one of the Tyrian shekels from its indented position holder within the case's blue felt interior.

'What do you think happened to the rest of them?' mused the detective.

The box had been designed to hold three rows of ten coins, thirty positions in all. Over half of the positions were vacant. Blake's thoughts turned cold at the notion of one of these coins being put under Alina's skin. He closed the box without answering the detective's question.

'Was this in the safe?' asked Blake, picking up a leather-bound notebook from the table.

'Yep. Looks like an old diary,' said the detective. 'It's got a title page. Says it belonged to a Nicholas Hawksmoor.'

The detective's words nearly knocked Blake off balance.

'Hawksmoor?' said Blake, the strength leaving his voice.

'That's right. It says it, just inside the front cover.'

Blake opened the book and read out the words, handwritten in faded copperplate lettering.

The Diary of Nicholas Hawksmoor.

A knot formed in his throat as he skim-read the yellowing sheets. Paging to the end, his attention was drawn to the final entry.

Diary Entry of Nicholas Hawksmoor
15th May 1733

Over fifty years of sand has passed in the hour glass since I first found the book in Mr Cooper's shop. Now my fingers are so disjointed, that I cannot steadily hold a pen, and my breaking health reminds me how ill I can afford to be slow in the completion of my commission. Since the binding of my soul to the Dark Lord's, I have never slackened in my diligence to perform my endeavours. I have prepared the road for His coming. On that day, the world will shake with His power.

Today the steeple of the church of St John Horsleydown was topped with my glorious weathervane. Those lank-jawed churchmen of the parish think that the vane depicts a flaming comet; little do they know the true representation of my work. The blazing star portrays the Dark Lord's descent from the heavens, cast out by God Himself millennia ago. The Druids, those masters of pagan knowledge, knew the location of His fall and where His dark power had entered the ground. At this place, known today as 'The Minories' after the great Abbey of the Minoresses that once stood there, they built a great circle of unhewn stones. This circle was imbued with powerful white magic to imprison the Dark Lord's power within the ground.

Then came the Romans, first landing on these shores in AD 43 and ruling for the next 400 years. Under the orders of Constantine the Great, the circle was destroyed and at its centre was erected an imperial mausoleum. This was indeed the great monument that I discovered over fifty years ago.

To symbolise Rome's dominance over the Druids, a magnificent statue was made to adorn the mausoleum. The carved stone statue portrayed a powerful imperial eagle with a writhing serpent in its beak. The serpent denoting any power, temporal or spiritual, that dared to stand in opposition to Roman authority. Such was its potency that Constantine's mother, Helena, sent cursed artefacts from the Holy Land to be placed in the mausoleum in order to banish them from the sacred soil of Jerusalem, including the thirty pieces of silver.

Constantine couldn't have realised that in destroying the magic ring of stones built by the Druids, he would allow my master's agents to be released from their captivity to do His bidding. These demons are everywhere; I can see them with my eyes and hear their scheming with my ears. They enter the weak and take possession of their faculties to carry out His dark purposes.

But I have been chosen to fulfil a greater calling. To build the very instrument to allow for His return. Four black churches, built in a perfect square alignment around the Minories, the precise location of His falling from the heavens. The Druids built a circle of white magic to keep my master caged; I have built a square of black magic to release Him from His prison. It was written in the book that a time will come when the alignment of the stars, planets and moon will match the dark geometry of my churches. Four blood moons, four black churches and four human blood sacrifices to bind them together in the blackest of magic. This is the key to unlock the prison chains of His captivity, and I will be exulted high above His lieutenants for bringing it to pass.

Blake's mind swirled. He had been right all along; the Hawksmoor churches were built according to a diabolical scheme. What's more Ricard was killing according to details set out in Hawksmoor's diary.

Just then Blake's phone buzzed. Still deep in thought, he answered it and recognised Rosalind's faint voice. He withdrew the phone from his ear and gave the detective a 'give me a minute' gesture.

'Roz, can you speak up? There's a lot of noise in the background.'

'Vincent, it's Rosalind, your sister,' her voice sounded slurred and detached.

'I know it's you. Is everything okay? Where are you?'

'Going to get my medicine soon. Then everything is going to be okay,' said Rosalind in a scrambled whisper.

'Speak up, Roz, I can barely hear you,' said Blake, raising his voice.

'Too many people here,' said Rosalind. 'Wanted to let you know.'

'What did you want me to know?' said Blake. A pang of anxiety rose in stomach.

'I'm going on a trip.'

'Have you taken something? Rosalind, listen to me. Have you taken something?' Blake gripped the phone hard.

'It's okay, Angelo is getting me my medicine and then we are going on a trip together.'

Blake's eyes snapped shut as if he were recoiling from a blow.

'Angelo? Angelo Ricard?' he said, his breath catching audibly in his throat.

'Yes, Angelo Ricard.' Rosalind's voice had almost fallen into a whisper.

A sickening feeling invaded Blake.

'Rosalind, listen to me. It's really important. Ricard is a very dangerous man. He kills women. Rosalind, do you understand me? You need to get to the nearest police station. Where are you now?'

Straining to hear above the ambient noise on the line, Blake's face suddenly blanched as he heard a public address announcement.

'Because of the large number of passengers travelling through Bank Station this evening, please allow extra time for your journey.'

Then a sharp grating sound burst through the phone's speaker and the line went dead. Blake quickly redialled Rosalind's number and waited. The line went dead again. No ringing, no answerphone. He dialled again, this time with his heart pounding in his throat. Nothing.

'Shit,' he said sharply, his head dropping into his hands. Looking to the floor, he saw something resting against the table leg, its distinctive blue colour standing out from the cream carpet. He leant down and picked it up. It was a silver ring mounted with a turquoise stone. Blake's heart leapt into his mouth. It was Rosalind's; her American boyfriend had given it to her. He immediately remembered what the curator of the Scotland Yard museum had said: occult killings often required the removal of jewellery to prevent metal from interfering with the dark energies called upon during the ritual. Ricard's previous victims had all been stripped of their jewellery.

'Fuck!'

Blake turned around to the detective, who was staring at him with a concerned frown.

'Listen to me. Phone DCI Milton. Tell him that Ricard has got my sister and they are heading his way.'

Seconds later, Blake was skidding out of the room with the architectural plans of Bank Tube Station in his hands.

CHAPTER 56

Rosalind ducked her head under the doorway and followed Ricard out of the narrow passage. She felt confused as her eyes adjusted to the pale light of her surroundings. Their way forward appeared blocked by a wall of tall metal pillars. Stumbling, Rosalind reached out to steady herself against the line of cold metal columns in front of them, her senses dulled by the cocktail of narcotics flowing through her blood stream.

'We've come out at the back of the church organ,' whispered Ricard, readjusting the backpack on his shoulder.

'Ahhh. These are the organ pipes, right? You always take your girlfriends to places like this?' She blew out a breath. 'When do I get my medicine?'

'In a second. Remember, keep your voice down. We shouldn't really be in here.' Ricard's face displayed annoyance.

'Okey dokey,' she whispered loudly, raising a finger to her pursed lips.

'This way.' He motioned her to a door at the side.

After Rosalind took a few shaky steps towards the door, Ricard took her elbow and steered her forwards.

Stepping through, Rosalind looked up at the lofty interior of St Mary Woolnoth. Shafts of ghostly moonlight shone down from the arched lantern windows cutting a line high up along one of the walls. Something about the interior dimensions of the space further disoriented her. She reached out towards the hefty wooden pulpit by her side and glanced around. Her gaze slowly lowered. The floor space was occupied by rows of pews all facing an altar at the back of the church. The altar was topped by a gilded canopy supported by two twisted wooden columns.

'Okay, now we're here. What was it you wanted to show me?' Her whispered tone was becoming impatient.

Taking her by the hand, Ricard led Rosalind over to the altar. He carefully placed his backpack on the richly decorated altar cloth and opened it. After rummaging for a moment, he picked out two objects and arranged them on the altar. Rosalind's eyes suddenly came alive at the sight of the fully loaded syringe and a length of rubber tubing next to the bag.

'Before I show you what we have come here to see, can I offer you some refreshment?' he said through a lop-sided grin. 'You sit up here,' he said, tapping the altar with the palm of his hand. Rosalind didn't need any more encouragement, and in a moment she was sitting on the altar with her legs swinging in anticipation. Soon the rubber tube was being tied tightly around her arm. With perfectly steady hands, Ricard directed the needle into a well-worn vein in Rosalind's forearm. As he released the tourniquet and squeezed the plunger, a dark slow smile crept up his face.

She let out a shudder as the hit of pure heroin surged in her bloodstream and took several shaky breaths as her body recoiled from the intensity of the rush. Within seconds, the strength had run out of her body and she slumped backwards against the rear wall. Whilst the world was blinking in and out of her vision, she thought she could see a knife twist before her eyes. She tried to struggle, but moments later, its long pointed outline had melted into the darkness of her unconscious. As Rosalind's eyes turned distant, a strong gust of wind rattled the large wooden entrance doors to the church. A storm was coming.

CHAPTER 57

The taxi driver put down his radio and shouted over his shoulder to Blake.

'Sorry mate, just confirmed it with the control room, this is as far as I can take you. It's the mayoral election. It looks like half of London is going to be out marching tonight. Don't blame them though, it's about time we had someone sticking up for Joe Public.'

Blake grabbed the plans of Bank Tube Station and tossed the driver forty pounds through the hole in the taxi's reinforced glass partition.

'Keep the change,' said Blake, already pushing down the door handle.

'You sure? Cheers mate. Holborn station is just there, up on right,' he said, pointing towards the illuminated Underground sign in the distance.

Blake hit the ground running, buffeted by the strong wind blowing down Kingsway. Rosalind's phone had gone dead, and Ricard was with her. The thought of the two of them together kept stabbing at his heart like a spike. Soon Blake's progress towards the station had slowed to a crawl. The pavements were thick with people heading to join the march. He tried to push against the tidal drag of the herd moving in the opposite direction. He ploughed onwards, struggling to gain ground towards the entrance to Holborn Tube Station. His head craned up above the throng and towards the road. Seeing the slow-moving traffic, he changed directions, this time setting off at right angles towards the road. Once free, he started to thread his way through the vehicles. Ignoring the horns of complaint, he sprinted his way along the central reservation of the main road.

Close to the station entrance, he hopped back onto the pavement and into the stream of people coming this way and that around the station. Soon he was through the ticket barrier, and seconds later he stepped onto the long escalator heading down to the train platforms deep underground. He tried to hustle his way past the people on the top of the escalator, but they wouldn't move. As he stood there with his shirt pasted to his back, a message announced its arrival with a vibrating buzz in his pocket. He fished out the phone and scrolled through to the message. It was from Dr Desai.

VINCENT, JUST TO LET YOU KNOW SARAH IS FINE AND THE POLICE ARE TAKING GOOD CARE OF US. VIJAY.

Without warning Blake's shoulder was shoved from behind. A party reveller who had had far too much to drink slumped forward into the lady directly behind Blake. The force of the shunt sent Blake's phone flying from his hand like a sling shot. With a gaping mouth, all Blake could do was watch the object's downward trajectory. It bounced several times off the metal barrier dividing the up and down escalators before finally hitting the ground in an explosion of broken plastic and electronic components. His neck turned rigid with anger. Making a fist, his teeth bit into the side of his hand.

He could feel the grains of sand running out of the hourglass. If he didn't get to Rosalind soon, she would be dead. Taking on long breaths of air, he waited for the escalator to complete its agonising journey downwards. As soon as Blake's feet hit firm ground, he was like a racehorse out of the stalls. Storming past the sign directing commuters to the Central Line, his pace increased to an out-and-out sprint, the plans in his hand whipping the air.

Up ahead, he heard the sounds of passengers disembarking from a train. He flattened himself against the wall of the platform and piled past the line of commuters coming his way. With his heart driving fast, he heard the rattle of the train doors start to move together. He was closing in, body-swerving commuters like a rugby forward on a lone run towards the try line. No matter what, he was getting onto that train. Throwing his body against the side of the closest carriage, he rammed his free hand into the space between the uniting doors and, through clenched teeth, grappled them open again. Reclaiming his composure, he coolly stepped into the carriage as the doors closed behind him. Despite the carriage being full, a small perimeter of free space quickly appeared around him.

Bank Station was the third stop on the Central Line heading east from Holborn. First Chancery Lane and then St Paul's. Blake used the time to scan the Bank Station plans. By the time the train's on-board loudspeaker announced their arrival at Bank, Blake had a pretty good idea of where to head for. With his thumb firmly fixed on the area of the plans circled in red pen, he exited the train before most of the passengers had even got out of their seats. Whilst most commuters headed for the escalators, Blake ran in the opposite direction searching for the stairwell. Skidding around the base of the stairs, he grabbed hold of the handrail and started bounding up the corkscrew staircase two steps at a time. Just before the top and with his heart pounding, he slowed his ascent and checked the plans. He peered around the next corner and the door appeared in his view, just as predicted in the drawings. It looked like some kind of service access door. Wiping the sweat from his forehead, he eyed the sign warning of no unauthorised access. He ignored it and tried the handle. It opened with a creak and Blake stepped inside, closing the door behind him.

CHAPTER 58

DCI Milton turned his flapping coat collar against the wind and strolled back to his patrol car parked on the corner of Lombard Street. Settling into the driver's seat, he reached over and retrieved his coffee standing upright in the passenger footwell. Taking a sip of the brew, he looked out onto the strange profile of St Mary Woolnoth. To his mind, it looked like a castle, the building's imposing tower facade capped with a pair of squat balustrade turrets blackened by years of traffic exhaust.

All the other churches he had seen in his life, stretching back from his Sunday school days in his native Jamaica to the grand European cathedrals he had visited during his travels, shared a common theme. They were designed to elevate the senses upwards towards heaven. St Mary's was different. Its squat, foreboding exterior seemed to drag the senses downward into the building's foundations.

And then there was its strange name: Woolnoth. It almost jolted the senses. According to Blake, the name 'Woolnoth' came from a wealthy benefactor, one Wulnoth de Walebrok who was known to have made financial contributions in the twelfth century for the church's upkeep. *Money is usually behind things, as true today as it was back then*, he mused to himself.

Milton retrieved his phone from his pocket and speed-dialed Blake's number. As before, there was no answer. An uneasy feeling swept through him. According to the officer at Ricard's Belgravia residence, Blake had sent word that Ricard and his sister were heading their way. From then on, Blake appeared to have slipped off the grid. No contact, no further instructions. Milton didn't like it; he didn't like it one bit. Where the hell was he? Since the announcement of the mayor's victory march, things had gotten a whole lot more complicated. People were streaming out of Bank Tube Station hoping to join the march eastwards.

Swapping his phone for a handheld police radio, Milton requested a status update from his team stationed around the perimeter of the church. The building had been completely sealed by padlocks. No one was getting in or out of that church; not on Milton's watch. He ticked off the names of his tactical response team in his head as they reported in over the radio. The last to give a status check were the two sharpshooters hunkered down on the third floor of the office building opposite.

CHAPTER 59

Blake emerged from the passageway with his senses on red alert. The door marked on Ricard's plans had led to a tight spiral staircase that continued upwards through the fabric of Bank Station to what he now took to be part of the church of St Mary Woolnoth directly above the station. He took on a deep breath and slowly eased the door open. It took a second for his eyes to grow accustomed to the poorly lit surroundings. His confusion evaporated as he realised that the large metal tubes in front of him were in fact a section of organ pipes. Scanning to his left, he found another door. He slowly twisted its handle and stepped into the open space of the church.

His face almost cracked at the sight of Rosalind prostrate on the altar. He rushed over to her. She was parchment white, her skin shining with sweat. Blake's eyes travelled around her face; the flesh looked collapsed and empty. Dark shadows filled the craters of her cheeks. He bit back a gasp of emotion, and then he noticed the faint rise and fall of her chest. Thank God, she was still alive. He pulled at her shoulder, trying to raise her out of her stupor. Then he noticed the syringe lying at his feet. He tapped it to one side with his foot, and readied himself to haul his sister onto his shoulder.

Forcing his hands under Rosalind's armpits, he strained to get her torso upright. A sound like scraping metal came from underneath Rosalind's listless body. Wedging her steady with his hand against the back wall, Blake looked down to the altar where the sound had come from. Originally concealed by her body, what he saw laid out on the altar sent terror twisting inside him. There, resting on the surface of the altar cloth was a Tyrian shekel and a knife, its blade six inches long, razor sharp and pointed at the end.

Just at that moment Blake heard the distinctive click of a bullet being chambered behind his head. Then came the jab of a muzzle against his neck.

'Dr Blake, you really are becoming a thorn in my side,' said Ricard. 'Turn around slowly and don't even think about moving that knife.'

He did as he was instructed and came face to face with Angelo Ricard, the Hawksmoor serial killer. Blake stood with his hands behind his head as Ricard patted him down for weapons. The only object of interest that Ricard could find on him was a brown plastic tablet bottle, not even a phone. With a sinister grin, he returned the bottle to Blake's jacket pocket.

'Painkillers? You're going to need a lot more than painkillers when I'm through with you.'

Motioning with his gun, Ricard directed Blake to sit down in the first pew on the left-hand side. With the barrel pressed firmly into his temple, Ricard handcuffed Blake's hand to one of the thick loops of cast-iron ornamentation that adorned the end of each pew. Blake railed against the restraint, trying to gauge the strength of the cast-iron fixing. It was rock solid.

Ricard turned the pistol over in his hand. As he did so, he looked up at the enormous disc of the moon through the window. Silvery grey clouds sped across its face like rolling tumbleweed.

'It will soon be time,' said Ricard, with a menacing smile curling up on his lips.

'Wait, you don't have to do this,' pleaded Blake.

'Don't have to? You have no idea how long I've waited.' He checked his watch. 'The New Age is just minutes away.'

'You think your killings are going to bring about a New Age?'

'Can't you feel it closing in on you, Dr Blake?'

Blake didn't answer and pulled at the handcuff.

'He has chosen me as His vessel,' Ricard said darkly. 'The war is just about to begin and all those who don't submit will be cut down like weeds.'

'I beg you, don't kill her,' said Blake, shaking his head.

Ricard was indifferent to Blake's pleading. 'Soon, she will be marked with the coin and her soul will be offered up as a sacrifice to Him.'

'This makes no sense. Why all of this?'

Ricard turned around and stared back at Blake. 'For a guardian of the Logos, Dr Blake, you seem pitifully uninformed.'

'A guardian of what?' exclaimed Blake.

'I've seen the mark on your finger. I saw it on the first day we met at Boodle's. You can't get away from what you are becoming. The demons have seen it. Ema Mats should have finished you off. I did my homework on you, Blake. I wasn't going to make the same mistake.' His eyes widened. 'When I heard that a physio had joined the shelter, I realised she might be useful to me. I searched her out and performed the ritual on her. Once the coin was inside her body, she was under my master's control. Arranging her placement at your daughter's hospital was relatively straightforward.'

'But you had her shot.'

'Somehow you repelled the Dark Lord's spirit from her. Once the secret was uncovered, you both had to die.'

'But why the coins?'

Ricard paused, mulling something over. 'You really have no idea, do you? I suppose, considering your present circumstances and that we have some time to spare, you deserve a little further explanation.' Ricard took a few steps closer, and Blake slipped his free hand into his coat pocket to search for the tablet bottle.

'Once a demon is released into the world, it only has a short time to find a host before it dies. Normally, a mortal person would have no control over the demon's choice, but with the coins and the right initiation, things can be somewhat more directed.' Ricard gave a sadistic smile. 'A cursed coin is like a beacon signalling to the dark forces that inhabit the void. Like a bright light attracting a moth. Once a host is subverted, its thoughts and actions can be manipulated and its soul harvested for the cause.' Ricard paused. 'Unless it is repelled by another form of ancient power,' he said dismissively.

'So where did these coins come from?'

'Two thousand years ago in Jerusalem, a payment was made using them and they became cursed.'

'What payment? The Temple Tax?'

'Don't you read your bible, Dr Blake? "Then one of the Twelve, the one called Judas Iscariot, went to the chief priests and asked, *What are you willing to give me if I hand Him over to you?* And they set out for him thirty pieces of silver." Matthew 26 to be precise. The payment was thirty Tyrian shekels.'

Blake's face dropped as confusion swirled in his mind.

'The coins were kept by the Sanhedrin, the ruling council of the rabbinical courts for centuries afterwards, until they were acquired by St Helena, mother of Constantine the Great. Afraid of their power, Constantine ordered them to be sent away and kept safe in Britannia, a territory at the very edges of the Roman Empire. Years before, Constantine had campaigned here under his father to rid the province of the troublesome Picts and the Druids. So the coins were brought to Londinium and a mausoleum was built to house them.'

'In the Minories,' said Blake slowly. 'Four Hawksmoor churches, all built to be aligned towards the Minories at the centre,' said Blake. 'But why the Minories? What's there?' he pressed.

'My master,' said Ricard, his face framed in an eerie gauze of silver moonlight. For a moment there was silence. 'My master is there. It's all in your bible, Dr Blake,' he tutted. 'Luke 10:18 I believe is the scripture. "I saw Satan fall like lightning from heaven."' Ricard raised his arm and slammed it down onto the altar, imitating a bolt of lightning.

It was as if all the air had been sucked out of the room.

'You mean ...' Blake's words stuck in his throat, '... the Minories is the place on earth where the devil hit the ground?' Blake couldn't quite believe what he was saying.

'He sends his agents out into the world from there to do his bidding. Haven't you ever thought why the area around the Minories has always had such a dark reputation? Jack the Ripper, The Radcliffe Highway Murders, the rotting slums, the seething vice. They were all part of His grand design.'

Ricard checked his watch again. 'In two minutes, He will come from the earth and be reborn in my body. He will choose me. Great power will be bestowed upon me, through Him.' Ricard's eyes were alive with unyielding wickedness. 'I will sacrifice countless souls in His name. The streets of London will run red with blood.'

CHAPTER 60

A shadow came alive between the two squat balustrade turrets that topped the church of St Mary Woolnoth. The lone figure of Enoch Hart moved out of thick shadows and threw a rope down the side. His form then melted back into the darkness. A second later, the ex-SAS soldier stepped out over the lip of the turret and performed a lightning quick carabineer rundown along the upper section of the tower. He landed expertly onto the flat-roofed extension of the church's eastern flank. Once safely disconnected from the rope, he moved towards the row of large arched windows, keeping to the shadows of the wall.

Under the cover of darkness, he quickly un-shouldered the L118 sniper rifle from his back and laid it down at his feet. Next he removed a circular glasscutter from the utility pack clipped to his belt and set to work on the window. Moments later, a circle of three-hundred-year-old glass was eased out from the windowpane with the help of a small handheld suction cup. There was no time to ready himself. The oversized moon hanging heavy in the sky was already blood red, and a slither of blackness had started to blur its edge. The eclipse was beginning.

Hart picked up the weapon and quietly drew the bolt in and out. He dropped down into a one-legged kneeling position and eased the barrel of the weapon into the hole in the window. He could hear voices clearly below even though the wind gusted around him. Blinking through the telescopic sight, he saw Angelo Ricard. He was at the altar and carried a large knife. Something caught Ricard's attention, and momentarily he stepped away from the altar. Suddenly the crosshairs of the telescopic sight picked up the body of a woman lying prostrate on the altar. With his eye still trained on the woman, Hart made a small adjustment to the sight's magnification ring. His scope eye flicked erratically from side to side as he tried to detect evidence of blood on the woman. He couldn't see any.

While Hart waited for Ricard to return, his finger slowly tightened on the trigger. He started reciting words to himself. 'Demon, know the power and strength of Jesus Christ, who defeated Satan in the desert, overcame you in the garden and vanquished you on the cross.' The words were taken up on the breeze into the cold night air.

Blake followed Ricard's gaze up to the blood red moon looming menacingly through the window. An edge of darkness had already invaded the corner of the moon's discus. Seeing that the eclipse had begun, Ricard focused back onto Blake. They locked eyes. Ricard's face had transformed into a sneering stare, and his irises had turned unnaturally large and black. In that moment, Blake knew he was looking straight into the presence of pure evil.

Ricard stepped closer towards Blake, his lips turning back into a snarl. 'First it will be your sister and then you, Dr Blake.' His teeth snapped at the air, sending spit out from his mouth. 'And I can assure you, you are going to die screaming.'

Blake was up on his feet, fighting to get free of the handcuffs. 'I'll kill you Ricard, I swear it.'

'It's time Blake, it's time.'

Ricard approached the altar and picked up the long knife. Grabbing a fistful of hair from the back of Rosalind's head, he raised her up. Licking his lips, he traced an imaginary line across Rosalind's ash-white neck with the tip of the blade.

The police sharpshooter positioned in the office building overlooking the church repeated his radio call into DCI Milton. This time there was weighted tension in every one of his words.

'He has a rifle and he is aiming it into the church, over.'

'Understood,' said Milton into his handheld radio. The circuits of his brain were working at full capacity to assess the unfolding situation on the roof of the church. It must be the killer, he said over and over in his mind.

'Requesting authority to proceed?' said the police marksman.

DCI Milton swallowed hard, his hand gripping the steering wheel of the patrol car.

'Sir, I need a decision now. Can I have your authority to take the shot?'

A single bead of sweat slid down the side of Milton's face.

'Sir?'

The DCI pressed the talk button and gave the command.

'Take the shot.'

CHAPTER 61

The flat retort of a rifle shot sounded from the office buildings opposite the church. A bullet droned past Hart's ear and slammed into the masonry two feet away from his head, sending sharp fragments of stone into his face. As he recoiled from the impact, the barrel of his gun scraped against the sides of the glass hole in the window. Two more shots rang out. This time, both found their target. The first blew a hole in Hart's shoulder, sending out a crimson mist into the air; the second tore into his ribcage in an explosion of cracking bone. The windows behind him blew out in a supernova of glass splinters.

Dropping the rifle, Hart staggered to his feet as white-hot pain spread across his body. With faltering steps, he edged forwards. Then his feet buckled and he toppled over the edge of the wall. He hit the ground with a bone-crunching smack, sending panicked pedestrians in all directions.

Milton had watched the scene unfold from his car and was now running in the direction of the church. A lone figure broke from the crowd and ran towards Hart's moaning body. It was Mary. With tears streaming down her face, she huddled down next to Hart's crumpled frame and leaned towards his lips. With his strength ebbing away, he whispered something to her. He clenched his teeth and repeated his words. Then a dreadful pain lanced through his chest, and he gasped and fell still.

By the time Milton arrived at Hart's lifeless body, Mary had evaporated into the confusion of the crowd. He checked Hart's pulse but found none. His eyes quickly scanned around the body. Spilled out onto the pavement were the contents of the half-open utility pack still clipped to Hart's belt.

Milton quickly examined the items. What he found sent deep wrinkles of concern pinching across his forehead. A phone, a purple stole, a small red bible, medallions of various types, a brass crucifix, and a small bottle labelled 'holy water'.

CHAPTER 62

A volley of bullets obliterated the large arched windows in the side of the church, and a shower of glass fragments rained down onto the stone floor below. With it came a sudden rush of wind from outside that blasted cold air through the church.

Ricard jerked his head upwards towards the windows, but in an instant his attention recentred on the face of the blood red moon disappearing in shadow. The wind whipped up the side of the altar cloth, and Ricard's black eyes turned back to Blake.

'He is coming. Nothing will stop us,' he hissed venomously.

Turning back to the altar, he regripped the back of Rosalind's hair and readied himself for the climax.

'Understand Blake that the guardians have failed and the New Age is about to begin,' he shouted over his shoulder, his voice crackling with malevolence.

Blake thrashed in his seat, his arms flailing to get free from the restraint locking his wrist to the pew. His head was spinning, and his veins boiled with anger. In desperation, he screamed up at the sky, but his words were whipped from his mouth by the wind blowing through the centre of the church.

Suddenly, an idea flashed into his mind. Grabbing into his pocket, Blake yanked out the tablet bottle. He unscrewed the lid and poured out its contents into the palm of his free hand. His fist closed around the cone of white powder that had formed in the well of his hand. Shooting up from his seat, Blake launched the ground remnants of the London Stone into the air towards the altar. Almost instantly the powder was gone, carried forwards in a gust of air.

Ricard slowly raised the knife, and allowed himself a breath to savour the moment. Soon he would feel the power of his master, coursing through his veins. Everything would come to pass as laid out in the book.

A shudder ran down Ricard's body, followed by an airburst of pain all around him. As the fine particles of London Stone stuck to the exposed parts of his body, they began to burn into his skin. He gasped with shock and excruciating pain. After drawing particle-laden gulps of air into his lungs, he felt his chest blaze with agony. He staggered backwards from the altar, and his eyes began twitching erratically. Ricard screamed a vile hideous scream and dropped the knife, sending it clattering to the floor. He fell to his knees and grabbed furiously at his neck.

The loud crack of a pistol shot reverberated through the church. The bullet from Milton's service pistol punched a hole straight through Ricard's temple, blowing out brain and skull from the back of his head. The force of the bullet lifted Ricard's body backwards, and he landed spine-down onto the stone floor. For a second, Ricard's hand juddered by his side, as the electrical signals from his brain began to shut down. But moments later, he gave out his final breath.

With his gun leading the way, Milton sprinted out into the open space of the church. After following Blake's urgent instructions to check on Rosalind's condition, Milton made his way back to his friend, his shoes crunching on broken glass.

Relief flooded into Blake's face. 'We nailed that son of bitch,' he said. 'One other thing.' He paused. 'Can you also call for a locksmith?' he asked, rattling the handcuff around his wrist.

Milton stared at Blake for a moment and then looked over at Ricard's dead body. 'What the hell has been going on?' asked Milton, massaging the back of his neck.

Blake smiled and leant back in the pew. 'It's complicated,' he said.

CHAPTER 63

Another blast of applause erupted from the massive crowd that had assembled around the brand-new Minories Hospital. Captain Lambton, the new mayor of London, couldn't hide his delight as he leant against the lectern. It had been one hell of a battle. He had fought tirelessly against the establishment, daring to hope that change was possible. His landslide victory represented a massive mandate by the people for a new beginning in London.

He tried to settle the crowd, but instead his smiling face just set off another burst of applause. Undeterred, he looked out onto the sea of people and began his closing remarks.

'Behind us stands the Minories Hospital. Just last year, this place was derelict land, and now look at it. With vision and hard work, we have transformed this waste ground into a state-of-the-art hospital for all of London. Come join me, and let's build more new hospitals for our great city.' A huge cheer swept through the crowd joined by a chorus of shrill whistles. 'I urge you to bring what you've got to the cause. Everyone is welcome. On this historic day, I ask you to join me to build a better London for all. Thank you.'

A wave of celebration surged through the exuberant crowd. All at once, the revelry hushed and heads started lifting towards the sky. The atmosphere felt charged, and thunder broke overhead with an enormous roar. Murmurs of nervous laughter rose in the audience, followed by a small round of applause that travelled quickly across the assembled crowd.

An eerie shadow began to travel across the red moon, and it fell dark—very dark. Around and above him, Lambton could feel electrical static. The hairs on his arms and head stood rigid. He looked up towards the moon, but it had completely disappeared, reaching its point of total eclipse. Then a fork of lightning stabbed down from the sky hitting the ground just behind the stage. With it came a terrific clap of thunder, as if the very structure of the sky had been ripped apart.

Quaking, the figures on the stage looked in the direction of the impact. A smouldering crater several feet across had been punched into the hospital car park behind the stage, as if a meteorite had fallen and struck the earth.

In the shadows, a strange black shape emerged from the steaming hole and advanced across the car park. Moments later it surrounded the stage. Lambton gripped the lectern as he felt a bone-chilling presence at his shoulder. A terrible fear spiralled inside him as the black shape enveloped his body like a shroud. He attempted to cry out, but the sound became trapped in his throat. A knot tightened itself around his heart, and for an instant his eyes turned pitch black.

Slowly, Lambton's fingers slackened their grip on the lectern, and his lips curled into an unnatural smile.

CHAPTER 64

'Don't worry, it's on DCI Milton,' said the bartender of Ye Olde Mitre Tavern.

Returning his wallet to his pocket, Blake thanked the man and watched as he finished off the creamy shamrock design on the second pint of Guinness.

Blake loaded a small circular tray with the drinks, making room for the packet of pork scratchings that completed his order. He tossed the packet onto the tray and started to zigzag a path across the room to Milton, who was seated in an alcove.

Blake delivered the tray to the table and fell heavily into his chair. At that moment, rays of dusty light shone out from between the gap in the curtains behind them, illuminating the back of Blake's head and shoulders. The feeling of warmth on his neck was immediate and slightly uncomfortable. He shuffled his chair around to get out of the light. 'Still no new leads on Ricard's henchmen?'

'Don't worry we'll catch up with those bastards soon enough,' said the DCI sternly.

'So, what did you want to show me?'

Milton took a large gulp of his Guinness, draining a third of the glass, and then slid a light blue police file across the table.

'These are just some of the things that we found on Ricard's home computer.' He drew closer to the table, glancing around to make sure they weren't being overheard. 'A word of warning; there are things in there that are quite close to home. I just thought you should know.'

'What things?' Blake reached over and started flicking through the file.

'Bloody hell,' he said, his frown deepening. 'Sarah's hospital records. How did he get hold of these?'

'If you go on, you'll see that your sister's medical files from her rehabilitation clinic in the States are also in there.'

Blake skimmed the pages and absorbed the details. 'So that bastard knew about Roz's problems all along. She was vulnerable, and he preyed on her,' he said, his indignation rising. He felt his heart skip a beat. 'Shit, this is the employment record of Sarah's previous physiotherapist. She was involved in some sort of car accident. I remember Sarah's hospital consultant mentioning it. That's why Alina replaced her.' He paused.

Milton saw the instant of comprehension in his eyes.

'You don't think?' Blake asked.

'It's not beyond imagination to think Ricard was involved,' said the DCI as he rubbed his hard-set jaw. 'We're looking at it right now.' Milton took a drink from his glass. 'From what we can piece together, it looks like you've been on Ricard's radar for quite a while. All the time he was making preparations, just in case you got too close.'

Blake's eyes flicked over Milton's face as he tried to process the information. He dropped the file back onto the table. 'So when I turned up at Ricard's office and explained my theory about which of the churches would complete the Hawksmoor pattern, he decided to come after me?'

'That's what it looks like. I guess Alina got caught in the crossfire.'

Blake sank his head in his hands for a moment. The two men drank their drinks, each lost in their own thoughts.

Remembering he hadn't eaten anything since the previous night, Blake reached over for the pork scratchings. With a blank and impassive expression, he opened the packet with his teeth and started munching.

'So we were wrong about Hart from the beginning,' said Blake, feeling the alcohol begin to unstiffen his muscles.

Milton nodded. 'I was convinced he was our man. It was obvious: a trained killer, obsessed with angels and demons,' said the DCI, his words laced with regret. 'He was some piece of work though. Almost a one-man army.'

Blake glanced down to the dark mark circling his index finger. He quickly flushed the thought away with another gulp of Guinness.

'You found Mary yet?' asked Blake, half-teasing his friend.

Milton smiled a little and flared his nostrils.

'That bloody tramp has disappeared again, along with her dog. Hell knows where she's gone.'

Blake chuckled as he picked at the scratchings. 'She's outrun you again.'

The policeman ignored the dig. 'Those things are going to kill your sorry ass,' said Milton at the sight of Blake finishing the packet.

'I'll take my chances,' snorted Blake with laughter. He stared back at his friend, whose stern expression had cracked into a smile. A moment later, Milton's shoulders were trembling as he tried to contain his amusement. Eventually he couldn't hold it any longer. The DCI threw back his head and gave out a tremendous belly laugh. The sound of Milton's booming baritone voice filled Ye Olde Mitre Tavern.

CHAPTER 65

The afternoon sun began its downward arc over the London skyline. With her eyes narrowing against the sun, Mary smiled up at the whispering tree that marked the corner of Redcross Way. She pulled her coat close around her shoulders and rubbed the neck of the black dog by her side. The animal nuzzled into her leg and then barked back up at the rustling leaves.

'Come on,' she said. 'It's time.'

As they approached the memorial gates of Crossbones Graveyard, Mary began to loosen the white handkerchief around her neck. As the knot fell away in her hands, her thoughts turned to Enoch Hart, the man who had delivered her from darkness. He had risked everything and had paid the ultimate price. With her eyes gleaming with tears, she tied the material onto the metal gate. It joined the countless other ribbons and trinkets that had been fixed there as a memorial shrine to London's forgotten dead.

The black dog lay down at Mary's feet and rested his muzzle on one paw. She knelt by his side and laid her hand on the dog's head. 'It's up to us now, my friend,' she said in a hushed whisper.

The dog cocked his head sideways, his black shiny eyes blinking up to Mary.

'Just before Enoch passed away, he told me things about the rod and the Logos.'

The wind blew past their faces, flapping the long lines of ragged ribbons tied to the gate. In the swirling breeze, the dog barked up at Mary.

As Mary drew closer to answer the dog, her words were carried up into the bright London sky.

CHAPTER 66

Sarah repositioned the cap on her head and dipped the roller into the paint tray, loading it liberally with blue emulsion. As her face broke out into a wide grin, she glanced up at her dad.

'Go on, but don't make a mess,' said Blake while struggling to hold his deadpan expression.

'Okay, let's do this thing,' said Sarah.

With her tongue pointing skywards, Sarah swept the roller over the living room wall. With each arc of her hand, a little more of Blake's hand-crafted map disappeared under the fresh paint.

He took one last look at the four Hawksmoor churches marked out on the wall before the configuration was lost under a coat of blue. His thoughts briefly returned to the Hawksmoor diary that the police had recovered from Ricard's wall safe. Reading it in full after the shootout at St Mary Woolnoth had sent an icy tremor shuddering down his spine. It had almost felt like Nicholas Hawksmoor had reached out to touch him. He wrestled with the thought for a moment and then blinked it away.

'Dad, when are we going to visit Auntie Rosalind?' asked Sarah as she accidentally wiped paint on her nose.

'I'm at the clinic again tomorrow while you're at school and then, all being well, we'll both go next weekend. Okay?'

'Okay.'

Rosalind had been making good progress at a modern drug rehab facility on the south coast. Blake had arranged the place with the help of DCI Milton. It was a safe and caring environment, and Blake visited her whenever he could. Things between the two of them were the best they had been in years. It felt as if she had started to pull her life around.

Sarah stopped painting, seemingly pleased with herself. 'Time for you to take over and do the top bits,' she said.

'Okay, boss,' he said, his eyes crinkling with amusement at the sight of Sarah's blue nose.

A thumping noise came from the front door. Blake glanced at his watch.

'They're an hour early aren't they?' Blake had promised to take the Desais out to lunch as a thank you for all their help looking after Sarah. Had he mixed the time up?

Brushing himself off as he approached the door, he opened it with an expectant smile.

'Dr Blake?' said the man on the doorstep holding a clipboard and wearing a bright-red polo shirt.

'Yes?' said Blake.

'I'm from the garage,' said the man. 'The guys in the workshop have done a fantastic job on your car, I hope you don't mind me saying. I saw the state of it when it came in. Looked like it had been through a war.'

Sarah arrived at Blake's side, rubbing at her nose.

'Just need you to sign a few papers.'

Blake signed the forms, and tapped his foot impatiently on the ground as he did so.

'Dad, I can see it,' said Sarah, pointing excitedly to a red car parked half-way down the street. Blake's beloved Alfa Romeo 155 sparkled in the midday sun. It looked as good as new. As the keys were dropped into his hand, Blake's eyes flashed with excitement.

'Have a great day, Dr Blake,' said the man, turning to leave.

'We will,' said Blake, pulling down Sarah's cap over her eyes.

AFTERWORD

The Four Blood Moon Prophecy

The Four Blood Moon Prophecy postulates that the occurrence of blood moon tetrads (a series of four consecutive lunar eclipses, coinciding on Jewish feast days, with six full moons in between and no intervening partial lunar eclipses) have historically coincided with globally significant events for Israel and the Jewish people. There have been a total of eight Blood Red Moon Tetrads since the time of Christ.

Nicholas Hawksmoor (1661 – 1736)

Nicholas Hawksmoor was an English architect of extraordinary vision. He worked alongside the principal architects of the day, Christopher Wren and John Vanbrugh, and yet his legacy is like no other. His London churches are mysterious and strange places and often use pagan rather than Christian references for their inspiration.

At the age of eighteen, and with a reputation as a competent draftsman, Hawksmoor travelled to London and entered the service of Christopher Wren. Hawksmoor was a brilliant student and absorbed much from his master.

Effectively working as Wren's apprentice, he became involved in the reconstruction of St Paul's Cathedral, Wren's London churches during the 1680's, the Royal Naval Hospital at Greenwich, and (with Vanbrugh) the building of Castle Howard and Blenheim Palace.

In 1710, the Fifty New Churches Act was passed by Parliament to serve the growing population on the fringes of the expanding city. With Wren now 79 years of age, the commission appointed Hawksmoor as one of its surveyors. Due to mounting costs, only 12 churches were completed. Hawksmoor was solely responsible for the architecture of six of them and collaborated on a further two with fellow commissioner

John James. Miraculously, all six of Hawksmoor's unique city churches have survived to this day.

Hawksmoor's Six London Churches:
St Alphege, Greenwich (1712–1714)
St Mary Woolnoth, City of London (1716–1724)
St Anne, Limehouse (1714–1730)
St George-in-the-East, Wapping (1714–1729)
Christchurch, Spitalfields (1714–1729)
St George, Bloomsbury (1716–1731)

Collaborations with John James:
St Luke Old Street (1727–1733)
St John Horsleydown (1727–1733)

Now regarded as one of the great masters of the English Baroque, Hawksmoor derived his style from a study of antiquity, particularly the seven ancient wonders of the world. He researched engravings of buildings from ancient Rome, Egypt and Greece and took his inspiration from ancient pagan traditions. He is known to have had a rich and eclectic library including books on subjects ranging from Solomon's Temple to the design of the great Islamic mosques.

Hawksmoor's churches are unsettling, brooding edifices to a pagan world. His buildings often employ architectural optical illusions that imbue them with an impression of size and weight much greater than their physical reality. Hawksmoor's striking churches evoke powerful emotions and often awaken feelings of unease in the beholder.

In contemporary fiction, the myth surrounding him has been further fuelled by writers such as Iain Sinclair, Peter Ackroyd and Alan Moore, whose work explores a possible connection with the troubled architect and the occult. I am hugely indebted to these authors, who led me to discover the enigmatic Nicholas Hawksmoor for myself. Even now, Hawksmoor's churches have the power to disturb and disorientate the senses.

St George-in-the-East

St George-in-the-East is one of six Nicholas Hawksmoor churches built as part of the Fifty New Churches Act of 1710. The Act was endorsed by Queen Anne, who was eager to 'bring religion to the godless masses of London'. It is located on Cannon Street Road, between The Highway and Cable Street, in the East End of London. Striking in profile, the white-stoned church projects the usual power and spatial ambiguity characteristic of a Hawksmoor church. With its extraordinary lantern tower and four distinctive 'pepperpot' turrets, it casts a powerful silhouette more in keeping with a fortress battlement than a typical Christian place of worship. The lantern is composed of eight supporting columns, each surmounted by a Roman altar design, a favourite theme of Hawksmoor that he also employed at St John Horsleydown.

During a bombing raid on London's docklands during the Blitz of May 1941, St George-in-the-East was set on fire by a Luftwaffe bomb. The interior of the church was gutted, but the tower, walls and distinctive 'pepperpot' turrets survived. The roofless ruin was restored in the 1960's.

The Site of St John Horsleydown

St John Horsleydown was built between 1727 and 1733 near the south bank of the River Thames in Fair Street (now known as Tower Bridge Road, just south of the junction with Tooley Street). The church was built as one of the last churches of the Commission for Building Fifty New Churches set up by an Act of Parliament in 1710.

The church's design was a joint effort between two architects: John James designed a simple square church body, to which Hawksmoor added an unusual spire. Hawksmoor's steeple took the form of a tapered column, making it look much taller than it actually was, and topped by a weathervane depicting a flaming comet.

The church was severely damaged by a bomb on 20 September 1940 during the London Blitz, but parts of the building remained in use for years afterwards. The church eventually closed in 1968, and the London City Mission (a Christian outreach programme) bought the site from the Church Commissioners in 1974 for £37,811. The church's crypt was emptied of its dead and the bodies moved to Brookwood Cemetery and Naismith House.

Redevelopment of the site by the London City Mission quickly followed. Interestingly, the Mission's modern red-brick headquarters was built directly on the stone foundations of the original Hawksmoor church.

Christchurch, Spitalfields

Christchurch was built as part of the Fifty New Churches Act of 1710. It is considered by many to be Nicholas Hawksmoor's architectural masterpiece. Built between 1714 and 1729, its bone-white exterior once dominated the landscape but is now somewhat hidden by the chrome and steel of London's financial district. Like many of Hawksmoor's London churches, it possesses a strange, overpowering quality that echoes power, both temporal and otherworldly.

The church site has a dark and grisly past. No area of London was ravaged more by the effects of the plague than the surrounding parishes of Aldgate and Whitechapel. In an attempt to dispose of the bodies, huge pits were dug, into which thousands of unfortunate victims were thrown. Hawksmoor's church was built on one such plague pit.

Christchurch's association with death continued into the 19th century, as the dark streets around the church turned into the killing fields of Jack the Ripper. In 1888, five women, all prostitutes, were horrifically murdered in close vicinity to Christchurch. Police witnesses often established the time of events with reference to the well-illuminated church clock.

Christchurch fell into disrepair. By 1960, it was nearly derelict with services held in the church hall because the roof was declared unsafe. In 1976, an independent charity was formed to restore the building and bring it back to use.

As part of the restoration efforts, the church's burial vaults were cleared. Between 1984 and 1986, nearly 1,000 bodies were removed from the labyrinth of interconnecting tunnels and cellars beneath the church. At the time, there were serious fears that some of the sealed coffins in the crypt might contain people who had died of bubonic plague or smallpox.

The site was immediately closed down when the exhumed body of a man clearly displayed the physical signs of smallpox. The vault was sealed for 6 months whilst the body was tested in an American laboratory. The results of the analysis confirmed the smallpox virus was dead and did not present a risk.

St Mary Woolnoth

Wedged into a triangle formed by the junction of Lombard Street and King William Street stands the remarkable church of St Mary Woolnoth. The site has been a place of worship for over two thousand years, and the present church stands on the site of a Roman Temple dedicated to the Roman goddess Concordia. The current Christian church is at least the third to have been built on the site. A church dating back to 1445 was badly damaged during the Great Fire of London of 1666 and was completely rebuilt by Nicholas Hawksmoor between 1719 and 1727.

Famed for its fortress-like double-towered facade and spatial ambiguities, it has a strange, almost threatening, appearance. The church's external dimensions emphasise the downward pressure of gravity, as opposed to architecture that reaches up to the celestial skies. Christian iconography is noticeably absent on the exterior of the building.

The interior of Hawksmoor's St Mary Woolnoth is based on the motif of a perfect cube, a very unusual design device for a Christian church. Several commentators have connected the form of the church with that of the cubic stone or 'perfect ashlar', a central symbol in speculative Freemasonry.

St Mary Woolnoth is also unique because it has an underground station beneath it. The construction of Bank Station between 1897 and 1900 required the clearing of the church's subterranean vaults and the transfer of its interred dead bodies to a cemetery in Ilford. The lift shafts and staircase shaft for the station are built directly beneath the church floor.

The Pyramid at St Anne's Limehouse

St Anne's Limehouse was designed by Nicholas Hawksmoor as one of twelve churches built to serve the needs of the rapidly expanding population of London in the 18th century. The building was completed in 1727 and consecrated in 1730.

Standing in the graveyard of St Anne's is a bizarre four-sided pyramid of Portland stone. Each face of the pyramid is divided into five panels. The top panel of one of the sides is inscribed with the words 'The Wisdom of Solomon' and under it is carved a raised but highly worn coat of arms. Some early commentaries concerning the pyramid also state that under the coat of arms were carved a number of Hebrew words, but these have since been lost due to weathering.

The Minories

The name refers to the area formerly housing the Abbey of the Minoresses of St Mary of the Order of St Clare, founded by Edmund Crouchback in 1293. (At the time, the nuns were known as Minoresses.) Today a small side-road off the Minories is still named St Clare Street.

In September 2013, the Minories was the site of a magnificent Roman discovery. During the last few hours of an archaeological dig in the foundations for a new 16-floor hotel, a 1st-century-AD stone Roman eagle was unearthed. Described by archaeologists as one of the best examples of Romano-British sculpture in existence, the two-foot-high carved stone monument portrays a powerful eagle with a writhing serpent in its beak. The statue is made from Cotswold limestone and is believed to symbolise the struggle between good and evil. Unusually the snake is depicted as having a row of sharp teeth.

The only other example of the eagle and serpent motif from the Roman Empire was found in Jordan in 1937 and is now in the Cincinnati Art Museum, US. The eagle found in the Minories is thought to have been an adornment to an imposing mausoleum, as a Roman burial ground existed there, just outside the City walls.

Prehistoric London

The square mile known today as the 'City of London' contains millennia of human history buried within its soil. In this area once stood a fortified enclosure. The enclosure (or 'Caer') was arranged around two hillocks about 35 feet high and positioned either side of a stream. Today, the present street named Walbrook runs very close to the course of the stream. To the north was a swampy moorland stretching to the foot of an immense forest that was later known as the Middlesex Forest. Parts of this ancient forest still remain at Hampstead, Epping and Hainault.

According to legend, on the western hillock, at the location of the present St Paul's Cathedral, stood a mighty stone circle of unhewn monoliths. The Druidic circle, the seat of the Archdruid, links the site of the nation's most important Christian church to a pagan religion stretching back thousands of years. The stone circle has long gone, and no trace has ever been found, apart from perhaps the remains of a single stone pillar, called the 'London Stone'. The stone once stood in the middle of Cannon Street. A second Druidic circle is rumoured to have stood where Westminster Abbey now stands.

Menhirs, or large isolated standing stones, are commonly found in connection with many British circles. Perhaps the best known is Stonehenge's 'Hele' (from the Greek *helios* for 'sun') or Sunstone. The name of Christopher Wren is expertly chiselled into one of the 40-tonne sarsen stones that make up the prehistoric stone circle of Stonehenge.

The London Stone

This unassuming block of Clipsham limestone can be viewed through an ugly iron grille incorporated into the front of a sportswear shop on Cannon Street. Known as the London Stone (or Brutus Stone), it measures only 53 cm wide, 43 cm high, and 30 cm front to back. But contrary to its small physical size and rather incongruous setting, it is an important relic of London's long history. According to a medieval saying, 'So long as the stone of Brutus is safe, so long shall London flourish'.

No one knows for sure where it came from and how it became so important in the folklore of London, but it is likely that this mysterious lump of masonry has been in the city from at least 1198 and probably for significantly longer. The object that remains today is just a fragment of the original much larger stone, which stood taller than a man.

Those seeking esoteric knowledge have always been drawn to the London Stone and its mystical aura. Dr John Dee, mathematician, astronomer, astrologer, occult philosopher, and adviser to Elizabeth I, was beguiled by the object. According to legend, Dee hacked off a piece of the stone for his own personal experimentation. In his poem 'To the Jews', William Blake postulated that it was a sacrificial stone for Druidic worship.

Ratcliffe Highway Murders

By the turn of the 19th century, the Ratcliffe Highway, which led east from the Tower of London through the district of Shadwell, had acquired a legendary reputation as a centre of criminal activity. Now simply known as 'The Highway', it was a principal traffic artery in and out of the city. A series of shocking murders along The Highway in 1811 sealed its place in infamy.

Around midnight on the evening of 7 October 1811, a man entered a draper's shop on Ratcliffe Highway and murdered the shop owner, Timothy Marr, his wife Celia, their 14-week-old son, and the shop boy. The nature of the frenzied attack was unprecedented and shook London to its core: Marr and his wife were battered to death with a heavy maul and slashed with a ripping chisel; the skull of their young apprentice was cracked open and its contents smeared about the walls; the head of Marr's son was almost completely severed from his body. As the four victims were buried beneath a monument at St George-in-the-East, panic spread across London like wildfire.

Twelve days later, another grisly killing spree erupted in the neighbourhood and bore a striking resemblance to the first: skulls smashed in and throats cut through to the bone. These horrific murders took place at the King's Arms public house on Gravel Pit Lane, which ran from Ratcliffe Highway down to the nearby River Thames. The landlord, John Williamson; his wife, Elizabeth; and a barmaid, Bridget Harrington, were all found slain after the crazed attack.

Shortly afterwards, a 27-year-old sailor named John Williams was arrested and imprisoned at Coldbath Fields. The night before his trial, he was found hanging in his cell

Extraordinarily and to satisfy the public's concerns, the Home Secretary ordered Williams's body to be paraded through the streets on an open cart. As the cart passed the second murder site, the coachman stopped the procession and whipped Williams three times across the face. Finally, the crowd passed by the church of St George-in-the-East to a hole dug at the crossroads between New Road (now Commercial Road) and Canon Street Road. Williams's corpse was bundled into the makeshift grave, and hundreds watched as his body was decapitated and a wooden stake hammered into his heart.

The Ripper Murders

Between August and November 1888, five brutal murders took place in a one-square-mile area of Whitechapel in London. All the victims were prostitutes, and all, except for one—Elizabeth Stride—were horrifically mutilated.

The ghastly crimes of Jack the Ripper (also known as the Whitechapel Murderer or 'Leather Apron') around a specific area of London's impoverished East End have gripped the world's attention for over a century. The identity and motivations of England's most notorious serial killer still remain a mystery.

Much has been written about the horrific scenes that met the police on those dark nights in 1888. A number of small but possibly significant details surrounding the case have been far less reported. Does a further examination of these items shed light on the shocking intent of the unknown killer that terrorised London in 1888?

- The first four victims were killed at the four points of a cross.
- The murders took place within one square mile, whereas most serial killers cover a much wider geographical area.
- All victims (apart from Mary Jane Kelly) were left on public display, whereas most serial killers conceal their victims.
- Coins were placed by Annie Chapman's body.
- Two brass rings were taken from Annie Chapman's hand during her attack.

Crossbones Graveyard

Close to the popular tourist landmarks of the Shard, Shakespeare's Globe Theatre and Southwark Cathedral lies a tiny piece of wasteland, tucked away at the junction of Redcross Way and Union Street. This piece of land now used as a storage yard hides a tragic secret. Under the tarmac lie the bodies of over 15,000 people.

The prostitutes that worked in the area were refused burial in consecrated ground due to their sinful profession and were found land away from the local parish church, which became known as Crossbones Graveyard. The graveyard was also the final resting place for many of London's paupers and outcasts. It was finally closed down in 1853 due to lack of space and the large number of bodies being buried there.

Today a memorial gate can be found at the site of the graveyard (opposite the Boot and Flogger pub), where people pay their respects to London's outcast and forgotten dead. As a makeshift tribute, countless ribbons and trinkets have been tied to the gate, and a small memorial service is held there monthly.

Boodle's Club

Boodle's is a private members' gentlemen's club founded in 1762 by the Earl of Shelburne, who later went on to become Prime Minister. The club was named after its austere headwaiter, Edward Boodle. It occupies a special place in the pantheon of British gentlemen's clubs, and many of the most established are still in the third of a square mile known as St James's. The area boasts a network of hidden passages, alleyways and courtyards to explore.

Boodle's is the second oldest gentlemen's club in the world, with the neighbouring White's gentleman's club being the oldest.

Hunterian Museum

Some exhibits of the Hunterian Museum collection wouldn't look out of place on the set of a Hollywood horror film. The home of an unrivalled collection of human anatomical and pathological specimens, historic surgical and dental instruments, paintings, drawings, and sculpture, the collection was the lifework of surgeon and anatomist John Hunter (1728-1793). Part of the Royal College of Surgeons since 1813, the Hunterian Museum is not for the faint-hearted, as you'll see body parts preserved in jars, but it is also a fascinating place and full of surprises.

Fountain Court

Fountain Court is a peaceful courtyard oasis hidden way from the hustle and bustle of London. It provides a great spot to rest weary bones after a long day exploring the city. A small fountain has been here for around three hundred years, but the surrounding gardens have a much older history, possibly dating back to the late 12th century, when the Knights Templar established themselves in the area. Renowned for the quality of their roses, the gardens provided Shakespeare with the setting for the dispute scene in Henry VI, Part 1 that heralded the War of the Roses.

Ye Olde Mitre Tavern

Ye Olde Mitre (a mitre is a bishop's hat) is located near Hatton Garden (the centre of the capital's gemstone industry) and is hidden off a back alley to Ely Court. This area was the London residence to the Ely Bishops from 1290 to 1772 (Ely being a part of Cambridgeshire). The

Ely Bishops were very influential and often seen as a seat of great power. In 1546, Bishop Goodrich had the tavern built for his London servants, and it has been there ever since.

Scotland Yard's Crime Museum

Known as the 'Black Museum,' Scotland Yard's Crime Museum contains a fascinating array of grisly exhibits. Access to the public is limited, but the museum boasts a fine display of Ripper artefacts (including the handwritten notes of the chief detective in the case), nooses, weapons and death masks.

Constantine the Great (272 – 337)

Constantine the Great was Roman Emperor from AD 306 to 337. He is an important figure in the history of Christianity and is cited as the first emperor to officially embrace the religion. He was responsible for many celebrated building projects, including the Church of the Holy Sepulchre in Jerusalem (on the purported site of Jesus's tomb) and Old Saint Peter's Basilica in Rome. The medieval church upheld him as a model of faithfulness, but Constantine was no saint, as he was responsible for the murder of his wife and son.

Constantine's father was Flavius Valerius Constantius, a Roman army officer who in AD 293 became Caesar, or the deputy emperor to the Western Empire. His mother Helena, Flavius's consort, had a profound influence on his life and later on the development of the Christian church.

In 305, his father Constantius was raised to the rank of Augustus, or senior Western Emperor, and Constantine was recalled west to Britannia to join his father's side in the campaigns against the Picts. When his father died a year later, Constantine was claimed emperor by the army at Eboracum (modern-day York).

St Helena (246-50? – 327-30?)

St Helena was the mother of the emperor Constantine the Great. Through her rediscovery and endorsement of early Christian historical sites and her pervasive influence on her son, Helena had a profound effect on the early evolution of the Christian church.

It is thought that Helena's conversion to Christianity came after her son's spiritual experience at the battle of Milvian Bridge in AD 312. In the following years, she was given access to the resources of the treasury to locate relics of the Judeo-Christian religion and set out on a pilgrimage to the Holy Land, no mean feat for a woman in her late seventies. Helena left Jerusalem in AD 327, bringing parts of the True Cross and other holy relics back to Rome. It is likely that she died in AD 330 with Constantine at her side. Her skull can be seen on display in the Cathedral of Trier in Germany.

Tyrian Shekel

At least half a century before the birth of Christ, the silver shekels produced in the Phoenician city of Tyre had become the predominant coin in the Judaeo-Phoenician region. First instituted by Moses (described in Exodus 30:11-16), every Jewish man 20 years and over was expected to pay a tax for the upkeep of the Temple. The Jewish Talmud required the tax to be paid with a coin of high purity silver, and so Tyrian shekels (renowned for their high silver content) became the only accepted coin for the payment of the tax.

When Judas Iscariot betrayed Jesus for 30 pieces of silver (described in Matthew 26:14-15), it was almost certainly with Tyrian shekels taken from the Temple Treasury.

Thanks for joining Vincent Blake in
THE DEVIL'S ARCHITECT.
He returns in THE LOGOS CODE.
The Most Dangerous Weapon is the Truth.

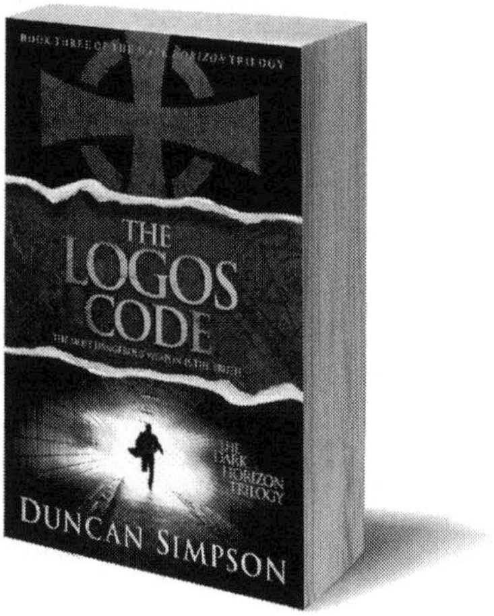

When a prominent Freemason is gruesomely murdered, Vincent Blake - London's leading stolen-art investigator - is called in to investigate. The events surrounding the killing are bizarre and shocking. The closer Blake gets to discovering the truth behind the murder, the more sinister his search becomes. Events soon spiral out of control, and he is drawn into the frontline of a secret holy war.

Pitted against a chilling adversary, haunted by the ghosts of his past, and driven to find the truth, Blake is thrust headfirst into a vortex of deception, stolen treasure, Templar codes, sacred geometry and forbidden knowledge. Gradually, he realises that the knowledge he is hunting for conceals an even greater secret - one so profound, it could trigger events foretold in the book of Revelations.

Join Blake in a life-and-death race across London as he follows a trail of cryptic clues left centuries ago by the founding members of London's Royal Society. Blake's greatest discovery will become the world's greatest threat, as the future of all things hangs in the balance between heaven and hell.

ALSO BY DUNCAN SIMPSON
THE HISTORY OF THINGS TO COME

The mind of a genius can hold the darkest of secrets.

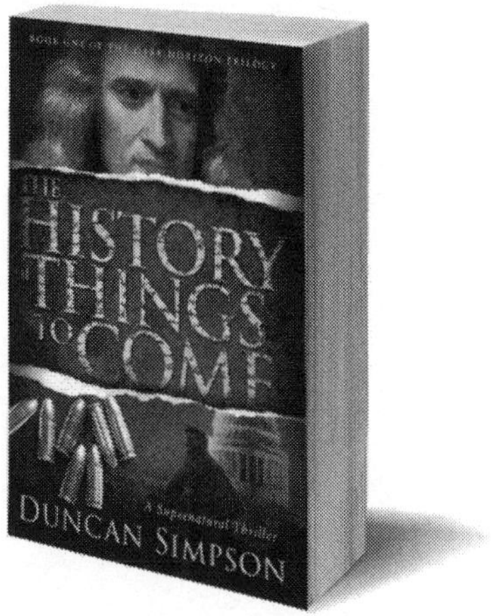

A Bosnian gangster is gunned down in a packed London restaurant. In his possession is a notebook once belonging to Isaac Newton. This is just the latest in a series of shocking crimes connected to objects once belonging to the famous scientist. The police are stumped and the pressure for an arrest is mounting.

Enter Vincent Blake, London's leading stolen-art investigator. As Blake sets out to solve the case, a series of devastating events threaten to destroy everything he holds dear. Broken but undeterred, he comes upon a shocking discovery: within the coded pages of a mysterious crimson book, annotated in Newton's own handwriting, is an explosive revelation. Possessing this secret knowledge turns Blake into a marked man.

Caught in the crosshairs of two sadistic hitmen, Blake is propelled into a breathtaking race through London and its dark historical secrets.

With time running out, will Blake solve Newton's deadly puzzle before the world is plunged into a catastrophe of biblical proportions?

ABOUT THE AUTHOR

Duncan Simpson spent his childhood in Cornwall, England. As a teenager he gained experience in a variety of jobs, from working in a mine to doing shifts as a security guard in an American airport. After graduating from the University of Leeds with a physics degree, he spent a year backpacking around the world. On returning to the UK, he embarked on a successful career in business. Along the way, he became the finance director for a technology company and a partner in a leading management consultancy firm.

The Dark Horizon Trilogy was born out of Duncan's lifelong fascination with the relationship between science and religion. A keen student of the history of London, he loves exploring the ancient stories and myths surrounding the city. When he's not writing or consulting, you'll find him playing guitar in a rock band, running by the Thames, or drinking tea with his wife and three children in their home in Berkshire, England. He can be reached through his website at:

www.duncansimpsonauthor.com

BIBLIOGRAPHY

The following works particularly inspired me during the writing of this book:

Ackroyd, Peter, 2001, *London: The Biography* (Vintage).

Ackroyd, Peter, 1990, *Hawksmoor* (Abacus).

Baguio, Matt, 2010, *The Rite* (Simon & Schuster UK)

Beresiner, Yasha, 2006, *The City of London: A Masonic Guide* (Lewis Masonic).

Coverley, Merlin, 2008, *Occult London* (Pocket Essentials).

De la Ruffiniere Du Prey, 2003, *Hawksmoor's London Churches* (The University of Chicago Press.

Duncan, Andrew, 2009, *Secret London* (New Holland).

Gilbert, Adrian, 2003, *The New Jerusalem. Rebuilding London: The Great Fire, Christopher Wren and the Royal Society* (Corgi).

Gordon, E.O., 1985, *Prehistoric London* (Covenant Media Productions)

Guard, Richard, 2014, *Lost London* (Michael O'Mara Books).

Hague, John, 2013, *Four Blood Moons* (Worthy Publishing)

Hart, Vaughan, 2007, *Nicholas Hawksmoor* (Yale University Press).

Hebborn, Eric, 1991, *Drawn to Trouble: The Forging of an Artist* (Mainstream).

Hollis, Leo, 2009, *The Phoenix: St Paul's Cathedral and the Men Who Made Modern London* (Phoenix).

Howard, Rachel & Nash, Bill, 2009, *Secret London: An Unusual Guide* (Jonglez)

Jardine, Lisa, 2002, *On a Grander Scale: The Outstanding Career of Sir Christopher Wren* (HarperCollins).

Jennings, Humphrey, 2012, *Pandaemonium, 1660-1886* (Icon Books)

Johnston, Author, 1965, *Francis Bacon* (B. T. Bratsford Ltd)

Long, David, 2007, *Tunnels, Towers & Temples: London's 100 Strangest Places* (History Press).
Pennick, Nigel, 2012, *Sacred Architecture of London* (Aeon Books).
Robinson, John L., 1989, *Born in Blood: The Lost Secrets of Freemasonry* (M. Evans).
Sinclair, Iain, 1998, Lud Heat and Suicide Bridge (Granta Books)
Winn, Christopher, 2007, *I Never Knew That About London* (Ebury Press).

And finally, a number of the biblical quotations referenced in this novel are taken from *The Holy Bible, New International Version,* 1996, (Zondervan) and from *The Authorized (King James) Version,* reproduced by permission of the Crown's patentee, Cambridge University Press.

ACKNOWLEDGEMENTS

Thanks to my readers and community at www.duncansimpsonauthor.com and also to my friends on Facebook and Twitter.

Thanks to my production team: Amy Butcher of the Book Butchers for copy-editing and proofreading; Juan Padron for cover design; and Jake Muelle at Creativindie for interior print design.

As always, my biggest thank you goes out to Katie, my master editor. I am constantly in awe of her love, patience and keen eye. Thank you for allowing me to dream and for riding shotgun on the journey. She is the brightest star in my sky.

TEAM BLAKE

A big thank you to the committed and loyal readers that make up 'Team Blake'. I am especially indebted to the following for their help, all above and beyond the call of duty:

RoseMary Griffith, Lynne Jones, Salvatore Carbone, Paul Turner-Smithson, Rise St Arno, Carol Oakley, Sharon K McQueary, Andrew J Norley, Lynn Osborne, Tina Lunsford, Mats Tage Axelsson, Carla Blanck, Randall Krzak, Debra Belmudes, Jackie Halle, Harry Kanth, Ward Donoho, Sheelagh Rogers, Rebecca Partington, Robert Young, Jane Parsons and Lee Button.

YOU CAN MAKE A BIG DIFFERENCE

If you've enjoyed this book, it would be fantastic if you would consider sharing the message with others. In particular, writing a short review can be a powerful way of spreading the word and getting attention for my books.

It would be awesome if you could spend just five minutes leaving a review (it can be as short as you like) on the book's Amazon and Goodreads pages.

Thank you very much.

Duncan

Other things you can do:

- Recommend the book to those in your small group, book club, workplace, and classes.
- Head over to www.facebook.com/duncansimpsonauthor, LIKE the page, and post a comment as to what you enjoyed most about the book.
- Recommend the book to those in your small group, book club, workplace, and classes.
- Mention the book in a Facebook post, Twitter update, Pinterest pin, or blog post.

Get in touch:

For more information and updates on new releases, join Duncan's mailing list at: http://www.duncansimpsonauthor.com

Website: www.duncansimpsonauthor.com
Twitter: www.twitter.com/dsimpsonauthor
Facebook: www.facebook.com/duncansimpsonauthor

FREE!

STARTER LIBRARY

Message from the Author

Building a relationship with my readers is the very best thing about writing. I occasionally send out newsletters with details of new releases, special offers and other exclusive material relating to the Vincent Blake thriller series. If you would like to be part of my readers group just sign up at:

www.duncansimpsonauthor.com

For signing up you will receive FREE digital copies of the following with my compliments:

1. The History of Things to Come (e-book)
Book One of The Dark Horizon Trilogy
The mind of a genius can hold the darkest of secrets.

A Bosnian gangster is gunned down in a packed London restaurant. In his possession is a notebook once belonging to Isaac Newton.This is just the latest in a series of shocking crimes connected to objects once belonging to the famous scientist. Naturally, it's a case for Vincent Blake, London's leading stolen art investigator.

2. Secrets From The Dark Horizon (e-book)
A Reader's Companion Guide to the Dark Horizon Trilogy
Discover where the truth ends ... and the legend begins.
Designed as a pocket reference book, Secrets from the Dark Horizon brings alive the legends, locations, facts, and background material to the series. Jam-packed with fascinating research and chock full of informational tidbits, the guide opens a window on 3,000 years of history. With this book in hand, you will follow Vincent Blake in his breath-taking race through London and its dark historical secrets.

Plus Exclusive VIP Bonus (pdf)
The highly confidential security dossier on Vincent Blake.

I hope you love them.

Duncan
London